BOOKS BY JOHN DWAINE MCKENNA

THE NEVERSINK CHRONICLES

THE WHIM - WHAM MAN

COLORADO NOIR

Colorado Noir

John Dwaine McKenna

RHYOLITE PRESS LLC

Published in the United States of America by Rhyolite Press LLC

P.O. Box 2406

Colorado Springs, Colorado 80901

www.rhyolitepress.com

McKenna, John Dwaine

Colorado Noir / John Dwaine McKenna

1st ed. September 2013

Library of Congress Control Number: 2013912121

ISBN 978-0-9896763-0-4

PRINTED AND BOUND IN THE UNITED STATES OF AMERICA

Cover design and book design/layout by Donald R. Kallaus

Author photo, © Donald R. Kallaus, 2013

Cover photograph: *Nightscape Colorado Springs, c. 1949* George W. Murray

Courtesy, D. Kallaus collection

For ***Mabel Jocelyn***,
who taught me to read.

CONTENTS

THE ALUMINUM MISTRESS

The Aluminum Mistress

AFTER THEY GOT TO KNOW HER BETTER, all the guys at the shop tried, but it was impossible to guess how long the old woman had been living on the streets—because she was stingy with personal information, wary, and tough as a feral cat.

The first time she was spotted by Santos and Little Davie, she was rummaging through the trash cans in the alley out back of the Southside Tire Company, down on South Nevada Avenue. Santos, the parts runner, saw her when he turned to flick his cigarette butt away. "Hey, check it out," he said, nudging Little Davie and pointing at the woman with his chin.

Little Davie, one of the tire busters, opened his eyes and eased his chair back down on all four legs from where he'd been leaning on the wall, enjoying the sun, and said, "What . . ."

"Check it out, man. Over there." Santos pointed with his chin a second time.

The old woman had her butt pointed at them as she leaned over into the trash, busy fishing something out. She was wearing men's work pants with a big stain on the right buttock that went halfway to her knee.

"Ugh," Little Davie said. "Got an ass on 'er like a pack mule."

"Whad'ja think she's doing in there?"

"Getting breakfast?"

"Naw, she's not," Santos said. "I bet she lost something."

"Looks to me like she lost it in her pants."

The woman straightened up and turned around, put her left hand on the small of her back where it ached. She was a medium-sized woman, thick in the waist—no doubt from the effects of a poor diet and being of postmenopausal age. She wore an old corduroy coat and her gray hair hung in greasy strings from underneath a navy-blue watch cap that, like her, had seen much hard campaigning.

She turned and faced Santos and Little Davie. "There ain't nothing wrong with my hearing," she said. "I ain't looking for breakfast neither. I'm hunting cans. Aluminum cans. Either one a you heroes got any? Or are yez too busy running your mouths about old ladies out here in the alley. And why ain't you working?"

Santos was silent, watching the old woman as she pushed her three-wheeled bicycle down the alley toward them. There was a large cardboard box behind the seat tied on with rope and half-full of aluminum cans that rattled as she came up to Little Davie.

"And you . . . you oughta be 'shamed of yerself, talking like that . . . I ain't got no ass like no friggin' plow mule neither. You kiss your momma with that mouth, boy? Well, doo-ya?" She said it just like Clint did in the movies.

Little Davie, who went about 340 and stood six feet seven inches tall, was out of his chair and had his back against the overhead door as the woman came up to him, pushing her bike. With his head down like a five-year-old caught stealing cookies, all Little Davie could say was, "No, ma'am. Very sorry, ma'am."

"You got any cans?"

"Nuh—no."

"You got any?" she said to Santos.

"No, I don't."

"Can you get some?"

"Sure," Little Davie said.

"Save 'em. I'll be back tomorrow and get 'em," she said. "Name's Elaine. I gotta go. I ain't got no silver spoon in my mouth ya know. Gotta go." She rode off, heading south down the alley with the box of aluminum cans tied on her bike.

Santos was lighting another cigarette when Caleb's voice came over the intercom: "Santos to the front desk. Santos to the front desk. Little Davie, your tires are here. Time to go ta work, hoss." Santos trotted off to the front counter to answer the owner's son's call. He knew Caleb was a nice guy, but he also knew that it was a good idea to be respectful of him.

Casting off thoughts of the old woman, *What was her name . . . oh, yeah . . . Elaine, that's it . . . Elaine.* Little Davie lumbered back to his station, not looking forward to changing a set of ten tires on an old Mack dump truck. They were ten-hundred-twenties, the old-fashioned eight-ply kind that have spring-steel snap rings, rubber liners, and inner tubes—the kind that have to be disassembled with a pair of twenty-four-inch pry bars, a three-pound hammer, and a four-inch chisel, then reassembled outside, in a special cage made from two-inch steel pipe set in concrete, just in case the thing exploded when 120 pounds of air pressure went in. He sighed and looked up at the "halo" forming around the top of Pikes Peak . . . a bad weather sign. It was the Ides of March. It could get as cold as deep winter—maybe it would even snow. No, he wasn't looking forward to the rest of the day. It was a nasty job. He sighed and gathered his tools.

But, in true Colorado Springs fashion, the implied bad weather never materialized. The clouds dissipated around the peak and disappeared. The following day was warm, the sun bright in a cloudless blue sky.

Little Davie stepped outside for his break at a quarter past ten, the same as he did every day, to the parking lot behind the garage bays by the alley. Drinking coffee from an insulated stainless steel mug, he nodded to Sonny Edmonds, the owner of Southside Tires, who was washing his horse trailer. "Hey, Sonny, you're about to wear the paint off that thing."

"Naw. It's the horse piss does that," Sonny said as he threw the sponge in the wash bucket and picked up the hose, started rinsing the sides and top of the trailer.

"You getting ready for the Range Ride?"

"Nope. It ain't 'til July, the week before the rodeo. That's when all the fat cats 'n' old farts go off and play cowboy by riding horses around Pikes Peak. It's supposed to advertise the Pikes Peak or Bust Rodeo, but I think it's just an excuse for all us good ole boys to go off and play cards, drink whiskey, and maybe make a few business deals. How are you bearing up, after all those truck tires yesterday?"

"Oh, just fine, Sonny, just fine. I got a couple blood blisters from the snap rings is all."

"When didja finish?"

"Little after six thirty. Caleb and I were out of here before seven."

"I'll tell Caleb to give you a couple of easy jobs."

"Thanks, you don't have . . ." He stopped talking when he saw the old woman on the three-wheel bicycle pedaling down the alley. She spotted Little Davie and headed straight to him.

"Girlfriend?"

"No. Well, sort of."

"You got cans for me?" she said.

"Yeah. Hang on a minute," Davie said and disappeared in the garage.

The old woman got off the bike and stood by it, watching Sonny. Behind the cat eye tortoiseshell glasses, her eyes were as bright and alert as those of a spring robin.

"What'cha got in the box?" Sonny said as he dried his hands on a paper towel.

"Cans. Aluminum cans. You got any cans?"

"No, not right now I don't."

"Well, if you get any, save 'em for me. I'll be back to get 'em."

"Okay," Sonny said. "I'll do that. Say, I'm thirsty. Think I'll go get a soda pop. You want one?"

"Sure, if you got orange. I only like orange."

"Okay. You watch my stuff. I'll go get us one."

"Don't take too long. I ain't got no silver spoon in my mouth. I gotta go."

"Okay. I'll be right back."

When Sonny came back with his Diet Coke and an Orange Crush for the homeless woman, she was teaching Little Davie the finer points of aluminum-can crushing.

"See, what I do is twist 'em like this," she said, holding the can top and bottom and twisting them in opposite directions, collapsing the sidewalls. "Then I squash 'em with my fingers like this." She held the can at the top and bottom with her thumbs and fingers and squeezed the can down to less than half of its original height, showing remarkable strength in her blue-veined hands. "That's so I can carry more of 'em," she said as Sonny handed the orange soda to her. "I'm not getting very many today. I think somebody's been watching me. Stealing 'em before I get there."

"You think so?"

"Oh, yeah, they're worth money ya know."

"Really?" Sonny said, giving Little Davie a wink.

"Oh, yeah, why I'm collecting them."

"Maybe I ought to keep 'em if they're valuable."

"You said you'd give 'em to me."

"Oh, yeah. Guess I did. What do you think, Davie?"

"I told her I'd save them for her."

"He did too. A bagful. I been showing him how to crush 'em."

"Well, okay then. I guess we'll have to save 'em for you," Sonny said.

"Well, I gotta go. I ain't got a silver spoon in my mouth."

Sonny said, "Hey, what's your name, so I know who we're saving the cans for?"

"Elaine," she said. "Name's Elaine. Be sure and crush 'em down. Don't let nobody else have 'em. I gotta go. I ain't got a silver spoon in my mouth ya know. Gotta go."

"See you later."

Elaine disappeared down the alley, heading south, just as she'd done the day before. Little Davie drank the last of his coffee, watching her go.

"Looks like you've got a new girlfriend, Davie. The mistress of aluminum cans."

Little Davie shook the last few drops from his mug and said, "I think we both do."

That afternoon, Sonny took a thirty-five-gallon cardboard container that car-wash soap had been shipped in, and put it next to the soda machines in the customer lounge. He wrote "ALUMINUM CANS" on it with a black marker, then added "FOR ELAINE" underneath. Caleb strolled over from his perch behind the front counter.

"What's up, Pop?"

"Figured I'd put this here. Save soda cans."

"For the old lady on the three-wheel bike?"

"Yeah."

"Santos told me he sees her all over downtown, riding her bike, hauling aluminum cans. He said he's pretty sure she's living in an abandoned Rio Grande boxcar on Sierra Madre Street, next to the old lumberyard."

"Funny old gal. Tough, too. She jacked Little Davie up a couple days ago."

"Yeah. Santos told me."

"At least she's doing somethin' besides begging on the street. There's bums everywhere in town, begging."

"Lotsa folks are plenty pissed off about it. That's for sure."

"I don't figure it'll hurt none to help the old girl out, though," Sonny said. "I hope business picks up."

"Me too, Pop. But it will once we get through with tax season. And I did sell a set of mag wheels to a GI with his tax return money this morning."

"Keep it up. We got a lotta mouths to feed around here."

"Sure, Pop."

Elaine came the next day, and the ones after that, until she was expected every morning around ten thirty. As time passed, she became kind of a rough mascot for the place, even though her personality—as well as her demeanor—was a long way outside the norm. Warm and fuzzy she was not, but her behavior somehow made the mechanics and service technicians want to care for her, like a feral cat who accepts handouts but won't allow itself to be domesticated. Maybe her attraction was her absolute honesty. With Elaine, what you saw was what you got . . . no more and no less, no better and no worse.

By the first of July, Elaine had Sonny and Caleb, Roger the front-end alignment man, Little Davie, and all eight mechanics saving . . . and properly crushing . . . aluminum cans for her. Even Eloise and Bertha, the two ladies in the bookkeeping department, were bringing their soda cans in from home for her.

Elaine, like a wild kitty, had an innate sense of people: she knew, or sensed somehow, which of the men at the garage to trust, and which ones to avoid. And despite their rocky beginning, she always favored Little Davie over all the others. Davie was her guardian angel, and she was his pet. When the chain broke on her trike, Little Davie fixed it. When she got a flat, he repaired it for her, as if she were one of his children, which, come to think of it . . . maybe she was.

On Monday, the second week of September, Elaine didn't show up at ten thirty like she had each and every other workday since March.

Little Davie came back from his coffee break and went straight to work mounting and balancing a set of radials on a three-year-old Lincoln Town Car. He didn't say much, just kept to his workstation, banging on wheels and tires with a little more force than was necessary.

Out front, Caleb was busy writing work orders and selling his fifth set of tires since noon the day before. When Sonny came back from a visit to his Northside Tires store over on Academy Boulevard, he parked in front on Nevada Avenue and came in the main door. It was just after lunch.

"Hey, Caleb . . . whaasup?"

Caleb didn't look up from the repair order he was writing. "Be with you in a minute, sir." He totaled the ticket, then glanced up and said, "Oh. Hey, Pop, been busy up here. You better go see Little Davie. Elaine's missing."

"Missing?"

"Well, she didn't show up this morning."

"Maybe she's busy doing something else."

"You know better than that, Pop."

When Sonny walked out into the ten-bay garage, he could tell something was wrong. Six mechanics had showed up to work that day, but only two were working. The other four, plus Little Davie and Roger, were all out back in the fenced-in parking area standing around Elaine, who was sitting on a white plastic lawn chair holding a can of Orange Crush to a lump and scratch on her head. She was rocking back and forth like a little kid who needs the bathroom.

"What the matter?" Sonny said.

Little Davie looked up from his crouch next to the distraught old woman. "Some son of a bitch knocked her off her trike a couple of hours ago. She's been wanderin' around tryin' to find it, and finally made her way in here. We got her to sit down and relax, so she could tell us what happened."

"She know who did it?"

"No."

As Sonny was about to say something else, Santos drove into the lot with his white parts truck. He leaned out the window and said to Little Davie, "I saw her bike."

Little Davie leaned over and whispered something to Elaine, then stood up and got in the truck with Santos. His bulk, barely fitting in the small cab, made the pickup list to one side. "Show me," was all he said.

Elaine stopped rocking and watched them go. Sonny sent the mechanics back to work and sat down on a metal milk crate next to her. "Such a pretty day, think I'll just sit here awhile. That be okay with you, Elaine?"

She opened her orange soda and took a sip, saying nothing, her eyes as big as raisin cookies. They sat there together for almost an hour before Santos and Little Davie came back with Elaine's three-wheeler in the pickup bed.

When she saw them, Elaine stood and said, "My bike. That's my bike. I gotta go now. Gotta go. I ain't got a silver spoon in my mouth ya know." As soon as Santos stopped and Little Davie put the bike on the ground, Elaine laid claim to it. "That's my bike ya know."

"Yes, I do," Little Davie said. "Are you okay to ride it? Are you dizzy or hurt?"

"Yes. No. And no. I gotta go. I'm after cans. Aluminum cans."

"Oh, yeah. Here's some bills and change from Roscoe. For your last load that was stolen from you."

"You know Roscoe?"

"Everybody knows Roscoe, if they're selling scrap metal in Colorado Springs."

Elaine took the cycle, got on the seat, then got off and checked the box and rope on the back. She fussed with a couple of knots, then put her arms around Little Davie. With her face sideways against his chest, and her eyes shut tight, she gave him a quick squeeze. Then she got on her trike and rode south, like every other day. "I ain't got no silver spoon in my mouth ya know. Gotta go." It was the only time any of them could remember she'd touched anyone, or allowed anyone to touch her. She was odd that way.

"What did you say to her?" Sonny asked Little Davie.

"Said I was gonna go get her bike."

"What happened?"

Little Davie just shook his head and said, "I need to go back to work."

"Yeah," Sonny said. "You think I oughta pay you full wages for today?"

"Didn't think about it. Probably not. Don't really care, Sonny. Guess it's up to you anyway," Davie said as he started inside.

"Course I'm gonna pay you. I oughta give you a bonus. It was a damn fine thing to do." It was later in the afternoon before Sonny heard Caleb and Santos talking about it at the front counter.

"Dude. It was awesome." Santos said. "Do not, and I mean not *ever*, make Little Davie mad. I never seen nothing like it, and I seen a lot of fights in my time."

"You guys were gone for quite a while," Caleb said.

"It took some time to find him. I saw him on Eighth Street, so that's where we headed, over to Wally World, but no luck. So we went north, checking behind the shopping centers and fast food joints. Then Little Davie said to start back and we went over to Colorado Avenue, spotted him by chance at Roscoe's."

"The guy who buys junk?"

"Yeah. Anyway, Davie says, real quiet-like, 'Pull into Roscoe's. In front.' Then I saw him too. So I pull in, right in front of the guy. He was on Elaine's bike, getting ready to take off. Had one foot on the ground and the other one on a pedal. Anyway, Davie jumps out, doesn't say a word. Walks three steps and grabs the old bum that's got her bike. Davie took hold of him by the shirt with one hand and the nuts with the other and jerked him right off of the seat, smooth-like, and in one motion pitches him about ten or twelve feet over in a pile of Roscoe's junk." Santos lit a cigarette and took a drag, put the lighter in his shirt pocket.

Caleb lit up too. "Little Davie never said anything?"

"No. Not at that point. He picked the trike up and set it in the parts truck. Meanwhile, the old buzzard don't know enough to quit. He came up with a three-foot piece of water pipe, gonna bash Little Davie in the back of the head with it. When he gets almost up to him, Little Davie spins around, fast-like, you know, and backhands the bum. Right in the chops." Santos dragged on his cigarette, tapped the ash. "Dude, I seen blood 'n' teeth fly. Two or three of 'em and the old buzzard goes on his ass again. Only this time Davie's right on top of him. You can't believe how fast that man can move. I see Davie pick him up by the front of his shirt and he says, 'If I was you, I'd hop my ass right on over to the rail yard there and catch me the next freight train leaving town. Not go messing around or hurting old ladies who never done nothin' to you. You *sabe*? Don't let me catch you around here again, *pendejo*. I'll put you under a moving train.'"

"You heard him?" Caleb asked.

"Yeah. He was about five inches from the guy's face when he said it in a real conversational tone . . . like it didn't matter to him, one way or the other. But his voice was just as cold as the fifteenth day of December. I believed him. I think the old buzzard did too. He staggered off toward the train tracks."

"Damn," Caleb said.

Sonny just grinned and went back to his office thinking, *I just love it when a fellow marine puts the old training to use, semper fi, Little Davie. Semper fi.*

Business at Southside Tires was good, and September's weather continued sunny, warm, and mild, but with an underlying cold edge to it that let everyone know winter was out there lurking, waiting for the unwary—like bad news from home.

It came on the twentieth of October. The jet stream dipped down, bringing a blast of arctic air and a severe cold front right as warm, moist air blew up from the Gulf of Mexico. The two fronts crashed together over southern Colorado, and overnight, Colorado Springs went from the Fourth of July to the dead of winter. Temperatures dropped fifty degrees in a few hours, accompanied by two feet of snow. Unprepared, the city was paralyzed.

At Southside Tires, the phones were jammed with customers wanting snow tires, car-start services, or tow trucks so they could come in and get their cars winterized. The whole place was a madhouse, and by three thirty in the afternoon they had sold out their entire stock of ice and snow tires . . . a whole warehouse full.

Little Davie, Roger, and four mechanics were all tire busting, mounting and balancing snow tires as fast as they could. And although sold out, they hadn't run out . . . and would all be working overtime to get every customer on the road. It was so busy for so long, no one noticed that Elaine had failed to show up for the second time.

The storm hit on Wednesday morning, a little after midnight. That day and most of Thursday continued at the same cold and frenetic pace for everyone at Southside Tires. It wasn't until Friday that the extra storm activity settled down and the normal, heavy pace of work returned.

A Springs Police Department detective named Parker showed up, late that Friday afternoon. He and Sonny disappeared into Sonny's office, and moments later Sonny's voice came over the intercom: "Little Davie to my office."

Out in the shop, Davie Clark laid the tire he was changing on its side and wiped his hands on a red shop rag. He dusted his pants with his hands as he climbed the stairs to Sonny's office. He heard Sonny's voice from the open door as he went into the room.

"No apparent reason . . ."

"Not that we know . . ."

Little Davie walked in, and whatever was about to be said next, wasn't.

"Davie, this is Detective Parker. He's here because of Elaine."

"She okay?"

"No. We found her bludgeoned to death on Tuesday evening in that old boxcar she was living in, just before the storm hit."

Davie sank down on a plastic chair that groaned under his size and weight. "Aw, shit," he said, "aw shit."

"Sorry to tell you, man—I know you looked out for her."

"She never hurt nobody. She's autistic. She's just a poor sad old homeless woman who's collecting cans for a living. Who the hell would hurt someone like her? She never done nothing to nobody."

"I know," Parker said, "that's the rub. It's sad. Homeless people, once they're living rough, out-of-doors like she was, have a life expectancy of about two and a half years before disease or crime kills them. If there's any good news, it's that we have the perpetrators. They're a couple of teenage thrill killers. The little bastards are brothers. One's eighteen and the other's twenty. It won't matter what kind of high-priced, high-powered legal talent the parents bring in, either. They still had the weapons and some of the old woman's blood on them. The little fuckers turned on each other and started squealing as soon as we got 'em in separate interrogation rooms. The damndest thing is, they were born with silver spoons in their mouths. They live in a gated community down on the southwest side of the city. Mumsie and Papa inherited money. She's an heiress to some kind of health-and-beauty-aids fortune. He's helping her spend it, and they're both lushes."

"Were they jacked up on drugs or something?" Sonny asked.

"No. They weren't. Just a couple young punk shitheads is all I can say. They confessed. Said that they did it just because they wanted to see what it felt like to kill someone. We have 'em on tape. They'll do time, no matter what. That's all I can tell you," Parker said. "I've got nineteen years in law enforcement and I've never seen a crime that makes less sense."

"How'd they . . . ?" Sonny said.

"Baseball bats," Parker said. "They sneaked up on her as she was sleeping. She never had a chance. Never woke up."

Little Davie looked at Parker with eyes that could have drilled a hole in half-inch steel plate. "Any chance I might have a few moments of quality time with the two of them?"

"None. I've already said more than I should have. I did it because I've known Sonny more than forty years. We went to grade school together."

"Oh."

Little Davie Clark, a man who'd "walked the walk" on the deserts of Kuwait and Iraq during two tours as a combat infantryman; a man with two purple hearts, a bronze star, and a silver star with a "V" for valor; a man who'd been treated at Walter Reed Army Medical Center for two months after returning Stateside; a man with 250 scars on his body from bomb fragments and small arms rounds; a man who dearly loved his country, could not understand what had become of his country, or the place he lived. It was the place where he'd been born and raised. A place known as "Little London," or "Newport in the Rockies," where the rich were very, very rich, and the poor were exquisitely so. And while the rich lived in million-dollar mansions behind high walls and gated entrances watched by old men in guard uniforms, the poor camped in the parks, under bridges, and in abandoned, rotting boxcars adjacent the decaying, old part of the downtown. As the rich talked to their brokers or accountants and clipped their bond coupons from Granddaddy's fortune, the poor searched through the garbage for aluminum cans and counted their pennies and begged for handouts, while the rest of the city just wished they would disappear.

Oh, yeah, Little Davie thought, *some of them are crazy, or drunks, some just don't give a shit. But so are the rich crazy or drunken or uncaring. Only difference is they're called "eccentric." Eccentric my ass* . . . So he sat there with his head bowed, a humble and proud man, wrapped in grief . . . surrounded by ghosts and memories of old ladies and silver spoons, bewildered, unsure where to direct his growing anger . . . and wondering what kind of a world his children were inheriting.

THE GHOSTS OF CHRISTMAS PRESENT

The Ghosts of Christmas Present

Yazzie and Darrel Lee had fallen on hard times . . . their circumstances so reduced that by the first week of December, they were living under the bridge at Cimarron Street and Interstate 25.

They were both drinking men, prone to lapses of memory and blackouts, their livers hard and their brains pickled from years of hundred proof and cheap beer.

Yazzie's health problems were more complex. Teenage glue sniffing, plus a jones for pharmaceuticals of any description had left a legacy of brain and nerve damage, which caused him to go into involuntary convulsions every so often. Without preamble, his eyes would roll up in his head until only the whites showed, he'd convulse for a minute or two, first going rigid, unable to move, shaking and clacking his teeth so violently that he'd cracked his molars a couple of times, but then he'd recover, and carry on as if nothing had happened. He called the attacks "brain-pukes" and laughed them off. Other than that, he was as regular as anybody . . . and great fun to party with. You just had to empty the medicine cabinet and lock the stuff in the trunk of your car whenever he was around.

Their hard times began when Darrel Lee went on a monolithic bender and fell four or five payments behind on his rent, which pissed off the manager of the Campers Hamlet Trailer Court to no end, because fifty-five dollars was due each and every Friday for Darrel Lee's ancient eight-by-fifty-foot Holiday Rambler mobile home. There were no exceptions. Payday was Friday, rent day was Friday—by nine o'clock p.m.—or a five-dollar-per-day late charge was added. After seven or eight—or maybe it was nine or ten, nobody knew for sure anymore—weeks of missed rent days, plus thousands of dollars worth of unpaid late charges, dodges, diversions, and general hoodwinking on Darrel Lee's part, Pete Hardon, the owner, CEO, and general manager of the Campers Hamlet Trailer Court, decided he'd had enough. Entertaining as he was, as likable a cuss as you'd ever want to meet, Darrel Lee wasn't ever gonna pay up. He had to go.

Well good luck with that plan. If you thought the jumpin' and dodgin' was bad before, well, "you ain't seen nuthin' yet," as the circus barker said. Once he got wind of the pending eviction, Darrel Lee became like smoke around there. He'd lived in Campers Hamlet for nearly nine years and considered it his home. There were nice big cottonwoods for shade, and there was Fountain Creek along the south side. It flooded the campground once or twice each summer, but the water never came up much past the porch, and it was always gone in a few days. Of course there was the mud and mosquitoes afterward, but that mess all went away in a couple of weeks, and mosquitoes never bit Darrel Lee. Yazzie was a different story, though, and he had bites and sores and scabs all summer long from their constant attacks on his flesh. Darrel Lee no longer noticed the 25 or so coal trains that passed through every day on the Burlington Northern Santa Fe tracks situated less than seven hundred feet from his front door. He was so used to them— and the rumble and shaking as the 125 car unit trains went north to Wyoming and south to Texas and Oklahoma all day every day, and all night every night—they weren't even on his radar screen anymore. And the truth was, unless the wind was blowing the wrong way, or the air was real wet and heavy . . . of a morning, say . . . he no longer smelled the sewage treatment plant that was located a half mile down the road. Traffic from the garbage trucks wasn't much of a bother as they headed in an unending stream for the transfer station. It was down on Las Vegas Street, which ran alongside the railroad tracks, and Darrel Lee never used it. He just drove past it on Nevada Avenue, turned in at the tire recapping plant, took a shortcut through their business, and just like a rabbit in a briar patch, he was in Campers Hamlet and home. *It's a great place to live. I love it*, he thought to himself, *and there ain't nobody gonna throw me out of it neither. Yessir, by God . . . nobody.*

It took another eighteen weeks of chasing the ever-more elusive Darrel Lee before Mr. Hardon got the sheriff to evict him. But even that didn't quite work. Darrel Lee moved into a lean-to he'd built on the side of the Holiday Rambler. He set up cots for himself and Yazzie, installed his Coleman camp stove and ice chest, and used an old clothes dryer for heat, stealing the electric to run it by splicing into the overhead power poles using some Romex cable he'd scrounged up. Darrel Lee was handy with any kind of tool and resourceful as an Eagle Scout. Some that knew him said he could take an old car transmission and a lawnmower and build an airplane . . . or something. Yessir. Darrel Lee was right handy when he set his mind to it.

The beginning of the end for Darrel Lee started when Yazzie came to town last spring. Those two made quite a pair of boyos: one was bad and the other one worse . . . what one didn't think of . . . the other one did. They were drinking all the time too. It got so bad that they were drunk eighteen hours a day and passed out the other six, and that's when Peter Hardon engineered his revenge.

Yazzie and Darrel Lee left early one morning in Darrel Lee's old '66 Chevy pickup to go fishing on the Arkansas River, down by Florence, Colorado. They started drinking early and were well oiled by lunchtime, sleeping it off in the shade of an old iron bridge where they'd been fishing with worms. Yazzie woke first. He nudged his companion and said, "Yo.

Darrel Lee. Wake up, man."

Darrel Lee made a nasty noise, cleared his throat, rolled over and curled up with his knees pulled toward his chest, then put his hands between his legs and snored.

Yazzie tried again. "Hey. Wake up. It's near dark. We gotta go. C'mon, Darrel Lee." This time he shook his pal.

Darrel Lee woke up. "Ugh. Izzit party time?"

"No. It's gonna be dark soon. We gotta go home."

"Kay, Yaz. Okay. 'M gettin' up. Any beer left?"

"Nope."

"Shit."

They gathered up their fishing gear and the garbage sack full of empties, put everything in the truck, and started for home. Darrel Lee's pickup had a wooden topper on it that he'd made from salvaged plywood, but it didn't have a door, so they made sure the gear was tucked in behind the tailgate before they pulled out for the forty-five-minute drive back to Colorado Springs.

It was dark when they came up Nevada Avenue and turned in at the G.D. Brewster Tire Service. They made a beeline for Darrel Lee's lean-to with the headlights off and got the shock of their lives . . .

It was gone.

Not only was the lean-to gone, the eight-by-fifty-foot Holiday Rambler mobile home with the two-tone ivory-and-pink paint job was history too. Where Darrel Lee used to live was now a thirty-by-eighty-foot patch of newly turned and freshly graded earth, with bits of glass, flakes of paint, and some broken chrome letters that spelled "Holiday Rambler Corp., Brazil, Indiana" in two-inch cursive script. The trailer and lean-to . . . and their entire contents . . . had been broken apart and crushed that very afternoon and hauled to the dump in two ten-wheel dump trucks while Yazzie and Darrel Lee slept in the shade under the iron bridge. A big yellow-and-black diesel-powered excavator sat where the trailer and lean-to had been when they'd left to go fishing that morning.

"Sonofabitch," Yazzie said. "What happened here?"

Darrel Lee was too stunned to answer at first. *All my shit,* he thought, *gone. My clothes, gone. My tools, gone. My food, gone. Everything I had is gone. It's gone. It's all gone.* He looked at the bare ground where his home used to be and blinked several times in the dark to hold back the tears. He said, "The dirty bastard. The sorry little sonofabitching, shit-eating motherfucker. He won't get away with it."

"Who?"

"Peter-fucking-Hardon. That's who," Darrel Lee said as he put the pickup in reverse. He drove over to Walmart, and they totaled up their combined liquid net worth in the parking lot and found it to be exactly eighty-seven dollars and forty-two cents—all but fifteen dollars attributable to Darrel Lee, who'd been working for a house remodeler. He'd been tearing out lath and plaster walls in a Victorian house over on West Pikes Peak Avenue for ten bucks an hour, paid in cash, under the table. "Okay. I'm gonna get us some camping supplies," Darrel Lee said. "We'll have to go get a frying pan at Goodwill in the morning. You coming in?"

"Nah. I'll wait out here. Get some smokes and beer."

They camped on Fountain Creek that night, about a half mile south of the Campers Hamlet Trailer Park, where there was a group of other homeless folks in an enclave down there. Luckily it was only early October and the weather was still mild. It was too dark to do anything when they got there, so Yazzie slept in the bed of the pickup and Darrel Lee bunked on the front seat.

Sometime after three a.m., Darrel Lee eased out of the pickup cab and walked up the creek to Campers Hamlet. He crept over to the vacant lot where his home used to be and poured a pound of Great Western pure white granulated sugar into the fuel tank of the Caterpillar excavator. For good measure, he urinated all over the seat, the instrument panel, and the controls.

There, he thought. *That'll smell just dandy in the sun and heat.* He giggled all the way back to the campsite.

Yazzie heard Darrel Lee come back and get in the pickup, just as he'd heard him leaving an hour or so before. *I wonder what he's got up to . . .* Yazzie lay quietly in the truck bed, too cold to sleep. *I'll see if he says anything about it in the morning.*

They got up at first light, tired from lack of sleep, stiff and sore from the cold. Darrel Lee, his breath steaming in the damp said, "Let's go to 7-Eleven, get coffee."

"Yeah."

They drove up Nevada Avenue to the all-night convenience store and bought two large coffees, a box of powdered doughnuts, and five dollars worth of gas. Darrel Lee took a sip of coffee and a bite of doughnut.

"We're about out of money."

Yazzie said, "Yeah. We gotta get something better for tonight too. I didn't hardly sleep at all last night, for the cold." He waited to see what Darrel Lee was going to say next, to see if he said anything about last night's three a.m. ramble.

"I hear that. We'll have to get some sleeping bags or we'll freeze our asses off."

Yazzie sipped his coffee, watching Darrel Lee over the rim of the cup. He waited for more. When Darrel Lee didn't talk about where he'd gone last night, Yazzie was quiet, kept his own counsel. He decided not to mention just yet about the drunk he'd jackrolled out back of Wally World while Darrel Lee was inside. It had been way easy; happened almost by accident when Yazzie went behind the building to pee. There was a chain-link fence and a big ditch back there, separating the parking and delivery bays from I-25 southbound. Yazzie had finished urinating and was tucking himself back in when a voice came from the other side of the fence.

"Shay, pal. You wanna drink? C'mon an' have a drink with me."

"Where are you? Where you at?"

"I'm here. By the hole. I'm shel'bratin', and I ain't got nobody to shel'brate wif."

Yazzie found the hole in the fence someone had cut and saw a figure sitting on the edge of the ditch in the tall dry grass. The headlights of passing cars on the interstate illuminated them briefly and then disappeared in a flash of red taillights that looked like a ruby necklace in the distance.

"I see you," Yazzie said as he sat down on the drunk's right side. "Howdy," he added.

"Here, have a drink and shel'brate wif me." He handed Yazzie a near-full pint of Jack Daniel's Black Label bourbon.

"Damn, boy. You drinkin' the good stuff," Yazzie said as he took a big snort. "What're we celebrating?"

"Shel'bratin' the United States of 'Merica an' its sosh'curity shystem. Got my first sheck today. S'why I'm shel'bratin' tonight. Go 'head. Drink up." The drunk laughed to himself.

Yazzie upended the bottle again, but tongued it, not drinking. He said, "So, did you cash it?"

"What do you think?" The drunk said as he took another swig and handed the bottle back to Yazzie.

"I would've," Yazzie said as he propped the bottle behind himself, moved in close, and put his left arm around the drunk man's shoulder. Yazzie gave a look around, tightened his grip, and delivered two short, vicious blows to the man's right temple with his fist. He was out cold. Yazzie thought, *He won't even remember anything in the morning.* He gave the guy a third, harder shot for good measure. He went through the pockets, found the cash wad in the right sock and stuck it in his jeans, then rolled the guy into the ditch. He put the cap on the pint of Black Jack and stuck it in his hip pocket, headed back to the truck.

When Yazzie came to Colorado Springs and moved in with his old friend Darrel Lee, he'd just finished serving fifty-four months of a six-to-ten-year jolt at McAlester for assault and arson in the first degree. He'd put his time at the Oklahoma State Penitentiary to good use . . . being instructed in the finer points of criminality by the best of the best in the business. Yazzie had been an apt and eager student. "Never waste an opportunity" was one of the first dictums he'd mastered.

Yazzie took a doughnut out of the box, bit it in half, and washed it down with lukewarm coffee, waiting for Darrel Lee to say something. He didn't have to wait long.

Darrel Lee put the doughnut he was eating on the dashboard, sipped his coffee. "We're down to about the cost of a pack of cigarettes, Yaz."

"I figured as much," Yazzie said, feeling good about the 260 dollars he had in his left boot.

"So I'm gonna go over to that house remodeler, see if he's got anything for me to do today. Maybe he can use both of us."

"I'm down with that."

They drove over to the West Pikes Peak construction site to see if Joe Thomas had a day's work for them.

There was still an hour and a half before Joe came to work at eight, so Darrel Lee and Yazzie spent most of the time in the fifteen-yard roll-off, digging through the construction debris for stuff they could use. Darrel Lee, the smaller of the two, climbed in the trash and started tossing things out; Yazzie put them in the truck.

"That's all the lumber, Yaz. I'm gonna throw a couple of cement blocks."

"Pitch 'em."

"Coming at you."

The last items Darrel Lee tossed out were three stainless steel shelves from an old refrigerator.

"Best fireplace grilles made," Yazzie said as he picked them up. "Looks like plenty of firewood too."

"Oh, yeah," Darrel Lee said. "I can probably make better use of some of it."

They were sitting in the truck smoking as Joe Thomas drove up at eight o'clock. When he saw Darrel Lee, he pulled alongside and rolled down the window. "Darrel Lee, where you been?"

"Sorry, Joe. Had some business I had to take care of. But I'm ready to work if you can use me. I brung Yazzie here if you can use him too."

"You guys sober?"

"More or less."

"Mostly more or mostly less? I ain't got time for horseshit, Darrel Lee."

"We're sober, Joe. Ain't drank since yesterday."

"Nothin' today?"

"Nope. Scout's honor." Darrel Lee didn't know about the half-pint of Jack Daniel's Black that Yazzie had plundered and polished off this morning with his coffee and doughnuts while Darrel Lee was in the bathroom at the 7-Eleven.

"Your buddy—what's his name?"

"Yazzie."

"Yazzie strong?"

"Oh, yeah."

"He understand the deal?"

"Ten an hour cash. No benefits. Get hurt, your tough shit, you're outta luck."

"Sums it up. You understand, Yazzie?"

"Yeah, boss."

"Okay, you got the job. Get on the wrong end of a square shovel in there, shovel plaster in the wheelbarrow. Empty the wheelbarrow in the roll-off. Don't stop 'til I tell you to or there ain't no more plaster on the floor." They went in the building through a side door. It had a piece of plywood nailed on where a window used to be. "Over there," Joe said to Yazzie, pointing with his index finger at a well-used wheelbarrow and a short-handled shovel. "Get after it."

"Let the crying start and the heartache begin," Yazzie said as he picked up the shovel and began scooping up the piles of plaster bits and chunks and shoveling them in the wheelbarrow. White plaster dust started filling the room.

"What about me?" Darrel Lee said.

"Don't worry, sweetheart, I got you covered."

Darrel Lee found himself on the roof of the two-and-a-half-story house ten minutes later. With a five-gallon bucket, fifty feet of half-inch nylon rope, a two-pound hammer and a chisel, he was tasked with removing a pair of square brick chimneys. Brick by brick, he knocked them out with the hammer, put them in the bucket, and lowered the bucket to the ground. "Where you want the bricks, Joe?"

"Stack 'em on the pallet that's leaned against the back wall. Neatly, boyo, neatly. Don't make a mess."

"Be faster if you have Yaz empty the bucket when he dumps the wheelbarrow."

"Good idea, Darrel Lee, I'll tell him."

By lunchtime, Darrel Lee had torn the top seven feet of chimney down on the first one, and two feet off of the second one. He was sick from the sunburn and fluid loss. He looked like a greasy, gray boiled lobster when he came down for a lunch of powdered doughnuts and Pepsi-Cola. His clothes, hands, and face were black from soot, and he smelled as rank as ten-day-old garbage.

Yazzie was covered in lime and horsehair plaster dust. It was caked in his eyebrows and hair, plugged his eyes, ears, and both nostrils, and his clothes were coated so badly, he gave off puffs of white dust with each step.

When Joe saw them, he started laughing. "By Christ if the two of yez don't look like Casper and Sambo."

Darrel Lee, who grew up in a rundown trailer court in southeast Oklahoma City, the son of a sometimes-working, always hard-drinking racist father, took offense. He said, "Don't call me no nigger names."

"I don't use racial slurs, Darrel Lee. I just said you two look like Casper and Sambo."

Darrel Lee was sick, sore, and spoiling for a fight. He jumped up and charged at Joe Thomas, who stepped to the side and shoved Darrel Lee, who went face-first on the floor. Yazzie, who'd been there, done that and wound up in the penitentiary for it, got between the combatants as Darrel Lee came to his feet looking for more. He said, "That's enough, Darrel Lee."

"You better quit while you're ahead, boy." Joe said.

Darrel Lee felt all the anger and frustration of the last months boiling to the surface and combining with the fear of the unknown he'd been trying to push back into his subconscious. He said, "I ain't your nigger and I goddamn for sure ain't your boy, neither."

"Listen here, pal, I didn't come lookin' for you this morning. You don't like it, you can clear the fuck outta here right now," Joe said. He had anger in his eyes and a flush on his face. He stood like he was preparing to fight both of them.

"Maybe you better just give us our wages," Yazzie said, "and we'll go."

"Good idea." He peeled four twenty-dollar bills from the cash he'd pulled from his pocket and handed it to Yazzie, who was still standing between the other two men.

"Here's your money. Four hours each at ten per. Don't come back. I can't use yez."

"We won't," Darrel Lee said. "We damn for sure won't."

It was the last time either one of them worked for hourly wages.

When Darrel Lee and Yazzie got in the pickup, there was barely room to get their feet in. The front seat was filled with red chimney bricks.

"Damn, Yazzie, how many'd you get?"

"Coupla hundred. That ain't all. I got a claw hammer, a cat's paw pry bar, and a three-foot steel crowbar too."

Darrel Lee giggled and lit a cigarette. "I guess we better find a place to camp, get this stuff unloaded. We've got more than she can carry."

"I know a good place, down at the end of Chestnut Street, past the junkyards. The crick runs through there and we can walk to the store."

"Probably be somebody there already, don't you imagine?"

"Don't worry," Yazzie said, "I'll ask them to move."

"Think they will?"

"Oh, yeah."

There were no campers in the copse of elm and cottonwood trees where Fountain Creek came out from under the culvert south of Eighth Street, next to Highway 24 West. They set the campsite as far in the trees as they could, making it difficult to see from the highway. After unloading the bricks, old lumber, and cement blocks, they took a break and washed up in the stream. "We can sleep in the truck again tonight," Darrel Lee said, "but we gotta figure something else out. We've got about ninety-five dollars is all, and we gotta get sleeping bags and a tarp or something. We're gonna be screwed if the weather turns."

"Yeah. I hear ya there," Yazzie said.

"Got any ideas?"

"Let's go to the army surplus and get some sleepin' bags. And a tent."

"With what? They ain't gonna give us no tent just 'cause we're poor and good looking," Darrel Lee said as he chewed on a blade of grass, and watched the water heading east under the I-25 bridge, where it joined Monument Creek and went on south to the Gulf of Mexico.

"No, Yazzie said, "but they'll give it to us for this." He bent down where he was sitting on a cement block and pulled the money from his boot, showed it to Darrel Lee.

"Where'd it come from?"

"Wally World." Yazzie grinned like a young boy who'd just learned how to masturbate.

"Yeah." Then he told Darrel Lee how he'd gotten it.

"Aw, fuck, Yazzie. Fuck me backwards."

Thinking he was being criticized, Yazzie said, "Yeah, so what. Where the fuck were you last night, creepin' around? What was you up to?"

"I introduced Mr. Great Western sugar to Mr. Caterpillar excavator."

"Why?"

"It crystallizes inside the engine. Ruins it—the fuel and injector system too. Costs about twenty-five, thirty thousand to fix. Gotta overhaul or put a whole new motor in it."

"Well, shit. That's a helluva lot more than two hundred fifty dollars. What I got."

"You don't get it, Yaz. You don't get it." Darrel Lee looked at his friend for a long thirty or forty seconds, the fear and pain apparent in his eyes.

"Don't get what?"

"He's dead, Yazzie, he's dead. You killed him."

"How do you know?"

"There was a lady cop in the 7-Eleven this morning, when I went in to piss. She was talking to the clerk. They found him last night."

Yazzie looked out at the traffic for a moment, then said, "Guess we better not go to Wally World for a while."

Darrel Lee shook his head, and stared at the ground. He picked up a rock and threw it in the creek, shook his head again. "Let's go to the army surplus."

When they got in the pickup, Yazzie was as eager as a puppy with a yellow tennis ball. "Don't worry so much, Darrel Lee, nobody saw me."

Except all them security cameras on the building, Darrel Lee thought as he started the old Chevy truck in a haze of blue smoke. He kept to the backstreets getting to the army surplus on South Tejon Street. It was stuck in behind Luigi's Italian Restaurant and Nemeth's El Tejon Mexican. Glenn's was the store name.

They bought a pair of down sleeping bags, a six-by-eight canvas tent, and two mess kits—the kind with utensils inside. Yazzie was like a little kid, wanting to buy everything, but Darrel Lee restrained him. The last things they bought were a couple of hundred-foot skeins of quarter-inch rope and three rolls of duct tape.

Darrel Lee made two more stops: he went to a pawn shop, where he got a hatchet, a short-handled shovel, and a handsaw; and he went to the liquor store for three cases of Old Milwaukee and a quart of Jack Daniel's Black Label for Yazzie.

"Jeez, Yazzie, that shit's expensive."

"Yeah. It is."

Darrel Lee clenched his jaw, said nothing. They went back to their campsite and set to work with a purpose. By evening they had a wood platform Darrel Lee had built from scrap lumber, with the tent erected on top and tight. The platform was up on cement blocks with bricks dry laid in between to keep the critters out. The space had been filled with leaves, paper, Styrofoam, and plastic for insulation.

Yazzie dug drainage ditches and a fire pit in front of the tent flap and lined it with bricks around the outside.

"If you make the far side higher, Yaz, it'll reflect heat in the tent."

"Good idea. Every little bit helps."

The fire pit was about four feet across, and centered on the tent, about five feet away. It had the platform scraps in it and short pieces of a two-by-four. Darrel Lee, who'd gone through a six-pack while he was building the platform, poured a cup of gasoline from a gallon can he kept in the back of his truck and they had a cozy fire going before dark fell. They dined by firelight on hot dog and mustard sandwiches on white bread, washing them down with cheap beer and Black Jack bourbon. Yazzie had killed more than half of the bottle plus three or four beers by the time they got in their army surplus sleeping bags and passed out at ten minutes 'til nine. They didn't even notice all the traffic on the pair of four-lane highways intersecting at their bedside.

Just as the unrisen morning sun illuminated the sky a rosy pink that was scattered among broken gray clouds, Yazzie was awakened by a long-haul trucker coming down off I-25 southbound who hit the Jake brake, stopping for the light at Highway 24. He eased out of his sleeping bag and listened to the trucker running up through the gears as he disappeared over the Cimarron Street Bridge, and caught a faint whiff of diesel fumes as he pulled his boots on.

He put his fatigue jacket on over his T-shirt and walked up to Eighth Street, then crossed over the six lanes of Highway 24 to the all-night gas station and convenience store. He used the bathroom, drew two large coffees, and helped himself to handfuls of sugar packets that he put in his coat pocket. He put the two steaming cups on the cashier's counter, walked back, and got a package of iced cinnamon rolls.

"You'd better get lids for them," the woman in the booth behind the bulletproof glass said.

"Oh. Yeah. Guess I better," Yazzie said, flashing the boyish grin women found irresistible. He saw the woman had dirty blonde hair that hung to her shoulders, and the dead-flat look of defeat in her eyes. She also had tattoos on all ten fingers that she'd tried to cover up with rings, but Yazzie could read the "FUCKYOUALL" written there anyway. She had crude jailhouse tats that ran up both arms and the sides of her neck. *Damned if she don't look like she's been rode hard and put away dirty,* Yazzie thought as he paid for his purchases, stuck the rolls in a coat pocket, and went back across the highway in the early gray dawn. He could see his breath in the cold air.

When Yazzie got back, Darrel Lee was up and had the campfire going.

"Morning."

"Hey, Yazzie. Thanks." Darrel Lee took the coffee, put six packets of sugar in it, and stirred with a piece of twig from the kindling woodpile. He said, "How much money you got?"

"Dunno," Yazzie said, "about a hundred and twenty, I think."

"I've got a hundred and three. We'll have to get a few more things and you're gonna haveta quit that expensive shit you been drinkin'."

"Maybe."

"Maybe, my ass. We can't afford no thirty-dollar-a-bottle hootch."

Yazzie got his bottle out, saw there was about one-third of it left. He poured a big slug in his coffee. "Want some?"

"Oh, shit. Might's well."

They sipped their coffee.

"Good, ain't it?"

"Oh, yeah," Darrel Lee said. "It takes the heartache right outta life."

"Amen to that."

They killed the bottle with their cinnamon rolls as they got ready to face the world.

Over the next few days and weeks, they got their camp mostly squared away and were surviving in a Spartan kind of a way . . . and then the mid-October blizzard hit. Twenty-four inches of snow fell overnight, and they, like most of the rest of the city, were caught with their pants down.

Darrel Lee woke up before Yazzie on the morning of the big snow. The first thing he noticed was the cold. Overnight the temperature had dropped nearly fifty degrees, from the low seventies to the mid-twenties, and about two feet of snow had fallen. The snow was heavy; it was the wet kind that packed easy and turned to ice. He could see where the snow was pressing down on the tent ceiling, making it sag and hang down, almost to the point of collapse.

He burrowed deeper in the sleeping bag where it was warm. He needed to urinate, didn't want to get out of the warm, into the cold, knew he couldn't put it off much longer. *Ohhh, shit,* he thought as he unzipped the sleeping bag and found his shoes, started to put them on while trying not to wake Yazzie. He'd been wearing the same jeans and T-shirt for ten days and noticed he was a bit on the tangy side as he put on his sweatshirt and fatigue jacket, then opened the tent flap and crawled out. When he stood, the snow was past his knees.

This here is gonna be a ball-buster of a day, he thought as he went behind the biggest elm tree.

He rummaged around inside his truck, found the shovel and an old snow brush behind the seat, and retrieved the gallon gas can from the bed. There was about a pint left, he estimated.

By the time he trudged back to the camp, his shoes and feet were wet, and he was cold. He scratched his neck under his beard and cleared the snow out of the fire pit, found the driest wood in the pile, and doused it with most of the gasoline. When he lit it with his lighter, it made a whump, and the flashback burned the hair off of Darrel Lee's right hand. He was brushing the snow off of a cement block to sit on when Yazzie crawled out of the tent. "Where'd this crap come from?"

"I sure as hell didn't order it," Darrel Lee said.

"What did we drink last night?"

"Everything we had."

"Now I know why I feel like this."

"Why don't you go over and get us some coffee? I'll get the fire going."

"Okay," Yazzie said. "I need to shave anyway."

When Yazzie came back, he had two coffees, a box of cinnamon doughnuts, and a snow shovel.

"Where'd you get that?" Darrel Lee said, pointing at the shovel with his chin.

"Borrowed it from Miss Fuckyouall."

"Who?" Darrel Lee said, stirring six packets of sugar in his coffee.

"Miss Fuckyouall—it's what I call the heifer who runs the C-Store over there. It's what she's got tattooed on her fingers, one letter per each."

"She must be a piece of work."

"Yeah."

"She know you borrowed her shovel?"

"Nope."

Darrel Lee sneezed several times, then blew his nose on some paper napkins and tossed them in the fire. His wet shoes were steaming as he tried to dry them out close to the flames. He sipped his coffee and chewed on a doughnut, trying hard not to retch it back up.

Yazzie was on his third doughnut when he said, "You doin' okay?"

"Sure."

"You know, maybe we oughta go over to Marion House, the soup kitchen, have some lunch or somethin'. They tell me it's mighty fine and no questions asked."

"I don't accept charity, Yaz. I'll stand on my own damn feet. I ain't no bum."

"I'm just sayin' . . ."

"No. Don't ask me again."

"Kay, Darrel Lee. I just thought maybe some good food would help you. We been living on hot dogs and doughnuts."

"Don't forget Pepsi, beer, and whiskey," Darrel Lee said. "I ain't goin' to the fuckin' soup kitchen."

Yazzie finished his coffee, threw the cup in the fire, stood, and got the snow shovel. He cleared the campsite and woodpile, then said, "I'm gonna go shovel driveways and walks, make us some money."

"Good idea. I'll be better this afternoon," Darrel Lee said as he wiped his nose and opened his first Pepsi of the day.

It was Wednesday, October 25, the first day of the storm, and Yazzie did well. When he came back at seven o'clock that night, he brought a bag of hamburgers from the King's Chef over on Costilla Street, an eighteen-pack of beer, a quart of Black Jack he'd purchased—plus two pints of it he'd shoplifted—and best of all, $250 in cash.

"Damn, Yazzie, you are the man," Darrel Lee said as he took a bite of hamburger. Grease was running down his beard and disappearing under his chin, but he didn't seem to notice, or mind—he was already on his third beer.

"I'm gonna go out again tomorrow, see if I can't make us more money," Yazzie said as he took a barbarian-sized bite from his second hamburger and washed it down with Pepsi. The snow had tapered off during the afternoon, but the wind had picked up. Snow was blowing and drifting and the wind was beating the tent, making it flap and shake. Even their lantern was swaying back and forth on the center ridgepole. They finished their meal and snuggled into their sleeping bags to keep warm. Wrapped in their personal thoughts, they each had a pint of Black Jack bourbon for comfort. It was a long time before either of them slept, their breathing ragged . . . their dreams troubled.

The snow had come on Wednesday. On Thursday the city was iced over, and Yazzie didn't go out. Instead, they hung around the camp, drinking and eating beef 'n' bean burritos from the Mexican fast food joint across the street from the C-Store where Miss Fuckyouall worked. They felt secure for a day, but that icy Thursday was their last one of false prosperity.

The snow and ice melted off by the following Tuesday but the cold remained. Nights were the worst; the temperature dropped into the twenties and didn't rise much past the mid-thirties during the day. They'd scrounged, chopped, and burned all the dead wood in the camp area and were now forced to forage harder for more. They stole wood pallets whenever they saw one, but even with the old pickup truck to haul them, firewood was a daily problem they had to solve.

Other problems were piling up too: clean clothes, for example. When they first set up camp, all they had for clothes were the ones they were wearing. Everything else had been destroyed by Peter Hardon's Caterpillar excavator.

At first, they bought clothes at the Goodwill. As money became scarcer, they raided the Goodwill collection boxes and stole what they needed. They also became adept at trash diving, could spot usable items two blocks away.

Personal hygiene and sanitation were difficult to almost impossible. Yazzie, always vain about his personal appearance, managed to stay presentable by cleaning up and shaving over at the C-Store. He kept his hair short, cutting it himself at least once a week—as long as he was sober—and changing his clothing every four or five days. Darrel Lee, on the other hand, was Yazzie's exact opposite. Bald on top, he grew the rest of his hair long, past his collar, never washed or shaved unless pressed to clean up, because he smelled too bad. His beard was soon wild, coarse, and matted, his appearance growing worse and worse as the days and weeks passed. The pair's health was diminishing, as they were being ground down by the elements.

Then, in November, a couple of days before Thanksgiving, things really went sour. They'd been making money by stealing the copper ground wires from city light poles. Darrel Lee showed Yazzie how to remove the inspection cover from the base and pull the ground wire out, which they then sold to Roscoe, the scrap metal dealer over on Colorado Avenue.

With the price of number-one copper at four bucks per pound, they were living pretty good, as it only took a few hours for them to gather fifty or sixty pounds of it, which they sold to Roscoe the next day, no questions asked. The trouble was, their vandalism was costing the utilities department around twelve hundred dollars per pole to repair, and they weren't going to put up with it.

The city of Colorado Springs increased surveillance, asking all their employees to be on the lookout for the wire vandals. They began welding the inspection covers on, and the city council passed an ordinance requiring all the scrap metal dealers to obtain identification from all scrap sellers . . . which put Darrel Lee and Yazzie out of business.

They went to sell their blood plasma, worth thirty-five dollars per pint, which they could do every ten days. After mandatory blood tests for screening purposes, however, Yazzie was rejected. He tested positive for hepatitis B, which was incurable. Darrel Lee was okay to give plasma, but was told to sober up and wash up before coming back. He never did.

For a brief time, Yazzie considered resuming his career as a jackroller, but was scared of the consequences—including another trip to the penitentiary. He started panhandling in the downtown area on Tejon Street, making enough for them to keep drinking and smoking.

They went to the Springs Rescue Mission for Thanksgiving dinner and had their first real full meal since August. They resisted all attempts at proselytization, and carried off all the leftovers they could gather in a couple of plastic bags Yazzie brought for just that purpose. Going there, accepting a handout, seemed to take some intrinsic piece of Darrel Lee, a big bite out of his pride maybe, that he was never able to recover from . . . and their lives fell deeper into jeopardy by the day.

One big advantage Darrel Lee and Yazzie had had up to this point was Darrel Lee's forty-year-old '66 Chevy pickup truck, because it gave them freedom of movement, which allowed them more and larger opportunities for trash diving. They could cover large areas of town, from the shopping malls to residential areas, and carry more and larger booty back to their camp.

That advantage went away on Thanksgiving Day when the truck was impounded.

Darrel Lee and Yazzie went trash diving at the Citadel Mall, over on East Platte Avenue and Academy Boulevard. The Citadel Mall property covered one square mile of land and was a rich source of swag from the trash bins behind the mall stores. They never knew what they'd find— obsolete store displays, returned merchandise, almost new and barely damaged—the possibilities were endless. Once, they hit the mother lode when a thieving employee put a brand-new thirty-two-inch TV out in the trash, intending to retrieve it after work. Yazzie and Darrel Lee beat him to it. They ate and drank for two weeks on the proceeds of the television, which they sold to a used car dealer on their way home. But on Thanksgiving Day they had no luck and found nothing of value. They headed back downtown. Yazzie said, "Damn. I can't believe we got skunked. We never did before."

"It happens. If we don't get some money today we're gonna have to park the truck. We're out of gas and it's making noise in the front end. I can't fix it without tools."

"We gonna make it back t'camp?"

"Should, but just. She might not start again 'less we prime . . . Oh, shit. Hang on."

They were headed west on Platte Avenue, just past Prospect Street, when the right front wheel fell off and they slammed into the concrete retaining wall in the underpass. When they came to rest at the west side of the underpass, the right-front wheel and brake drum were shoved under the motor, and the right-front fender was shoved back where the wheel and tire were supposed to be. The hood was crumpled up by the windshield and the radiator was mashed over the engine. The street was covered with fluid.

"We're fucked," Darrel Lee said. "You hurt?"

"Nah. Whadda we do now?"

"Get out and walk away."

"What about the truck?"

"It's fucked. C'mon. Get what you can carry before the cops get here."

They climbed out the passenger side, pushing the door open past the mangled fender, where it hung like a torn ear. Walking away, heading south, the old truck reminded Darrel Lee of a sparrow that had flown into his mother's kitchen window when he was a boy, back in Oklahoma. He'd seen it, lying on the ground with its neck broken, head bent down and one wing outstretched, as if the bird were embarrassed by the mistake that cost it its life. It had been a good truck. He was sorry to see it go, and embarrassed, too.

On the hike back to their camp, Yazzie said, "Ain't you worried about the cops?"

"What for?"

"The truck. Leaving it there, with the plates on it and all?"

"Wasn't my plates. Belonged to the guy I bought the truck from. He left and went to Louisiana. Said he was gonna work on an offshore oil rig."

"Oh. Gettin' colder, ain't it?"

"Yeah."

Tired of citizen complaints, on the day after Thanksgiving in a rare display of cohesion and holiday spirit led by the mayor—a local stock tout with much ambition and no apparent leadership ability—the Colorado Springs City Council met in "executive session" and passed a no-camping ordinance. The word was passed from the city manager . . . a known credit-flake from California who'd been hired at a six-figure salary to sign the city's checks . . . to the chief of police, who passed it down to the cops in the cars. The result of which was, on the Tuesday after Thanksgiving, the cops and some city parks employees came and tore up Darrel Lee and Yazzie's camp.

There was no warning, no appeal, and no bargaining.

When they came at eight o'clock Tuesday morning to clean up and enforce the ordinance, there were two big cops and three city parks guys. The cops were pretty cool, gave Darrel Lee and Yazzie a half hour to clear out, and take whatever they could carry, they even told the park and rec guys to give the freshly dispossessed Yazzie and Darrel Lee some trash bags to carry their gear in. The cops stood around for a few more minutes, then got in their patrol car to keep warm.

The parks and rec guys, on the other hand, were clearly and thoroughly pissed off about drawing cleanup detail, and were trying to take it out on Darrel Lee, Yazzie, or any other poor unfortunates they were apt to encounter. All three made a show of putting blue rubber gloves and white face masks on, acting as if they were picking up radioactive bits and pieces of the Chernobyl reactor.

They kept looking at the cops out of the corners of their eyes and making their resentments known through snarky comments.

After awhile, Yazzie couldn't take it any more, picked out the biggest of the city guys, and said, "Whatsa matter, boy? Couldn't get it up for that pig you woke up next to this morning, or was she too tired from walking the streets all night?"

"What'd you say?"

"It was about the pig you woke up with. I asked if you couldn't get it up or . . ."

The parks and rec man lost it. He went apoplectic with rage and made a run at Yazzie, who managed to get behind the tent, out of sight. He also had a fist-sized rock in his right hand with which he clocked the big guy in the forehead. The parks and rec man was laid out flat, seeing nothing but night.

"Hey, boss," Yazzie yelled. "Got a man down. Man down over here." Yazzie bent over and used his thumb and middle finger to press on the carotid arteries, making sure he stayed out cold as his two coworkers rushed to help.

"What happened?" the first one said.

"Dunno," Yazzie said. "He came 'round the corner, next thing I knew he was on his ass. Musta slipped, hit his head on a tent peg or somethin'. Piece of firewood maybe." Yazzie pointed at several pieces of wooden pallet he and Darrel Lee had lying around.

The cops called the paramedics. They rolled in, sirens hot, in Engine Company Number Three's old red Oshkosh fire truck, followed by an AMR ambulance. The camp filled up with emergency responders while Yazzie and Darrel Lee gathered up what they could carry.

The parks and rec man started waking up when a fire department paramedic began taking his vital signs. "What happened? What's going on?"

"You slipped, hit your head on a tent peg," the paramedic said. "We're taking you in for observation." The EMTs loaded him in the ambulance and it disappeared, lights and sirens screaming, headed for Memorial Hospital.

Darrel Lee looked at Yazzie, who had a slight grin on his face. Yazzie made an almost imperceptible nod of his head, picked up a couple of trash bags, and they headed out, looking for another place to live. Someplace where they could rest easy and sleep warm, safe from predators and out of the elements . . . someplace dry.

With the weather getting colder, numbing their fingers and toes, with their breath condensing in clouds of steam that froze in their nostrils and formed ice on their eyebrows, mustaches, and beards, Darrel Lee and Yazzie trekked through lower downtown Colorado Springs all day. They only stopped twice, once at the soup kitchen where the warmth made their cold bodies ache . . . and their smell made people blink and step back when the odor hit them like a sonic wave, and the second time at the Drive-In Liquor store where they bought two pints of Ten High bourbon, spending their last twelve dollars in an attempt to keep warm.

With the temperature at ten above zero, they slept on the loading dock at the Ross Auction House that night, bunking on a pair of plaid couches left there for the next sale. They lucked out in the morning when the owner came in early. He took pity on them when Yazzie asked if they could do any odd jobs and paid them ten dollars each to sweep the loading dock and parking lot, which they did. He also told them, "Don't y'all make a habit of sleepin' here. Once was enough. Next time might not be so good. Understand?"

"Yeah," Darrel Lee said. "We do."

After a quick breakfast of oatmeal, toast, and coffee at the Marion House, and a bathroom break at the Penrose Public Library two blocks south, Darrel Lee and Yazzie walked around downtown, looking for a place to roost. They were each carrying two large black trash bags with what few possessions they still had, and they were wearing out.

There was an old abandoned Denver and Rio Grande boxcar next to the lumberyard that was closed and vacant, but it was padlocked and covered with yellow CSPD crime scene tape across the front.

"Looks like old blood all over the door and ground over here," Yazzie said.

"Yeah," Darrel Lee said. "This place has some bad juju. Let's get outta here."

They went south on Sierra Madre Street, crossed Cimarron, and holed up for a few days under the loading dock at the Roofing Supply, which was closed for the month . . . or maybe forever by the looks of it. The dock wasn't a very good place for them—it was dark, damp, rodent infested, and fireless, but it was out of the wind at least. They were rousted one morning when the nice ladies at the Red Cross shelter across the street reported them to the cops.

"Let's head west," Yazzie said, "check out our old camp. Maybe we can do something there, find stuff."

"Yeah," was all Darrel Lee said. Losing his truck had affected him in a bad way. Losing the camp a few days later had devastated him. Darrel Lee turned inward, didn't talk as much or assume a position of leadership like he'd always done. He didn't seem to care anymore whether he was alive or dead, hungry or tired; he did whatever Yazzie told him to do. It seemed as if Darrel Lee had lost his lust for life and was only interested in drinking until he passed out. He was going through Ten High as fast as Yazzie provided it.

When the cops came and told them to move on, Darrel Lee followed Yazzie in mindless fashion as they trudged up Cimarron Street toward their old camp. But as they passed beneath I-25, Yazzie saw it: the perfect spot for them to be for a while.

It was about forty feet up the embankment, under the overpass where the interstate highway crossed Cimarron Street, at the confluence of Fountain and Monument Creeks. There was a flat area up there, at least ten or twelve feet by eighty or a hundred feet. *By however wide the interstate is. Might be noisy, but I'll bet it's dry,* Yazzie thought.

When they got up there, they found the headroom was lacking, being less than five feet, and really, closer to four if the truth be told. But it would do, it would damn sure do.

They climbed up and Yazzie looked around, found a place for them under the exit lane for the southbound vehicles. They wouldn't be able to have campfires, *but,* Yazzie thought, *I don't wanna be hauling firewood up no forty-foot incline, neither.*

"Kay, Darrel Lee. Put the gear right there. We're gonna stay here."

Darrel Lee put his bundles at the spot Yazzie pointed to and sat, staring down at the creek and the cars and trucks headed east and west on Cimarron Street where it turned into Highway 24, west of the interstate. He lit a cigarette and said, "Pretty far to the liquor store."

"Yeah," Yazzie said, "but we'll manage it. Here," and he handed Darrel Lee a "short dog," a one-ounce bottle of Ten High, and got another for himself. Darrel Lee tipped his head back and emptied it in one brief swallow. He smacked his lips and said, "Ahhh. First of the day."

Yazzie held his up in a mock toast and said, "And here's to the day of infamy," then drank it down. They threw the empties to the side and as far back as they could. It was December 7 and the temperature was fifteen degrees.

They settled into a kind of routine for a few days, going to the Marion House for breakfast if they were able, if they hadn't got sick or too drunk the night before. Both of them were wearing down, they were losing teeth and had constant runny noses and sore throats, but they manned up, kept going.

After breakfast, they'd hang out at the library until lunch at Marion House, and by afternoon, warm and fed, Yazzie would panhandle around downtown with Darrel Lee as his silent, shadowy sidekick. Once they had some cash, they headed straight to the liquor store for bourbon and cigarettes. Then they were then good to go, drinking and smoking until lights out.

About a week before Christmas, Colorado Springs was in the grip of a severe arctic cold front. The temperatures plunged below zero and stayed there. All over the city, pipes were freezing and cars were refusing to start. The public schools all started their Christmas break a few days early, fearing an epidemic of frostbitten kids waiting for morning school buses. Patrols went out warning the homeless, urging them to seek shelter at the Red Cross, Salvation Army, or elsewhere. The patrols warned but couldn't force Darrel Lee and Yazzie into the shelters. They hated the idea of charity, after all, and their options were limited anyway, because the shelters refused those who were drunk or using drugs . . . fearing for the safety of the other residents.

On Christmas Eve, it was so cold that the snow on the ground made squeaking noises when they walked on it. Cars waiting at traffic lights trailed white plumes of exhaust that rose straight up in the air like a signal fire. Most folks were home for the holiday before dark. By six o'clock the downtown area was almost deserted, except for a few late shoppers, one or two bars, and Yazzie and Darrel Lee, trudging down Cimarron Street in the minus-ten degree air.

They were both skunked, having started early that morning, when one of the regulars at the Marion House passed around a bottle of peppermint schnapps right after breakfast. Yazzie had scored almost twenty bucks in less than an hour from some of the stockbrokers exiting the financial canyons at Tejon Street and Colorado Avenue. It was just before noon when he got the money, and they started drinking right after that.

Yazzie was leading Darrel Lee by the hand, stumbling across the bridge at Fountain Creek. They were almost to the northbound entrance ramp for I-25, where they had to get across the ramp, up forty feet of steep and icy embankment in the dark, cross sixty feet of icy snow-packed ledge, and, easy as pie, they were safe in their lair.

"C'mon, Darrel Lee, not much farther, you'll be home." Yazzie pulled his nearly catatonic friend by the hand, stumbling onto the on-ramp. That's when the black Chevy pickup with mag wheels and a throaty V8 rumble pulled in front of them and stopped. Yazzie could hear it slap into park, then sit there at idle, making a noise like a Doberman pinscher growling low in its throat.

I'm fucked, Yazzie thought. *Nowhere to run, can't drag Darrel Lee anyway . . .* He stood frozen, waiting for the gunshots he was certain would follow as the window slid down. But as Yazzie waited, nailed in place by fear,

Sonny Edmonds's voice came out of the window.

"You! Hey, you! You believe in angels?"

Yazzie, holding Darrel Lee upright, with his left arm over Yazzie's shoulders and Yazzie holding his left hand, didn't know if he had just met one or was just about to. He wondered, *Will I hear the gun go off . . . the one with the bullet that has my name on it?*

He said, "Yeah. I believe in angels."

"Well, here. Merry Christmas," Sonny said, as he reached out the window and handed the drunk, dumbfounded Yazzie a hundred-dollar bill, and drove up the ramp without another word.

Clutching the bill tight with his right hand, Yazzie had the semiconscious, nearly comatose Darrel Lee halfway up the forty-foot embankment when the attack came. He hadn't had a brain-puke for months, so it caught him by surprise as he struggled to hold Darrel Lee and the money.

When the seizure hit, Yazzie's eyes rolled back in his head and his body went rigid. He stood straight up, convulsing for an instant, then flipped over and slid on his back in the snow and ice, down into Fountain Creek where his head hit a boulder . . . crushing his skull and snapping his neck . . . killing him instantly. His right hand, hanging in the icy water, released its grip on the hundred-dollar bill. It disappeared in the current, heading south toward the Gulf of Mexico.

Darrel Lee came down on his belly, face-first in Yazzie's trail. Dazed and drunk, sick with pneumonia, cut and bleeding, he tried to gain some leverage to pull Yazzie's body out of the water, but was soon exhausted by the effort.

"Don'shu worry, Yaz. 'M goin' ge'shu out. Jus' need resh'a min . . ." were the last words he ever spoke. He died of exposure some while later, alone and unnoticed in the cold and dark.

A CSPD patrolman, on his way in for shift change on Christmas morning, spotted the bodies. The coroner's assistant said at the scene,

"It's no wonder the poor SOB died; it was down around thirty below last night."

With no IDs, the bodies unclaimed, they were cremated and buried in the public cemetery with a numbered headstone flat in the ground, identifying the remains.

The local newspaper, because of the tragic time and place of death, and mostly because news was slow and it had space to fill, had a cub reporter write a short human interest story . . . in a flash of sentimentality and Dickensian inspiration, she called them "The Ghosts of Christmas Present."

The story and photos ran on the front page the day after Christmas.

The hundred-dollar bill disappeared.

MOSBY'S RETREAT

Mosby's Retreat

THE MARLBORO MAN AND I were keeping each other company out on the loading dock by the delivery door, where I'd gone for a cigarette . . . smoking at the facility being forbidden . . . when a big gray cat appeared. He strolled up in the insouciant way that cats have—as if he owned everything in sight, including me. He hopped on the curb, took a seat beside me, and proceeded to survey his human companion from head to toe with a pair of luminous yellow eyes that seemed to contain equal parts mirth and gravitas. Finished, he cocked his head a bit and went, "Mee-row?" in a chirpy sort of way.

"Not bad," I said, "and yourself?" as I crushed out my cigarette on the sole of my shoe and fieldstripped it, letting the tobacco sift through my fingers and mix in with all the yellow, red, and orange leaves blowing by in their last dance before November.

The cat watched as I put the filter tip in the breast pocket of my field jacket and a piece of Trident in my mouth, then he stuck his right hind leg out and began licking it with enthusiasm.

He was still a pretty cat, even though he had a big scar over his right eye and his left ear was as tattered and torn as Old Glory flying over Fort Sumpter one infamous night in April 1861, and large and hard muscled—probably fifteen to eighteen pounds worth of badass fighter. He had gray fur that was the color of fifty-year-old tin siding, the kind tempered by time and hard weather, and a long full tail that every other tomcat in three counties was no doubt jealous of. I said, "Good idea.

You're looking a bit seedy, boy."

He looked at me . . . and yeah, I knew he was a he by the pouch he was carrying below the button under his tail. He stopped washing and gave me a hard stare that seemed to say, "Hey, sport, you try making a living on the streets for a few months and see how you do . . . see what you look like . . ."

As I stood up to go back to work, I reached out and gave him a pet and scratched under his chin, said, "Good luck to you, kitty. You'd better find someplace to hole up for the winter. It's coming soon." I looked up at the mass of Pikes Peak looming over the city, and pulled my collar up as I saw the clouds building around the shoulders of the mountain—they'd bring a storm, maybe even snow, this afternoon or evening. I opened the door I'd blocked with a pebble, picked it up and put it in my jacket pocket. I never even saw Mosby, as he came to be known, slip through the door behind me like the gray ghost he was named for. He disappeared, a shadow in the bowels of the Southwest Assisted Care Center, or SWAC Center, where I was working my way through the University of Colorado as an orderly. The little rascal had already found a place to live. It was a place where he'd do well and be loved. A place where all those he met would never forget him.

I went about my duties that afternoon and forgot about the little furry dude, concentrating on the patients—or residents as we're supposed to call them—and a midterm exam that was coming up in a week. I had this fall and the spring semester to finish, and then I'd get the bachelor of arts in English that I so coveted. I'd been on a six-year college plan and was ready to get on with life, wherever it led.

I had two classes the next morning, and came to work at one in the afternoon. I got there just in time to help finish up in the dining hall and get some of the infirm residents back to wherever they were supposed to be, doing whatever they did until five o'clock, when we started gathering them again for supper.

The SWAC Center was divided into two parts: the downstairs, where the mostly ambulatory, mostly cognizant residents lived, and the upstairs, where the ones unable to do for themselves in much of any way were housed. They were the late-stage Alzheimer's patients, the physically or mentally disabled, the poor souls who'd wander off, lost, helpless, and destitute if not looked after. That was the function of the SWAC Center . . . to care about the uncared for, to take the unwanted, and do for the unable. They're the victims of modern society and modern medicine, coupled with modern social welfare programs . . . victims of the two-wage-earner family and urban lifestyles where keeping abreast of the neighbors is more important than keeping Ma or Grandpa in the house. It's not right or wrong, it's just what it is . . . a sad, sad fact of modern times. Because the truth is, places like the SWAC Center are only warehouses. Places for the old folks to go, out of sight and mind, while we wait for them to die. Oh, sure, we dress the places up with rec rooms and gardens, fresh cookies on plates, televisions and arts and crafts to keep them occupied, but it's only a stopping place on the way to the cemetery. The average patient's average stay is less than eighteen months.

With our usual patient census of a hundred downstairs at two to a room, and forty upstairs, we'd lose between four and eight per month. Expressed another way . . . one or two residents of the SWAC Center died every week. Of course, some of those deaths happened at the hospital. We had a couple of staff doctors who did what they could, who sent a regular stream of our old folks over to Memorial and Penrose Hospitals where some of them passed away, but the majority died here. Me . . . I'd rather take a bullet in the head.

I could tell something was going on with the residents when I went in the dining room. They were all atwitter with gossip and innuendo, knowing looks and grins, sly, under-the-breath remarks to each other, winks and nods and chatter. It was as if an epidemic of mirth had broken out and infected all of them since I'd last worked.

I found out what had them so animated that evening after dinner. Mr. Lee told me. It had to do with a certain furry person, soon to be known to all as Mosby, the gray ghost.

Mr. Lee was my favorite resident in the whole place, and the one I'd known the longest. He'd humped a pack in the Central Highlands back in the sixties while on an all-expense-paid tour of the Republic of Vietnam, courtesy of our Uncle Sammy, and stayed for eighteen more years of fun and games with live ammunition in the big green machine. He came out in 1985 with a sleeve full of stripes, more medals than he could carry, and a handful of plates and self-tapping titanium screws holding most of the larger bones in his body together. After that, he joined the Colorado Springs Police Department and spent the next twenty-five years as a cop . . . eighteen of which he was a homicide detective . . . until the department forced him to retire because of his age and chronic emphysema. He'd busted me my second week at the SWAC Center, when I'd snuck out the delivery door for a smoke. We'd been friends ever since.

Around seven o'clock we were both outside, by the delivery door. I handed him a cigarette and took one myself. Mr. Lee was in his wheelchair and I was sitting on the curb. I said, "You turn that oxygen off?"

"Yeah."

"You warm enough? I can get another blanket if you want." The bad weather I'd thought was coming yesterday hadn't showed up, but it had gotten colder.

"Yeah. I'm warm enough. Gimme a light boy, quit bein' such a nag."

I pulled my lighter out, said, "Not naggin', but you oughta take the cannula outta your nose."

Mr. Lee pulled the plastic tube out of his nose and from behind his ears, dropped it in his lap. He didn't say anything, but I could tell he was irritable, out of sorts. I lit his cigarette, then my own. We smoked in silence for a while, listening to the night sounds of the city. Then he said, "I gotta quit this, smokin' these friggin' cigarettes. And you, boy. You gotta quit 'em too. Right now. Tonight."

He flipped half a Marlboro out in the parking lot. I watched it as it arced out and hit the ground in a blossom of sparks. I got up and retrieved it, pinched it all the way out and stripped it as I retook my seat next to him, my head tilted to the side to keep the smoke from the burning cigarette in my mouth out of my eyes. I said, "'M'gonna quit, soon as I graduate, just like I told you."

"Sure, sure, and you're still gonna love her in the morning. Better lissen'a me. There's a reason they're called coffin nails."

I took a last drag and put the thing out, said, "So tell me what's going on. Why is everybody buzzing, acting like tenth graders?"

He smiled. "Seems we've got a squatter in our midst, an unauthorized, nonpaying tenant partaking of the amenities here at the SWAC Center."

"A stowaway?"

"No, a squatter. Moved in and took up residence in the atrium, way in the back by the banana and rubber plants, behind the big rocks."

"What is it?"

Mr. Lee laughed, started coughing . . . a nasty-sounding wet cough that went on until tears leaked out of his eyes, while he hacked until he hawked up a big gob of greenish-yellow phlegm, shot through with streaks of blood, and spat it over to his left side.

"Sorry," he said.

"Forget it. You all right?"

"Yeah, I'll quit wheezing in a second."

"Want me to get you some water?"

"No. Just give me a second." He wiped his mouth on the back of his sleeve and tried to slow his breathing.

"You'd better put the oxygen back on."

"Yeah."

"It's getting worse, isn't it?"

He hooked the plastic tube over both ears and reinserted it in his nose. I turned the bottle back on, heard it hiss through the tube, saw Mr. Lee draw in through his nose and start to settle back in the wheelchair. I was looking at his face, watching to see if he was breathing okay, when he blurted out, "I've got late-stage lung cancer, boy. It's spreading to my brain and other organs."

I groped around in my head for some sort of an appropriate answer that would make him feel better . . . but what can you say, what could you possibly say, to make the situation any better when your friend has just said in a conversational way . . . *Oh, by the way . . . I'm under a death sentence.* The awkward silence lengthened until I managed to come up with a laconic and unsubstantial sounding, "I'm sorry. I'm very, very sorry to hear that . . . damn. Damn damn damn," I said in a voice that didn't quite sound like my own.

He didn't speak for a while, and neither did I. I didn't know what else to say. I'd never been this close to someone confronting their own mortality before. As the silence spooled out for a second, then minutes, I found myself trying to find something appropriate to say, but nothing came. Finally, Mr. Lee, who never used profanity, said, "I am well and truly fucked."

"How long . . .?"

"Coupla three months, maybe."

Neither one of us felt much like talking after that, so I pushed him back to his room and left him staring at an old 1940s black-and-white film noir on the classic movie channel, lost in thoughts known only to himself.

It was Mrs. Rosen who told me a few hours later, as I was lifting her into bed, about the gray tomcat that had moved into the center. It was she who told me the residents were sneaking him tidbits of chicken and fish from their plates, and that the cat was very standoffish, didn't seem to want to be petted or fussed over. She also said Professor Hoffmeister had come up with the name Mosby . . . for a Confederate colonel during the Civil War whose daring cavalry missions had caused the Federals to call him the Gray Ghost . . . a man who had such a string of successful raids that he, or any of his men, were to be "executed without trial if captured." Mrs. Rosen, I decided, would have made an excellent Civil War spy as she was a great conduit of information. I thanked her as I left her room, for bringing me up to speed.

The next five days were intense, with events happening one after the other.

Mosby came out of hiding, making his presence known to all by showing up for breakfast on Saturday morning. The residents, of course, had all heard about him and were eager to get a glimpse of the elusive little squatter. They welcomed him like an honored guest, with saucers of half-and-half, bits of bacon or ham, and poached egg. The residents were, for the most part, accepting of this new presence and vibrant young life among them.

The cat accepted the handouts with the same degree of humility as one of the Louies in pre-Revolutionary France . . . which made the residents even more eager to serve him. Go figure. I guess it's human or cat nature or something, but the residents and Mosby seemed to connect with each other somehow. I had no idea at the time of the profundity of their relationship, but would soon learn. Some things just can't be explained.

Animals were forbidden at the SWAC Center. The thinking among the owners was that if they allowed one animal, then everyone would want their Tippy, Spot, or Fluffy, and the center wouldn't be able to accommodate them all. And besides which . . . who'd care for the animal after its owner passed, or pay for its food and care? The owners, a group of physicians intent on padding their six-figure incomes, were practical about things like that. They had a business to run and profits to make, after all. I knew they were all humanitarians by the way they squeezed every nickel until old T.J. groaned from the pain, and by the raises in pay no one ever got, the maintenance they never did, or the equipment they never bought to ease the residents' suffering. But other than that, they were a great bunch to work for.

Emma Crotts was nominally in charge, she being the one on duty at the time with the most seniority, and she was having an absolute psychotic breakdown over Mosby's presence. She got me and Ray Moody out in the hallway and said, "What's a cat doing in here? Just who is responsible? Where'd it come from and just what are you going to do about it? I want some . . ."

Ray, who was a giant-sized man and a fellow orderly with whom I'd spent many a break—along with Mr. Jim Beam and the Marlboro Man—out on the delivery dock . . . said in his basso-profundo voice that sounded like it was coming from the center of the earth, "It ain't cho problem. You ain't in charge."

"I am at the moment."

"Naw. You ain't."

Before she could say something else, I said, "Ray's right, Emma. You don't have to do a thing."

Emma thought for a moment. "What do you mean?"

"Ignore it," I said, "then it's not your problem. It's Mrs. Moults's. You just go about your business like any other day and let her discover it for herself."

"Then it be her problem," Ray added.

I could see the lights go on in Emma's eyes. "Maybe that's a better idea," she said.

"Sure it is," I said, "the residents have known about it since last week. They've even named him Mosby."

"Mosby?"

"Yeah, for a Civil War guy. He was called the Gray Ghost because he was uncatchable."

She sighed and looked up at the ceiling, then said, "Okay. We'll do it your way, let Sarahanna Moults find out for herself."

Ray looked at me—I could see just a hint of a smirk about to break out and scamper across his face, and I knew what he was thinking because I was thinking exactly the same thing: Emma Crotts no longer had any moral authority over either one of us. I had to turn away to keep from laughing out loud.

Mosby's Retreat was secure until late Sunday afternoon, when it became apparent that Father Albert Dassetti would expire in the next few hours, and it looked to be a turbulent passage. He was afraid of what would come next. Father Albert, who was eaten up by cancer and down to less than ninety pounds, had started his personal Walk to Golgotha about two weeks ago. He'd taken less and less food, until finally, five days ago, he stopped eating altogether. The next day, he refused water, and by the day after that he'd slipped into the coma from which there is no awakening in this world.

I drew the low card from the deck we kept hidden at the nurses' station and was tagged as the hired mourner to sit with him until he drew his final breath. It was one of the amenities at the SWAC Center: "One of our trained, caring, and compassionate staff members will always be there to comfort and care for your loved ones if you cannot . . ." was right out of one of the SWAC Center's carefully prepared professional sales brochures. I'm sure it did good things for the psyches of the residents and the heirs, but truth was, it was the losers who did the morbid watch. That Sunday it was me. I hope Father Dassetti, wherever he is now, appreciated the effort.

Stopping by the lunchroom, I bought a couple of Snickers bars. I gathered my backpack with class notes and a couple of textbooks inside, and started up the stairs to his room thinking, *On the bright side, I'll get some study time.* Midterm exams started next week.

When I got to his room, a young priest who looked only a bit older than me was administering the last rites to Father Albert. As I watched from the door, the priest made the sign of the cross on Father Albert's forehead, then tucked a small catechism into the old man's left hand where it was lying on his chest, and whispered in his ear. As he stood and started removing his vestments and began folding them, he noticed me for the first time and said, "Aye. And you are family then?"

"No. I'm on staff here, sent to be with Father Albert in his last moments."

"Drew the short straw, did you?"

"Card in my case, but yeah. How'd you know?"

"Not my first time to administer the rites to one of our own. We don't attract much in the way of friends along the way."

"Oh."

"'Tis a lonely life and a lonely death if you're a traveler, never long in one place like this one, if one doesn't stay in a small parish."

He put the folded vestments into a small black case, and as he prepared to leave said, "Sure, and I don't think 't'will be too long then." He nodded and left.

I checked the catheter and the bag clipped to the side of the bed, then stepped into the bathroom to wash my hands after disposing of the latex gloves I was wearing. The shower curtain rustled, moved, and Mosby appeared. He looked at me for a moment, and went, "Mee-row?"

Before I could reply, he brushed past and jumped on the bed next to Father Albert.

I watched as I dried my hands. Mosby, at the end of the bed by Father Albert's right foot, went down into a stalking crouch . . . as if he was approaching a wild wren . . . and crept up with deliberate, measured precision, inch by inch until he had his front half on the old man's right thigh, then settled down with his front paws stretched in front, resting on the dying priest's hip and pelvis. With his tail straight out behind him like a banner and his ears at full alert, the cat watched Father Albert with all of the intensity he'd give a goldfish in a clear glass bowl. His eyes never moved, never blinked, and never turned away. Mosby looked like a miniature gray sphinx crouched on the bed.

Father Albert continued to draw short and ragged-sounding breaths that were more like gasps. Then his right arm moved, curving protectively around Mosby with his hand facing the cat's left flank. They both looked settled and peaceable, so after a few moments of dithering, I elected to leave well enough alone, and settled into an old green leather-and-chrome chair with my study notes. And that's when Sarahanna Moults showed up on a surprise visit with one of the owner-doctor partners in tow.

She was chatting away at the chubby doctor as they came in the room and stopped midword when she looked at the bed. I'd shoved my notes under the chair with the backpack when her voice carried down the hall, but Mosby was still there in all his sphinx-like glory as they came in. Her voice went up an octave as she said, "What . . . is a cat doing in here?"

"Well, uh . . ."

"Are you responsible for this—is it your idea of a joke or something? I want some answers." As she blasted me with questions she made a move toward Mosby, intent on grabbing or knocking him off of the bed.

Instead of running, the cat laid his ears back, squinted his eyes, and emitted a ferocious hissing, spitting growl. At the same time he loosed an attack with ten front claws . . . connecting with the closest offensive threat . . . Sarahanna's right hand and arm, laying it open as quick and easy as one of those Ginkgo knives you see on late night television: the ones that slice concrete or cucumbers with equal ease, one after the other.

Then the screeching went up a notch, and all three hundred pounds of the fat lady was singing. "Ohmygod, ohmygod, it attacked me! Ohmygod I'm bleeding I'm bleeding take me to the emergency room I'm going to have to get rabies shots ohmygod!"

I got her some tissues, while the doctor, whose last name was Gupta, said, "Take it easy, Sarah. It's a cat scratch, not dengue fever. Let me see it."

I went to the sink, got a couple of clean washcloths and a towel, handed them to Dr. Gupta, who began wiping arm and hand while Mrs. Moults made whimpering noises.

He said, "It's not serious. Come downstairs and I'll put some antiseptic on it and give you a tetanus shot to be on the safe side." He led her from the room without another word or glance at me, Mosby, or Father Albert.

Throughout the commotion, the cat had held his place next to Father Albert. As he settled back into position, he turned his bright yellow eyes on me and went, "Merr-row?"

"Fraid so, Mosby, this is the lull before the storm. She'll be back with reinforcements."

I couldn't honestly say if he was laughing or about to freak out, but he didn't seem too concerned as he turned his focus back to the old priest. I sighed, pulled out my study notes, and tried to concentrate. Father Albert did his best to keep on breathing . . . just for a little while longer.

All three of us were occupied when Dr. Gupta came back about half an hour later. I braced for the worst . . . Mosby and Father Albert ignored him.

Focused on my notes, I didn't hear him coming back down the hall, don't know how long he stood watching before he cleared his throat . . . causing me to glance at the bed and start to rise out of the chair before I saw him. I tried to recover and shove my notebook under the chair at the same time, but without much success. Finally, I just stood and dropped it behind me. I braced for the butt-chewing to begin, so it surprised me when he said, "I had to work my way through school, too. Don't worry so much, son. I understand."

I couldn't have been more surprised if he'd handed me fifty dollars and told me to take the afternoon off with pay. I must have looked like an idiot, moping around in there with my mouth wide open.

I'm not often without words, so twice within an hour must have been some kind of a personal record. I waited, watching as he moved to the opposite side of the bed, took a stethoscope from his shoulders where it was resting, and prepared to put it on Father Albert's chest. He said, as he put it in his ears, "Do you think that the Gray Mouser over there will take it personally if I touch the patient?"

I noticed he used the word "patient" instead of the required word "resident," figured Father Albert, if he still could think, didn't give a damn, and wondered if his reference to Fritz Leiber's Gray Mouser was intentional. I said, "No, he's very friendly. The residents have named him Mosby, for a Civil War general, and feed him tidbits from their plates."

"I see," he said as he bent over, listening to the fading contractions of a failing heart muscle. He looked under Father Albert's eyelids and felt his hand. Mosby, alert as a fresh trooper in a foxhole, watched with feline solemnity . . . Father Albert's right hand and arm curled along his side . . . as the doctor finished his examination. "I don't think he'll be with us much longer."

"He's been like that all morning."

Dr. Gupta picked up the medical chart from its holder at the foot of the bed and glanced at it, replaced it, and pointed at Mosby with his chin. "How long has the Mouser been here?"

"He was in the bathroom when I got here."

"How long in the facility?"

"Oh . . . ten days to two weeks." I figured Mosby's tenure here was about to end forcibly. Added, "Do you know who Falard is?"

"If you mean a certain seven-foot-tall barbarian, lives in a place called Lankhmar, yes, I do."

"Just wondered, when you called Mosby the Gray Mouser. I read a lot of sci-fi and sword and sorcery tales. Gray Mouser was one of my favorites."

"Mine, too, when I was a teenager."

Doctor Gupta came around the bed and looked at Father Albert and Mosby. He reached out, stroked the cat's fur. "He looks healthy enough, do you think I can examine him?"

"I dunno, Doc. I think so. I think he perceived Mrs. Moult as an enemy . . . a threat."

"Yes, I do too." He put the stethoscope back in his ears. "How about it Mister Mosby, are you willing?"

He put one hand on Mosby's back and the other on his chest, listened, then said, "No problem, his heart and lungs sound fine."

I wondered why he was even bothering to check the cat, found out a moment later when Gupta said, "I told the director she should keep him if he's healthy and the residents like him. It's been proven in studies that pets have a therapeutic effect on humans. We'll have to have him checked by a veterinarian, get his shots for rabies and distemper, but I think he'll be fine."

I backed up and leaned against the windowsill, wished I had a cigarette, said, "Doc, you think the other directors will go for it? No pets has been as strict policy as long as I've been here."

He looked at Father Albert before answering, saw the arm and hand curled around an attentive Mosby, "They will if I tell them to."

I thought he was going to say more, but Father Albert opened his eyes and made a noise in his throat. He made what I thought was a long sigh and opened his mouth . . . and then he died.

Doctor Gupta checked for vital signs, and finding none, pronounced him deceased, noting the time on the chart and then closing the eyes and mouth, crossing the hands on the body's chest, almost as if Father Albert were an Egyptian pharaoh instead of an ordinary parish priest.

Mosby turned, jumped into my chair, then down to the floor. He stretched, chest down and tail up, looked at me and went, "Mee-row, mee-row, err-row," then sauntered out the door and down the hall, his tail straight in the air like the mast on a sailing ship, the death pronounced . . . benediction given . . . soul in transit, his presence now superfluous.

The death of Father Albert set a pattern—a pattern that had Mosby there to comfort the dying. He stayed at the SWAC Center . . . even became a celebrity of sorts with a couple of write-ups in the local newspapers and a feature on the TV station a couple of years later.

Dr. Gupta was as good as his word. The owner-doctors decided to keep Mosby, after hearing what Dr. Gupta had to say and over the protests of Sarahanna Moults. She complained, griped, and whined, all to no avail. Mosby would stay . . . case closed . . . pending shots and a physical, which he passed with flying colors. She took a measure of revenge on the creature by having the vet castrate him at the same time. "They're happier afterwards. Neutering makes them much better pets," being her explanation. Mosby never forgave her for it.

December that year was a tough one on the residents, especially around the holidays. three of them expired before Christmas, including Mrs. Rosen. The old yenta went as the fourth Hanukkah candle was being lit. Professor Hoffmeister went two days after Christmas. All of them, seven in total, died with Mosby lying right next to them in every case. He'd show up about twenty-four hours in advance, never leaving their side until they'd gone over. And funny thing, every one of the dying—cat lovers or cat haters—had a hand or an arm touching his fur. For comfort, I suppose.

Sarahanna Moults, with Emma Crotts as an understudy, made a last try to evict Mosby, just after New Year's, claiming he upset the residents by anticipating their passing. She claimed the usually aloof cat scared the residents—that he only sat with them as they lay dying.

True, the residents rebutted once the word got around, *it's true he's aloof. He's a cat. It's what cats do; it's how they act. They're like that. But he's a friend to all of us, he comes to comfort and be with us without prejudice, in the most dire time of our lives. We know Mosby will be there for us, even if no one else will. He cares for us when caring is critical, when it matters the most.*

Day by day, as the dispute got more animated, it became apparent to me that the residents were united in their desire to keep Mosby, and determined to thwart Sarahanna Moults. It was a battle of wills . . . hers versus the collective of the residents . . . and she never stood a chance. The fight was over, nearly as fast as it started.

Through it all Mosby was living large. Thanks to various residents and their families, he'd had a great holiday season, full of gifts, cat toys, and a fleecy, down-filled cat bed from L.L. Bean where he spent most of his time snoozing, when he wasn't watching over one of our dying residents. He dined on gourmet cat food and the occasional can of albacore or sockeye, was treated like the royalty he knew he was. Then, in the eye of the storm the SWAC Center had become, in the early morning hours of February 20, Presidents' Day weekend, the unthinkable happened. We lost Mr. Lee.

A few days earlier, on Valentine's Day evening, he asked me to take him out the delivery door, on the dock, for a tête-à-tête with the Marlboro Man.

I bundled him up with coat and hat, put a blanket over his lap, and pushed him out there. I stopped, only to pull my hoodie over my head, turn the door alarm off with my key, put the pebble by the sill to prevent it locking behind us. I recall the night well . . . the details remain clear in my mind . . . and the heartache that followed does too.

It was clear and cold, the temperature down in the low thirties or high twenties. I didn't have any gloves for him, but made sure he was well tucked in, asked him if he was warm enough. He looked at me with brown eyes that seemed too old and too frail all of a sudden. I felt a chill down my spine as he said, "I'm okay, boy. Light me up." His voice was wet and froggy and weak, without its usual authority. The chill went around my coccyx . . . I felt my scrotum tighten . . . then it lodged in my stomach where a thousand bees were all trying to break out of jail.

I stuck two Marlboros in my mouth, lit up, and handed one to Mr. Lee . . . we each took a couple of drags in stone silence, watching the city lights of the downtown high-rises and in the houses climbing the foothills beyond. He was breathing in short, panting gasps, painful sounding and wet, as if he were laboring harder, but with less effect. He drew a long raspy intake, tossed his cigarette and wheezed, said, "'M'gone miss it, miss it all. And, boy . . . I want you to promise me you'll quit these goddamned cigarettes."

Before I could say yeah, soon as I graduate, the delivery door clacked open and Mosby strolled out, followed by Ray Moody and the featured guest that night, Mr. Yukon Jack. He came in a one-pint flask, easy to carry in a coat pocket, easy to conceal too. While Ray broke the seal and unscrewed the cap, I lit him a cigarette. And Mosby, Mosby went right over and jumped in Mr. Lee's lap. He snuggled up to the old man and started to purr . . . something we'd never heard him do before.

"Hello, kitty. What's news?" Mr. Lee said in his wet voice that gurgled out of his chest like a fart in the bathtub.

I passed a lit one to Ray. He took it with a nod, pointed with his chin at Mr. Lee. I shrugged, took the bottle and had a nip. It felt thick, syrupy, and sweet, and it burned all the way to my gut. I shivered, wiped my mouth with the back of my right hand . . . and started to hand it back to Ray.

"Boy, I ain't gone yet."

"Sorry. Shoulda asked."

Mr. Lee took a pull, handed it off to Ray, and we stayed like that for a while, huddled against the concrete block wall out on the delivery dock, smoking and passing a bottle under a cold, starry, indifferent sky. I noticed that Mr. Lee's hand, curled around Mosby's flank, looked just like Father Albert's had.

We never said much that night. I wish we had. Two days later, Mr. Lee came down with pneumonia. Three days after that he was dead, and the closest thing to a real father that I'd ever had was gone.

Numb, in a state of disbelief and grief, I stumbled through the next few days and nights like I was somewhere else in space and time. I, who was surrounded by death, who dealt with death every day in the form of the aged, the infirm unwell and feeble, had forgotten. I forgot. Death is uncaring. Death is impersonal. And . . . death takes us all in the end.

Mosby was there, of course, as he was whenever anyone passed. He was death's own usher. But I never did figure out if he was an observer, a comforter, or the Reaper himself, sent to ease a soul from its earthly shell. Hell, maybe he was all three. All I know for certain is that that cat was with everyone who died at the SWAC Center . . . and all of them had one of their hands wrapped around his flank as they left this world. And Mr. Lee was no exception.

I started growing up then, as I mourned Mr. Lee, the toughest and best man I ever knew, felled by a few micrograms of nicotine, taken just one puff at a time. Doesn't seem like much does it . . . not when you light up after a meal, the flame touching the tip, where all of that good-smelling tobacco is just waiting for the kiss of combustion . . . when you take the first drag, draw the smoke deep in your lungs, at peace with the universe for a few seconds. But that's the power of nicotine, and the power of addiction. We continue doing that which we know will kill us, because it feels so. Damn. Good.

Mr. Lee comes into my thoughts at odd moments, like a chance comment or just as I'm about to fall asleep at night. I see him in my mind on that last night, sitting on the dock with Mosby on his lap, both of them huddled against the cold, and I wonder. I wonder if he shouldn't have been out there. Maybe I should have taken him back inside. I wonder if I hastened his death and bear responsibility for his fatal bout of pneumonia. I think I'll think about it for a long time. I know I will.

Life has moved on, too. Next Wednesday is my last day at the SWAC Center. Graduation is on Saturday and I'll get my degree, take a few weeks off, before I try to find another job. The Colorado Springs Police Department is hiring new recruits, and I'm going to take the exam in honor of Mr. Lee; he always told me I'd make a good cop. And it's got a nice ring to it, don't you think. . . ? *"Officer Crowley Quinn, CSPD. How can I help you, ma'am?"* Yeah. It does.

Mosby is well. He's got a good thing going . . . I guess Mosby's Retreat has become Mosby's Home. He's still there with each and every resident who dies, and he still has it in for Sarahanna Moults. He spits and hisses and growls whenever he sees her . . . and he urinates on any articles of her clothing that he can find. Shoes, purses, or car keys—anything that smells like her gets the same treatment. Ray Moody and I are always careful to make sure her office door is closed, so Mosby can't get in there. Sure. We are. Always.

I promised Mr. Lee. Promised him I'd quit these friggin' cancer sticks when I graduated. It's the best thing to do, but I'm not sure I'm going to be able . . . the Marlboro Man's a hard hombre to ditch. Maybe Mr. Lee will understand. Hope so. I really really hope so.

THE RISING

Author's Note

The following narrative was recorded during the spring and summer months of 2012 by Dr. Richard Blade, a college professor, consulting parapsychologist, and hypnotist, at the Southwest Assisted Care Center in Colorado Springs, Colorado. It concerns the case of Lieutenant General Jeremiah Livingston Ross, United States Air Force (USAF) (Ret.), who was then eighty-nine years of age. General Ross has had a long and storied career with the USAF, and was in command of a number of forward-looking and secret projects at Schreiber Air Force Base (AFB), which concerned the uses of outer space . . . and the goals of which are classified ULTRA: the most sensitive of secret classifications. Speculation among knowledgeable, but unnamed, sources inside Schreiber AFB command, however, are saying that the general and his teams were working on the weaponization of space, using certain new—and as of yet undisclosed—advanced technologies of incredible destructive power. Due to the sensitive nature of those programs, the general is the only person in possession of complete details. Shortly after the narrative was made, however, both General Ross and Dr. Blade disappeared.

Problems arose, and Dr. Blade was called in when General Ross started becoming agitated during the monthly phase of the full moon. Under hypnosis, this is what emerged.

As far as confirmation of the facts herein, General Ross's WWII record is classified, as are the last fifteen years of his service, and as such are unavailable to me. General Ross himself is said to be gravely ill and cannot be interviewed or asked to comment, according to USAF spokespersons authorized to speak for him. It should be noted that, with the exception of the aforementioned phases of the moon, General Ross was in perfect health, and could easily pass as a sixty-year-old.

Dr. Blade is on sabbatical from the University of Colorado, where he lectures in high energy physics, math, and parapsychology, and unavailable for comment. I was told by the dean of faculty at the university that he is traveling in the Himalayan Mountains, somewhere in Tibet, Nepal, or China, where he has been a frequent visitor, researching a new book on the hypnotic practices of certain Tibetan Monks. Dr. Blade's return is overdue, and all attempts to contact him have been unsuccessful as of this date. However, the search is continuing.

Stamped "Secret," "Extremely Sensitive," and enclosed in a black folder with the ULTRA designation, the transcript was given to me by Dr. Blade's close personal friend and companion, Ms. Susie Miller of Colorado Springs, in hopes that publication will cause Dr. Blade to surface, or that verifiable news of him will become public. I have no idea how, or under what circumstances, she obtained it.

I leave it to the reader to draw their own conclusions.

John Dwaine McKenna
Colorado Springs, Colorado
January 2013

The Rising

HER NAME WAS *GALLOPIN' GERTIE* and she had to be the sorriest-looking B-17 in the entire Eighth Air Force, and out of thousands of airplanes, that's saying a lot. She was an old G model, with a chin turret and staggered windows for the waist gunners. I thought, *She must have been one of the first Gs sent over in forty-three. It's a wonder she's made it so long . . . she looks rode hard and put away wet . . . as Daddy used to say, and she's been drilled more times than a two-dollar whore in a mining camp.*

She had aluminum patches everywhere, and patches on top of patches in a few spots. One bomb door, the left and right ailerons, the rudder, elevators, two wing flaps, and three of her four Wright Cyclone engines looked like salvage from other aircraft because nothing matched color-wise. It is a fact that even in natural aluminum, all the B-17s were slightly different colors when seen up close . . . like at preflight inspection . . . what I was doing that day. I suppose it's due to weather conditions or age, but they're all just a tad different. Trust me; they are.

I'd gone over the aft and midsection. I ducked under the left wing and checked the landing gear, props, and hydraulics. They, like the rest of the old flying battle-ax, looked well and heavily used, but serviceable. I duckwalked and came out in front of the nose, then looked up at the cockpit where I'd be sitting tomorrow morning, worked my way around in front of the wing, and met *Gallopin' Gertie* herself.

Well, I thought, *she's damn sure interesting, but I don't think I'll be taking her home to the folks.* She was what we called "nose-art," a kind of informal name for the ship, and a mascot for the crew. It was our way of personalizing the Flying Fortress, and gave us a name to call her, rather than calling her by her tail number, or the cold military nomenclature: Bomber, B-17G. *Gallopin' Gertie* was a realistic looking, voluptuous, large-breasted woman whose long blonde hair slipstreamed behind her like a flag, wearing only a pair of red cowboy boots. Her right hand was holding her hat and her left was gripping a pair of tight reins, but they weren't attached to a horse. No, because Gallopin' Gertie was mounted astride a gigantic erect phallus, spanking a pair of giant testicles with her hat. "*Gallopin' Gertie*" was written underneath in large cursive script, and the legend "Fuck 'em All" was neatly printed in small letters near her head. It was a most professional-looking job too.

I couldn't help it, a big, shit-eating grin crawled across my lips and plastered itself all over my twenty-five-year-old face. I stood there, admiring someone's artwork and sense of humor, in the afternoon sun on an endless grassy plain, somewhere in the southeast of England. It was late June 1944, and "The Mighty Eighth" was carrying the war into the heart of Germany, bombing twenty-four hours a day, and locked in mortal combat with the Luftwaffe.

I was FNG, or Fuckin' New Guy, although no one would say that to my face. I was here to replace the previous pilot, who'd been struck and killed by a stray hunk of flak a few days previous on a mission to northern France. The war was in such high gear by then that the crew got a forty-eight-hour pass while *Gallopin' Gertie* was being patched up, and then it was right back at it. We were supporting the D-Day invasion, which was a little over two weeks old, and the ground troops who were fighting their way to Berlin . . . foot by foot.

I was getting on my borrowed bicycle to ride from the hard stand back to the hut I'd been assigned when a jeep drove up and stopped. A master sergeant who looked tougher than a ten-year-old jackhammer got out and yelled, "Hey! Who are you and what the fuck are you doing on my flight line?"

I noticed the cigarette butt in his mouth and his old, broken nose first . . . then I saw the .45 caliber Colt automatic pistol in his right hand. He was holding it down by his right leg, where I could see the hammer was pulled back in the full-cock position. The driver was also out and standing behind the jeep, next to the front fender, leveling an M1 carbine across the hood in my general direction. I had no doubt that it was cocked, locked, and loaded. I held my hands up in a nonthreatening position with the black-and-white English bicycle leaning against my thigh. I said, "Easy, chief. I'm on your side. I'm the replacement pilot for this ship."

"Name?" he said.

"Jerry Ross. Captain Jerry Ross."

"What's Jerry stand for?"

"Jeremiah. If you've gotta know."

"Where'ya from?"

"Colorado Springs."

"Where?"

"Colorado."

"What's there?"

"Pikes Peak."

"Anything else?"

I racked my brain, Seven Falls, Garden of the Gods, Broadmoor and Antlers Hotels . . . Finally, I said, "Lotsa stuff. Whadda ya want?" I was starting to get uncomfortable, and angry.

"What's behind Pikes Peak?"

"Woodland Park."

"Anything else?"

Finally I got it. "Cripple Creek."

He eased the hammer down on the pistol and shook his head at the driver, who pointed his weapon skyward and opened the breech, ejecting a brass cartridge that clattered across the hood. He retrieved it and got back in the driver's seat without a word, and stowed the rifle on some dashboard clips.

The sergeant sort of came to attention, and sort of saluted. I sort of returned it and he said, "Chief Master Sergeant Earl Van Horne, sir. This is my flight line and these are my birds. We just towed *Gallopin' Gertie* out here an hour ago."

"Were you working on her very long?"

"Ten men, about forty hours straight."

"Lots of damage?"

"She's a heartbreaker, but a tough old girl," he said, ignoring my question, then added, "Throw the bike in the back and jump in. We'll carry you back."

I was glad to accept the offer and jumped in with the cycle tipped on end next to me. I said, "Tight security, loose discipline around here."

"Security's tighter than a frog's ass, and that's watertight. But we ain't got time for all the candy-assed chickenshit that goes on in garrison, back Stateside. It don't look it right now, but this here's a war zone. Our mission is to bomb the livin' crap outta Germany. With all due respect, sir."

I knew what he'd just said made sense. Being a reserve officer, I didn't much care about all the spit 'n' polish part of the service. I'd be out of the army air force as soon as the war ended and go back to the family ranch. I said, "Where are you from, Sergeant?"

"Hereford, Texas. Up in the panhandle, south of Amarillo."

"How do you know so much about Colorado Springs?"

"Rodeo. My old man was a bronc-buster. I tried it too—it's how I broke my nose. Pikes Peak or Bust Rodeo, July 1931, on a hoss named Jumpin' Jiminey. Went in the army right after, soon's I healed up."

We pulled up in front of the Nissen hut barracks I'd be sharing with seven other flight officers. Sergeant Van Horne and I got out of the jeep and the driver retrieved the bicycle for me. I said, "Sarge, what's the deal with *Gertie*? Why do you keep patching an old wreck like her back together when there's so many new ones being sent from the States?"

He got a funny look on his face, like a sudden cramp from all the brussels sprouts they were always feeding us over there, and said, "She's special. The air crew is superstitious and real partial to her because she's a survivor . . . always makes it home. She may be all shot to hell, but she always comes home. She's flown more missions than any two other ships in the fleet, and she always comes home. Four different pilots have done their thirty mission tours in her. You'll be the fifth, if you make it."

"What do you mean, if I make it? Didn't you just say that four crews have done their full tours?"

"No. I said four pilots. Talk to one of the other officers about it. We got flights coming in. I gotta go to work, sir."

I could tell he wasn't going to say any more. I thanked him and took the bike, walked it back to the CQ—Charge of Quarters—I'd borrowed it from. When I got to the operations hut, the CQ, several other officers, and a couple of enlisted men were outside with their faces turned up, looking toward the eastern horizon, waiting for the return of the morning mission. I leaned the bicycle next to the door and joined the group watching the sky. It was a somber confederation, without ribald commentary or idle chatter, as we waited together for the survivors.

After the longest fifteen minutes of my life up to that point, a tech sergeant with field glasses said, "I see them. They're at five o'clock low." He pointed with his left arm and hand.

I looked, saw nothing at first, then tiny dots the size of pepper grains began appearing as the returning flights came nearer. The sergeant with the glasses started counting out loud as the dots got bigger, and we could hear the sounds of tens of dozens of twelve-hundred horsepower cyclone engines as the returning air crews homed in on the field.

It got real busy in a hurry. Planes landed in quick succession and taxied to their hard stands. Red flares, indicating wounded on board, started going off. Ambulances and fire trucks screamed out toward the strip to transport the wounded and the dead, or to put out fires that started when damaged aircraft pancaked in and dazed crewmen were pulled from the wreckage. Adding to all the confusion were trucks, ferrying air crews in for debriefing, and armorers, who were pulling a dozen .50 caliber machine guns from each bomber to clean, inspect, rearm, and reinstall before the next mission. Picture that and then you have an idea of the activity level I witnessed for the next couple of hours. That morning, eighty-seven B-17 Flying Fortresses had left on a mission to southern France . . . only seventy-five made it back—a loss of more than a hundred men and twelve aircraft. I found out later that my first day was typical of the appalling losses the Eighth Air Force was suffering. By war's end, the Eighth would lose thirty thousand men . . . more than ten times the losses of the U.S. Marine Corps in all the battles of the Pacific. But I didn't know that at the time. All I knew was that I had a date with old *Gallopin' Gertie* the first thing in the morning . . . and I was scared stiff.

I didn't sleep very well and was wide awake when the CQ made his wake-up call at 0300 hours. I got ready fast; I'd shaved the night before so I could save time dressing for flight duty. The B-17 was unpressurized and unheated, which meant that at twenty-five thousand feet where we operated we had to use oxygen and dress warm; the temperature up there was forty to seventy below zero, and the combat missions averaged ten hours. You do the math: ten hours of arctic temperatures in cramped quarters, unable to move about to keep the muscles loose and the blood circulating, it was impossible to stay warm.

Dressing for a mission meant a suit of long-handled underwear over regular shorts and T-shirt, and then a pair of wool socks, followed by what we called a "blue-bunny suit," a set of electrically heated long johns, and another pair of socks. Next was a pair of wool pants, a wool shirt, flight coveralls, fleece-lined leather flight jacket and pants, heated flying boots, wool scarf, and knit cap. Last was a leather flying helmet, a steel flak helmet we called "mouse ears," and heavy, fleece-lined heated gloves. A parachute, inflatable "Mae West" life preserver, and a heavy flak protector completed our equipment. I learned, after the first day, to hit the latrine and go to the mess hall at 0330 before putting the last of my flight gear on and going to the mission briefing.

At the briefing I met my copilot, Second Lieutenant Paul Johnson.

"Call me PJ."

"Jerry," I said, as we all stood when the briefing officer, Lieutenant Colonel Hillman, came in. We sat and focused on the mission information, which we learned would be to hit the rail yards at a place named Ulm, in Germany. We were told to expect flak and Luftwaffe fighter planes as soon as we entered Belgian air space. Nobody, other than Colonel Hillman, had much to say, and at 0440 I was out at *Gallopin' Gertie's* parking spot, watching the crew go through the preflight inspection.

When they finished, I called them together and introduced myself. It takes ten men to fly a combat mission in a B-17; I asked them to introduce themselves and promised to do my best to get all of us home safely. At that time in 1944, a combat tour was thirty missions, and less than half of us made it; the rest were killed or gravely wounded . . . and a few would be captured. The crew of *Gallopin' Gertie* had flown five missions when their previous pilot, First Lieutenant Robert Evans, had been killed on June 6 during a mission to Caen. PJ had flown the ship home with no other casualties. *A miracle,* I thought, but that was before, before I learned of the legend of *Gallopin' Gertie* and the rising of the moon. If I'd had the intuition and the means to check the previous flights of *Gallopin' Gertie*—by checking with sergeant Van Horne, for example—I would have found out that it wasn't a miracle at all. In fact, it was a regular occurrence on the flights of that infamous, bloodied, demonic Flying Fortress from hell.

The mission to Ulm, my first under fire, was a tough one. We hit resistance from Focke-Wulf 190 and Messerschmitt 109 fighter planes as soon as we crossed over the German border, but nothing except occasional heavy flak before that. Personally, I think every available fighter plane was called back in defense of the fatherland, although it's just an opinion.

We lost close to sixty percent of our aircraft that day. From Belgium to Ulm and back, the flak laid down before us was so heavy it looked like a macadam roadbed lofted into the sky, one smoking hot piece of steel at a time. The 109 pilots lined up in rows, ten to a row, and came at the lead bomber in each section, one after another, blazing away with machine guns and twenty millimeter cannon fire. It was a head-on, 650-mile-an-hour game of you-die-first chicken against our belt-fed twin .50 caliber machine guns.

The noise of all those guns going off at once was stunning, and indescribably loud. Imagine all the loud noises you've ever heard, then double it, double it again, and it still wouldn't come close to the actuality. The noise shock was accompanied by the smell of oil burning off the hot guns, cordite from the shell primers, and the stink of animal fear rising from my body as green and red tracers, every fifth bullet, crisscrossed in the sky in front of us . . . knowing that any one of them could mean personal annihilation. The sheer terror I experienced that first day was so powerful I expected my heart to stop beating at any second.

But it did not. We came through the conflagration and dropped our bombs. *Gallopin' Gertie* rose for the heavens with the bomb release, and I banked her away to the northwest in a predetermined escape pattern as we hightailed it out of there and headed for England. I couldn't believe it. I survived my first bombing run. Now all I had to do was make it home through all the fighters and flak.

And somehow we did. After almost eleven hours, I turned nose up, flaps down, wheels down, and landed her in smooth fashion as befits an ex-instructor pilot with a thousand landings behind him.

And one combat mission, I said to myself, *only twenty-nine to go . . . God help me.*

Gallopin' Gertie arrived home with sixty-five new holes to patch, and needing a new number-one engine and prop. On inspection, it had taken a hit from something, and would have to be replaced. I vaguely remembered Sergeant Black, the engineer and top turret gunner, calling out to me, "Engineer to pilot. We've got a small fire outboard number one."

I feathered it somewhere over Belgium, and she came home on three engines. Like a gift from God, we encountered no more fighter attacks, and the flak gunners all took a break as we came home a little lower and a little slower than normal, with the entire crew unharmed and unbroken.

I took a few extra moments to collect myself as the other crew members exited the ship. When I finally came out of the nose hatch, a little shaky in the legs and achy in the back from sitting through the long terrifying flight, Sergeant Van Horne was there with a clipboard. He said, "Nice landing, Captain. A real grease job."

"Thank you, Chief. I had to feather number one over Belgium. Had a small fire—probably oil on an exhaust port or something. Nothing else I can think of. She handles better than any B-17 I've ever flown."

He looked at me with a strange light in his eyes . . . like he was looking at something no one else could see, his head cocked to one side as if he were listening to something only he could hear. He reached in his pocket and pulled out a pack of Camel cigarettes, offered me one. "No, thanks," I said, "don't smoke."

He nodded and lit up. "Not yet anyway. Give it time. Number-one engine took a hit from something nasty. It's got a six-inch hole in it."

He motioned to me to step around to the right side of *Gallopin' Gertie* and pointed to the rudder in the tail section. It looked like it had been chewed by giant flying rats . . . ragged and in tatters, it was shot full of holes. Van Horne said, "Number one and the tail rudder will have to be replaced, probably some of her control cables too. We'll have to check 'em. I don't know how many holes she's got total, but I quit counting at fifty."

I had no idea, too scared I guess, that we had taken so much damage. "I'll leave it to you, Sarge. How soon will she be airworthy?"

"Best guess, about thirty-six hours, depending on how long it takes us to salvage a rudder. Should be flyable and mission-ready by day after tomorrow."

The gunners were all busy removing, disassembling, and cleaning the machine guns, so the armorers could take them to their shop to be checked, recleaned, and oiled before being reinstalled and reloaded with new belts of .50 caliber ammunition.

A jeep pulled up and took me, PJ, our bombardier and chin turret gunner Captain Lou Fanelli, and the navigator First Lieutenant Tom Norton to the debriefing. There, we'd go over what went right and what went wrong with the mission. The rest of the crew followed after a few minutes in a second jeep. We'd had nothing to eat or drink on the flight, but knew there'd be hot cocoa and coffee and corned beef sandwiches at debriefing. It was a small but much appreciated treat for all of us.

After debriefing, the whole crew staggered to our bunks and fell into the deep and dreamless sleep of the exhausted.

When I awoke the next morning at 0630, the mission to Ulm seemed like an old nightmare that would fade with time, but it didn't. After a quick washup and shave, I got some chow and looked for Sergeant Van Horne.

Gallopin' Gertie had been towed to a hangar that had overhead electric cranes running on tracks to do the heavy lifting needed to replace things like engines and tail rudders. I found Van Horne, clipboard in hand, watching as a couple of PFCs backed a deuce and a half, a two-and-half-ton truck with ten wheels, into the hangar. In the back was a twelve-hundred horsepower Wright Cyclone engine and a big three-bladed Hamilton Standard propeller that was more than twelve feet in diameter. It was lashed behind the truck cab with one blade pointed skyward, as if it was giving the finger to the Luftwaffe. *Gertie* had a couple of dozen men crawling all over her performing different repairs, and huge holes with wires and tubes hanging out where her number-one engine and rudder used to be.

Sergeant Van Horne guided the truck with hand signals, positioning it in front of the wing. He pointed at a couple of burly men standing beside a rolling metal staircase, "Smitty, Leroy, you two and Kowalski get over here and start on the engine. Keep the two birds in the truck busy too. Get after it. We got a war out there."

He turned and saw me, gave a laconic salute, and said, "Morning, Cap'n. What can I do for you?"

"I was wondering how you're coming along with repairs."

"We're progressing is all I can say right now, should have her ready to test late this afternoon, don't know yet if she'll be mission-ready by tomorrow. Check the postings tonight. They're on the CQ board at 1900 hours, and they list the next day's flight crews."

"Thanks. I'll do that."

"Try not to cobb her up so much the next few times you fly her, at least until the rising. I expect it then."

"The rising? What do you mean? What rising . . . ?"

"Come the rising, you'll know. Ain't no sense me tellin' you anything else about it—you wouldn't believe it."

He tugged out his cigarettes and lit one as he walked away without another word, the ubiquitous clipboard jammed beneath his left arm.

I watched him go, thinking, *He knows I'd bust his ass to buck private for such insubordination back in the States. Is he so good at his job he gets away with it, or just doesn't give a damn? Maybe he wants to get busted, relieved of responsibility.* All were questions for some other time and place, I guessed, because the truth was, I was still the FNG, and all I really cared about was getting through the war alive and in one piece. And if yesterday's mission was typical, getting home alive and in one piece was going to be damned hard to do.

Alone and bored, I moped around the base for the rest of the day. I unpacked my flight bag and squared away my quarters, then borrowed the CQ's bicycle. Armed with a hand-drawn map he made me, I found the Officer's Club and holed up for the afternoon, drinking cokes at first, beer as the afternoon wore on, trying to kill time. That's what war is, you know: periods of utter terror followed by periods of utter boredom in a never-ending cycle until you're either killed or go home.

Despite all the effort, *Gertie* wasn't airworthy the next day; she was having problems with two of her magnetos, causing a critical drop in power. Van Horne got new ones flown down from Scotland, but not in time for the next day's mission. It all turned out to be a moot point, however, when the 977th Bomb Group, as well as the rest of the Eighth Air Force, was grounded by old Mother Nature, who sent a massive weather system that blanketed the whole of southern England and all of northern Europe and kept us grounded for three days.

Sergeant Van Horne and his crew got *Gertie* put back together on the first afternoon of our three-day stand-down, and the aircrew and I gave her as much of a shakedown as we could without going aloft. We did fly her on a test hop during a short break in the bad weather at 1100 hours on the second morning, finding her combat ready in all respects. I released the crew with orders to be back in barracks at 2400 hours in case of a mission the next day.

The third day, we were called out at 0300 hours and went through our whole mission routing. We were tasked with a shorter run to Cherbourg, France, to bomb the V1 and V2 rocket launch sites. Because it had only about eight or ten antiaircraft installations, it was considered to be an easy "milk run," but it still counted as a combat mission that made one-thirtieth of our required and put us that much closer to going home.

We loaded up and taxied out, lined up for takeoff at 0640 hours, thirty B-17s holding, props spinning at idle in the golden light of the new-risen sun. At 0730, engines were shut down, and we waited. At 0940, a red flare was fired off and arced toward the sky and the day's mission was aborted. So much for milk run. The following day we drew the oil refineries at Merseburg. Merseburg, where the brownish-black flak was so heavy it looked like we could walk on it, and the Focke-Wulf FW-190 and the Messerschmitt BF-109 fighter planes swarmed up like clouds of insane hornets, spitting out machine-gun and cannon fire in such profusion that the green tracers looked like the streams from high-pressure fire hoses. But that terror wouldn't come until tomorrow. First, we had to kill time for the rest of today.

Monotony and boredom have been the enemies of soldiers everywhere for as long as armies have been formed, and we were no exception. And that's why, after all the guns were cleaned and oiled, the reports and letters home were written, the brass and leather was polished, and the weapons of war were loaded and standing at the ready, we did what soldiers do. We headed for the closest watering hole and drank stupid amounts of intoxicants. Drinking relieved us of the dull pain of monotony and numbed us to the stress and stark terror of our next combat.

When I got to the Officer's Club it was late midafternoon, about 1600 hours or four o'clock—teatime for the Brits—and still a bit early for happy hour. *But what the hell,* I figured, *there's a war on, right? We all have to make adjustments.*

I went to the bar and was waiting to order when someone touched me on the elbow. Paul Johnson, my copilot, invited me to join him and Lou Fanelli, *Gallopin' Gertie's* bombardier, at their table in the corner. I got each of us a fresh beer and headed over.

"Thanks for inviting me," I said as I put the beer on the table and sat down.

"Thanks for getting us back from our last mission," PJ said as he clinked bottles with me and Fanelli.

"Not sure how much I had to do with it," I said. "Seems like luck or something. Are they all so fierce?"

PJ looked at Fanelli before answering. Fanelli took a drink of his beer. PJ said, "Depends."

"On what?"

"Where it is, first of all. France isn't too bad unless you run into a lot of fighters. Now that we've got those P-51 Mustangs for escorts it's a lot better. It's the flak that gets us."

"Or other things," Fanelli said.

"Like what?" I said.

"Midair collisions, mechanical failure—I saw one of our guys in the low-flight group get hit by a bomb dropped from the high flight once. Saw a tail gunner die of oxygen deprivation when his regulator froze. Other stuff too. New gunners get excited, shoot into their own planes by accident."

"That happen very often?" I said.

"Too often," Fanelli answered.

"Weird stuff happens up there," PJ said. "Remember the guy who hit a flock of birds, crashed in Holland?"

"Yeah. He was a laggard from the earlier flight. Shot up, number one out and feathered, number three leaking oil real bad. Hit a flock of storks. Poor bastard was fifteen hundred feet below and in front of us. I saw feathers and crap going every which-a-way and he nosed down. From the angle and altitude, I don't think any of 'em made it out."

"You couldn't see what happened?" I said.

"No. We were going about a hundred seventy-five miles an hour faster than them and had a lot of battle damage ourselves. We were hotfootin' it for the channel."

"You made it?" I said.

"On a wing and a prayer. We made the field here and Hillman pancaked her in. *Sara-Anne* never flew again. She was salvaged. In fact, parts of her are in *Gallopin' Gertie*."

"You mean Colonel Hillman—Michael Hillman—who gives the mission briefing and the afternoon debriefings?" I said.

"Yeah. It was a long time ago," Fanelli said after draining his beer, "almost a year. He was a captain then. Like you."

"Didn't know he made rank so fast," PJ said. "He's been a light colonel since I've been here."

"For what, two months?" Fanelli said.

"Nine weeks. I'm gonna hit the head and get the next round," PJ said as he got up and headed for the latrine out behind the building.

I noticed Fanelli staring at the table, lost in thought. I kept quiet for a while and sipped my beer. After a minute or two, he pulled out a pack of Camel cigarettes and offered me one. "Thanks, no. Don't use them."

"Boy Scout, eh?" he said as he stuck one in his mouth and lit up with a pack of matches that advertised "Pennstibles, where the gents go to meet the girls." I couldn't read the address in London.

"You been here long?" I asked.

"Eighteen months, two weeks, three days," he said. "Seems like a lifetime. I was a second louie when I got here."

"How long have you had tracks?" I said, adding, "Captain's bars."

"Nine months, ten days."

"You're pretty precise."

"I'm a bombardier, a numbers guy. I got promoted while I was convalescing, up north of here."

"How long?"

"Nineteen weeks."

I didn't say anything else. I thought, *Musta been a severe injury, to get him laid up for so long. I wonder . . .*

As if he were reading my mind, Fanelli said, "I was shooting at one-oh-nines. They were in a line, coming up one at a time, blasting away at us, one right after another. The first two peeled off when the belly gunner and I started hammering away at 'em. The next one came up with his twenty millimeter cannon firing, and he didn't peel off. We both nailed him and he blew up right in front of us. Pieces of his ship knocked holes in our nose and took a few chunks outta me. I'm lucky it didn't de-nut me."

"Man, that's weird," PJ said as he put three bottles of beer on the table. "I always thought you had the biggest balls in town. How'd they ever miss such a target of opportunity?"

Fanelli grinned and reached out for one of the bottles. He said, "Good thing you brought us beer." He took a big swig and then added, "Two more and I'm outta here."

"Beers?" I said, noting all the empties in front of him. "We'll fly tomorrow for sure."

"Missions." He took another long pull on his beer.

I watched him swallow . . . saw his Adam's apple working up and down like a piston, pumping beer from his mouth down his throat, into his belly. As he lifted his chin to drink I saw an angry red ropy-looking scar that snaked down from his right ear and crawled a crooked path across his breastbone and disappeared down his shirt.

PJ moved some bottles, knocking two of them to the floor where they broke into a thousand splinters. A young man with a white apron and a cigarette tucked behind his ear came with a broom and metal dustpan and swept up the pieces. He said, "No harm then, mate," and went away, taking several empties off the table with him.

As conversation picked up again in the room, I said, "Speaking of weird, Van Horne, the crew chief said something odd to me, but wouldn't explain himself. Something about the rising. Either of you guys know what he's talking about?"

PJ squirmed in his chair and looked at Fanelli, who exchanged glances with the copilot, then looked off in the distance. Neither of them spoke, but it was plain that they were thinking . . . and plain that some unspoken thought passed between them. The length of the silence grew, became uncomfortable. Traffic in the club had picked up. The cacophony of voices, the plink and tinkle of glass on glass filled the void. Finally I said, "What, I say something wrong?"

"No," PJ said. "It's just hard to explain is all." His voice trailed off and he stared down at the table.

Fanelli took over. "It's not so hard to understand. It's just so goddamned unbelievable."

"Try me," I said.

Fanelli looked at PJ, who shrugged and looked away. The big bombardier peeled a corner off of the label on his beer bottle and coughed, then lit another cigarette. PJ took one too, and accepted a light. It was plain to see that they were both squirming. I waited for one of them to speak.

After another minute or two, one of them finally did. PJ started, "The thing is, you're gonna have to open your mind for a while, forget what you think you know. Can you do that?"

"Be open-minded and listen? Sure. That's easy," I said.

"It won't be when me and Fanelli start talking."

"I understand," I said. "And I will keep an open mind," not having any idea what I was getting myself into.

"Okay," Fanelli said. "What else did Sergeant Van Horne say to you?"

"Not much. He told me that the crew is superstitious about *Gertie*. That she's a survivor, always comes home to the base here. And that's why he keeps patching her back together."

Fanelli nodded. "He tell you she's flown more than a hundred sixty-five missions?"

"No."

"Or that she's come home several times with battle damage so severe, remaining airborne was a scientific impossibility?"

"Hell, no. What are you talking about?"

"Remember that open mind? 'Cause it gets worse," PJ chipped in.

Fanelli looked at me with eyes so dark and black, they looked like holes in space and time. His voice quavered slightly as he said, "I've been on her and come back with one of her horizontal stabilizers blown clean off."

"That's impossible," I said. "I've been a flight instructor for a year and a half. It's impossible."

Fanelli crushed out his cigarette, took a long pull and finished his beer. He said, "I know it's impossible but I've done it. Twice."

I absorbed that with slow deliberation and determination, like I was chewing on a tough piece of meat.

Fanelli watched PJ go for another round of drinks and lit another coffin nail before he dropped more bombshells on me. "Sergeant Van Horne tell you that he's afraid of *Gallopin' Gertie* . . .?"

"No."

"That she's a fucking cannibal?"

"*What . . .* "

I sat there in disbelief. It must have shown on my face, because when Fanelli looked at me again his eyes had the weight of the world in them. When he spoke, his voice was so soft I had to lean over the table in order to hear him. He said, "It's what Sergeant Van Horne was hinting at. The rising is the rising of the full moon . . . when *Gallopin' Gertie* goes cannibal and takes another one of us when she wants to wallow in blood."

I was still staring at him with my mouth hanging open in total disbelief when PJ came back with three more beers. He put them on the table. He looked at Fanelli. "You told him?"

Fanelli nodded.

PJ said, "Skipper, we didn't believe it when we first heard it either. But you'll see when the moon comes full next."

I managed to look away without saying a word, but my brain was smoking hot from the friction of all the thoughts whirling through my head, dancing about like cosmic dust motes in a solar flare. The thought that first surfaced and stayed dominant was, *These guys are insane. Stark raving mad. Flak-happy from too many missions.* I took a sip of beer, buying time to think before I spoke. I noticed that both of them were quiet, both staring down at the table; both appeared to be waiting for me to say something. I let the silence gestate, then said, "You flew on *Gertie* without one of her horizontal stabilizers?"

Fanelli said, "Yeah."

"When, what mission?"

"It was October fourteenth, nineteen forty-three. We were coming back from Schweinfurt, Germany . . ."

Holy crap, I thought, *the Kugelfischer ball-bearing plant at Schweinfurt was one of the most heavily defended places in Germany. The raids there, on August 17 and October 14, 1943, were already recognized as two of the toughest of the war . . . with some squadrons suffering a seventy-five percent casualty rate.*

". . . after we'd made the raid and dropped our bombs. We got out of there okay, but had constant fighter attacks all the way to the channel. One of them shot our left tail section with twenty millimeter cannon fire. Our left horizontal stabilizer was blown away. It was so chewed up and full of holes it just fell off."

"Did the pilot lose control?"

"Hell, yes. *Gertie* turned left and started down. She should have rolled over, but somehow she didn't. Lieutenant Nelson kicked in rudder and elevator, and somehow she straightened out enough that he was able to get us home. We were about fifty miles from the channel. We picked up three P-47s and they escorted us to England. It was the damndest thing. Nobody could believe it. She flew crabwise and wallowed like a hog, but she came home."

Fanelli stopped and drank more beer, and lit another cigarette from the butt of his last one. I noticed the yellow nicotine stains that covered the insides of the index and middle fingers of his right hand. As if he could read my mind for the second time that night, he looked at his hand and said, "I'm up to two and a half packs a day now. Didn't even smoke when I came here. I gotta get outta here while I've got some lungs left."

"You will," PJ said, "The next rising of the moon isn't until the sixth of July. You've got eight days to get your last two missions in."

"Yeah," was all Fanelli said.

They both got quiet then. Both of them turned morose and moody. It was as if they could see the disbelief in my face and eyes. I thought, *My God. They seem smart, educated, and informed. They can't be so ignorant and superstitious. Can they? This is the twentieth century . . .* I made a mental note to check with the medical officer after tomorrow's mission. *There isn't enough time left to help Fanelli before he completes his thirty missions, but maybe I can help PJ. I wonder what Fanelli was hospitalized for . . . and why for so long?*

Aloud, I said, "Tell me why you're afraid *Gallopin' Gertie*'s a cannibal?"

PJ took up the narrative. "Maybe vampire is a better description. Whatever she is, men die at the rising of the full moon."

"But . . . not the rest of the time?"

"Never," Fanelli said. "She always comes home without major casualties the rest of the time no matter how much she's been shot to hell and gone."

"Sounds more like a deal with the devil," I said, playing along. "Either one of you guys ever read Nathaniel Hawthorne, or a guy named Robert E. Howard?" They both shook their heads. "Too bad. Both of them wrote a lot of stories that mentioned the devil." I'd hoped at least one of them was a reader, then maybe one of them could see and understand that the nature and root cause of superstition was ignorance. *No such luck,* I thought. I said, "Does the rest of the crew believe this too?"

Fanelli said, "Everyone who's been on board for at least one full moon cycle."

That was everyone but me. *Well,* I said to myself, *I've got eight more days and one, maybe two missions before I'm baptized too . . . or eight more days to disabuse them of the idea. Sweet Jesus on a bicycle . . . what'll they think of next?*

The mission to Merseburg the next day was a double-barreled son of a bitch. I never prayed or cursed much before that mission, never smoked either. But I was doing all three, all the time, after it.

The flak around that place was the heaviest I ever encountered in all the missions I've ever flown in the entire course of my career, and I've flown a bunch. World War II, Korea, and Vietnam were all wars I've dropped bombs in, but nothing, not Berlin, nor Pyongyang, nor Hanoi compared in ferocity to the defenses of the oil refinery at Merseburg, Germany. Nothing at all.

We lost eighteen of thirty bombers to flak and fighters that day, an appalling casualty rate of sixty percent. I flew right wing to the lead bomber in our flight, and he and I were the only ones who brought our ships home. *Gallopin' Gertie* had sixty-five holes of various shapes and sizes, in addition to several from machine-gun bullets that were drilled through the Plexiglas of Captain Lou Fanelli's bombardier position. It was where a fighter plane in a screaming vertical dive had strafed us. It was an absolute miracle no one was killed and the wing-mounted gas tanks weren't hit. Fanelli had scratches and cuts on his face from pieces of flying plastic, but nothing of a serious nature. Other than a couple minor cases of frostbite, small cuts, bruises, and abrasions, our whole crew was unharmed . . . and *Gallopin' Gertie* was home again. It was Fanelli's twenty-ninth mission. One more and he could go home. The date was June 29, 1944.

It was my second combat mission, and I'm not ashamed to say that I was so damn happy to be back and still alive that I got down on my hands and knees as soon as I exited the nose hatch and kissed the ground. It was the only time I've ever done that in my life, and I have more than 150 missions and close to a thousand hours of combat flying time. Oh, yeah. It was that bad.

The crew and I went through our after-mission routines as if sleepwalking. All of us were hollow eyed and exhausted, our faces set, teeth clenched . . . staring at something just over the next man's shoulder, somewhere out of sight. We got debriefed, the bomb-damage teams analyzed our bomb-run photos, and the Red Cross ladies gave us shots of whiskey and peanut butter sandwiches. Even though I hadn't eaten anything for twelve hours, I had to force myself to eat such inelegant food. I kept it down is about the best I can say. Then I stumbled back to my hut and fell into my bunk to try to sleep in spite of the newsreel images flickering through my brain, replaying every moment of heart-stopping terror that was my second mission in *Gallopin' Gertie*, again . . . and again . . . and again.

When I woke at 0300, from habit rather than necessity, the word had already come down from Eighth Air Force Command and was making its way through our 977th Bomb Group with the speed of a forty millimeter distress flare arcing skyward.

"It's a fact, Jack," I heard the CQ runner say to one of the other officers in our hut. "The new mission requirement is thirty-five combat flights before your tour is done and you get'cher Lucky Bastards Certificate."

The groans could be heard all over the base as the news spread.

"This ain't no latrine rumor?"

"No. It's the real deal, sir. I pulled it off the teletype and decoded it myself at 0130 hours. It's typed and posted."

A Lucky Bastards Certificate was a kind of diploma given to those who'd completed, and survived, their tour.

Lou Fanelli is going to be devastated, I thought. I knew he'd been on the verge. *One mission just turned into six. Aw shit. Shit. Shit. Shit.*

And then a stray thought, like a lone coyote loping through the sagebrush, came into my mind: *and it's only six days until the rising.* I couldn't believe I'd thought that thought. *What, you gonna start believing in hoodoo now? Get hold of yourself, Jerry. You've still got a ways to go before you're done over here.*

Truth was, I was concerned about the state of Fanelli's mental health. I decided to look up the flight surgeon, talk to him about the situation. With one last mission, Fanelli could tough it out. Six more would be a problem. The guy was cracking up, in my estimation. It was imperative to get a handle on the situation, and put a lid on all the cannibal and vampire nonsense.

The flight surgeon was a major named Donald Cole. He didn't look much older than me, but the sheepskins hanging on his wall indicated that he'd graduated cum laude from Johns Hopkins University Medical School in 1937. Other degrees, awards, and certificates were hung there, including one I couldn't quite make out from where I was sitting, but I could tell it was issued by Oxford University just north of here, because I recognized the insignia.

Dr. Cole came in and introduced himself. He got right to the point, asked me why I was there. I explained my concerns about Captain Fanelli and then told him about the superstitious beliefs of the rest of the crew, concluded by asking his opinion about what he thought would be the best course of action. It was soon apparent I'd come to the wrong man at the wrong place at the wrong time to get help of any kind. Major Cole had skipped the lectures on compassion in medical school, or maybe, like Fanelli and Sergeant Van Horne, he'd seen so many casualties, he was burned out. He said, "You can't do anything. Forget about it and do your job, fly the plane." He looked at his watch, then at me.

"Nothing?" I said.

"Nothing. Every man on every flight crew and every ground crew has a lucky charm of some kind. There's all sorts of talismans over here."

I got the hint, stood, thanked him, and got the hell out of there.

Hey, Jerry, I told myself, *it's get tough or die time. Nobody gives a rat's ass about personal problems. It's kill or be killed. Keep your focus on flying each mission, get your thirty-five, and get out of here. If those guys want to believe in fairy dust or demons, it's their business. You're not here to make new friends.* I resolved to myself to be tough as the next guy and try not to get creamed in a B-17 at five miles high, somewhere over Europe in the year of our Lord, one thousand nine hundred and forty-four.

We didn't fly again until the second of July. It was my third mission and Fanelli's thirtieth; we flew the aborted run to Cherbourg, France, and bombed the rocket base there. It was the second time the place had been attacked, and we pretty much destroyed it, dropping the equivalent of twenty-five thousand tons of TNT. I don't think the place was ever operational again. Best of all, it was a coveted milk run. We experienced only token resistance and a couple of half-hearted attempts to kill us by a few lazy flak gunners. It was a piece of cake when compared to the first missions I flew.

I was elated when *Gallopin' Gertie* swooped down out of a steel gray afternoon sky with her nose up and flaps down like a big bird of prey. I was happy, but the crew was grim and tight-lipped, moving about their duties like the condemned, ordering a last meal. Fanelli, I could understand. The guy was hanging on by his emotional fingernails before he got another five missions dumped on him, but the other guys? And then it came to me. There were only four days . . . four more days until the rising of the full moon.

We flew a short supply drop to some partisans in France: explosives, some weapons and ammo, and a bunch of medicine and C-rations. It was in a remote part of the north French countryside, so there weren't any major defenses in place. It wasn't exactly a milk run, because we were harried by scattered gun emplacements and fighter squadrons all the way there and back, but the effort wasn't concentrated or sustained. I called it half-hearted. All the eyes and the attention of the world were on the ground troops who were fighting their way to the Rhine River and the heart of Germany. It was a good way to celebrate the birth of America on that July the fourth, 1944.

We flew again two days later. It was my fifth mission and Fanelli's thirty-second. It was the sixth of July . . . the rising of the full moon.

We were roused from our bunks at 0200 and went through our normal mission motions, knowing it was going to be a long day because of the early wake up. At the 0300 briefing, Colonel Hillman was as solemn as an owl when he revealed the day's mission behind the drape: Stuttgart,

Germany, was the destination; the petroleum cracking plant and oil storage tanks there were the targets. We'd be in the air at least ten hours and would land in twilight. Nobody said a word while he spoke. We were a respectful and grim group that morning, our solemnity matching that of the intelligence officer, Lieutenant Colonel Hillman. There was no small talk or joshing when I filed out of the briefing with PJ, Fanelli, and First Lieutenant Tom Norton, our navigator. Sergeant Van Horne put out the cigarette he was smoking and carefully fieldstripped it, then climbed behind the wheel of his jeep. He started the engine as we piled in for the three-mile ride out to where *Gallopin' Gertie* waited for us.

As he pulled up and stopped, Van Horne said, "A word in private, sir?"

I wasn't in the mood for either advice or personal problems, but the other three officers had already jumped out and joined the enlisted crewmen who were busy preflighting the plane. I said, "What is it, Sergeant? It's gonna be a long day . . ."

"I know," he said. "It's gonna be your toughest one yet. I just wanted to wish you well and give you this." He handed me a silver cross and Saint Christopher's medal on a silver chain.

"Why? I'm not Catholic, not very religious either. Besides, it's kind of personal, isn't it?"

"Yes, I guess it is personal, but you're gonna need help up there today and I'd like to see you get back intact. It's the rising and you're gonna change the way you see the world, and what you think you know about it. You may even get religion, or lose it. Others have. I'd take it and wear it if I was going up there today . . . that's for sure. But it's up to you."

He looked straight into my eyes as he said it. When he'd finished he turned forward, looking out the flat windshield as he reached in his jacket for cigarettes and matches.

To this day, I've wondered what it was that made me slip it over my head and drop them behind my shirt. I got a small shiver as the cold metal hit my bare skin, wondered what my old Episcopalian mother would say if she knew I was wearing what she called "papist claptrap." "Thank you, Sergeant. Would you mind giving me one of those cigarettes?"

He had the grace not to remind me of my antismoking attitude of only a few days ago. He cupped his hands around the match as he gave me a light. I inhaled and said, "See you when we get back," and walked to where *Gertie* and the crew waited.

I could almost hear Van Horne's thoughts, *"Sure hope the poor bastard makes it back alive . . . didn't take him any too long to take up smoking either . . . he don't know what he's in for."* Maybe he wasn't thinking those exact thoughts, but I'd bet I was close. He had a strange, uneasy look about him. Like he was about to puke his guts out.

I walked up to *Gallopin' Gertie*, where the crew was gathered in a silent clump, their shoulders slumped and faces downcast. They looked like a pack of whipped hounds. *Well,* I thought, *it's time to show 'em who's the alpha male . . .*

I stood for a few moments with my legs spread wide, my hands full of gear. I noticed that all of them were wearing full sporrans, the front and back steel-armored flak protectors, and about half of them were, like me, augmenting that protection with additional tapered sporrans that covered the thigh and lower abdomen and groin area . . . protecting what we air warriors modestly referred to as the family jewels . . . our most prized possessions. They did a pretty good job of protecting, but caused problems with our shoulders on long missions—like the one we faced that day.

I waited to speak, letting the silence grow. When the fidgeting stopped and all eyes were on me I said, "You all know there isn't anything easy about today's mission. Don't make it harder than it already is with a bunch of superstitious horseshit about the moon or what your personal mission number is. Stay alert and do your job. Stay focused. We'll have fighter escorts for part of the way and the weather is forecast to be clear and dry. Clear your weapons once an hour with a three-round burst and keep the chatter to yourself. Focus on your job. Any questions?"

No one had anything to say.

"PJ, did everyone preflight the ship?"

"Yes, sir."

"Problems?"

"No, sir."

"All right. Let's saddle up and get to the rodeo."

As I threw my parachute in and was climbing in the nose hatch, I heard one of the waist gunners—it sounded like Jones—mutter to someone, "See if he's still so full'a piss and vinegar when we get back, when the moon's rising in his face and *Gertie's* screaming for his blood."

The hair stood up on my neck, but I ground my teeth and let the remark pass. *I'll see Sergeant Jones when we get back.* I slipped my parachute behind me and took the left-hand command seat, started the preflight routine, and prepared to meet my destiny. It was 0400 hours . . . takeoff at 0520. It was going to be a day I'd never forget. The butterflies in my stomach felt like a whole flock of London pigeons fluttering around in there.

I forced myself to concentrate, kept my focus on the immediate task at hand: start up, run up, taxi out in line, and hold . . . waiting for the green flare that signaled the start of our mission and releasing the brakes, letting the four props bite the air and move us forward, slowly at first, gathering speed, until just at the last few feet of runway, *Gallopin' Gertie* lifted off and went airborne. She felt sluggish and heavy at first, pregnant with four, thousand-pound bombs in her belly, and several thousand pounds of high-octane aviation gasoline in her wing tanks, and twenty thousand rounds of belt-fed, .50 caliber ammunition for the dozen machine guns bristling from her body. She quivered and wallowed in the first few moments of flight, as if she were unsure whether she could handle such a heavy burden, but then she gained grace with increased speed and altitude, until we were north of twenty thousand feet at three hundred knots, headed for the heart of Germany. It was *Gallopin' Gertie's* last flight. It was my date with destiny: a day my life changed forever . . . it was the rising of the moon . . . a day that made me question God, science, and the nature of the universe itself.

We formed up over England and the channel. Individual planes found their wingmen and tucked into position, became squadrons, then groups of thirty or more, until we were an armada of hundreds, maybe even thousands of the most destructive air machines the minds of men had yet conceived. Bombers filled the sky in front of me, in back of me, above and below me. The contrails streaming out behind them looked like "squirts of white icing against a blue icing sky." Even higher, and slightly in front of the B-17s, the Mustang fighter escorts were trailing lace-like single contrails as they prowled the high range, spoiling for a fight with the quicksilver-fast Focke-Wulfs and Messerschmitts of the Luftwaffe.

We were in high, low, and middle groups of airborne attackers, intent on bringing death and destruction, carrying the "terrible swift sword" of the United States of America deep into the enemy heartland and killing him dead, dead, dead. At the same time our deepest wish was just to get the hell out of there alive and in one piece, and that was going to be damned-awful hard to do, because tens of thousands of Germans on the ground and in the air were trying just as hard to kill all of us.

As we crossed the coast over Holland, I was having trouble staying in position. *Gertie* kept pulling ahead of my wingmen. PJ and I set the throttles time and time again, only to have the engines surge by themselves somehow, and we'd creep ahead once more. We were admonished by the wing leader several times to hold a tight formation. It was in the midst of his third or fourth reprimand as we crossed into German airspace that they opened up on us with their eighty-eights and the sky bloomed with red-brown and black flak.

The shredded steel blossoms lay in front of us at first, like a dirt road across heaven. As quick as we saw it, we were on it, and steel shrapnel from the flak was hitting *Gallopin' Gertie* and sounding like rocks and gravel on a car's fenders as it was driven down heaven's dirt road. It stopped as suddenly as it started.

I keyed the 'comm and said, "Captain to crew, anybody hit?"

There was silence for a few moments, then, "Need help in the waist. Got a problem here."

I recognized Smith's voice. "Do you need medical?"

"Yeah."

"Sergeant Black, take a kit, go see what's going on." To PJ I said, "You take Blackie's place at the top gun. Keep your eyes and ears open in case I need you back down here to help fly."

Sergeant First Class Robert Lee Black came down from his perch in the Sperry Gun Tower that poked up through *Gertie's* back like a wart, clipped on a walk-around oxygen bottle, and headed down the catwalk through the bomb bay to aid the waist gunners. PJ stood up in the tower and plugged into the oxygen supply. He rotated the gun in a full circle and fired a short three-round burst to make sure the twin fifties were cleared.

Gertie seemed to calm down. The surging engines were running smooth, the flak guns were quiet, and I was able to fly in formation without a copilot. For the moment it could have been a training exercise. That all changed a few heartbeats later when Blackie came back . . . he had a lot of blood on his face and gloves when he leaned down between the seats to speak to me off of the 'comm.

"Jones is bad. Piece of shrapnel took his left leg off just above the ankle. The big artery's severed. I put a tourniquet on him but I couldn't stop the bleeding. He's not gonna make it back before he runs outta blood.

I told him he should bail out, maybe get help on the ground. He said, 'In Germany? No fucking way.' He wants to stay with the ship. I shot him with morphia, but there isn't enough. He's going into shock."

I nodded. There was nothing else to say or do. We had another six or seven hours still to go. Blackie said, "He's as comfortable as I can make him."

I nodded a second time, couldn't think of anything to say, settled for "Okay." I knew Blackie was thinking I was a heartless son of a bitch, couldn't do anything to change his opinion. He turned and tapped PJ on the leg, exchanged places, and we flew on into the fatherland.

There was a short respite from the flak guns and then they started again. This time they were accompanied by streams of fighters. I saw the puffs of flak bloom in front of us as the German eighty-eights laid out that same dirt road to heaven, then I heard *Gertie's* twin .50 caliber guns all start up firing at once as the fighter planes came closer, and last, I smelled the stink of expended brass casings, cordite, and smoking-hot oil as the empties from Blackie's long bursts showered down behind PJ and me.

We jinked left, right, and up and down as we did our best to keep in formation and avoid the shrapnel from the flak at the same time. The ship on our left, named *Little Evie,* took a direct hit in the nose from a burst of flak and fell off to the left, crashing into another bomber below us, sending both of them down in a death spiral.

PJ and I moved over and filled the gap, became wingman to the flight leader. In front of and below us, P-51 Mustangs were engaging Focke-Wulfs and Messerschmitts in running, twisting aerial ballets that were punctuated by the dash-dash-dash of tracer rounds, explosions, flames, and smoking-black trails down to earth, where they expired in deadly blossoms of orange smoke and falling debris. We looked for chutes . . . saw few . . . droned onward, headed for our own reckoning.

The quiet interludes between attacks grew shorter and shorter the closer we got to Stuttgart. The city was defended with concentric rings of eighty-eight millimeter antiaircraft guns for about one hundred miles or so, and we were under constant harassment from fighter planes as well. The flak road to heaven got longer and longer, stretching from wherever we were, all the way to St. Peter's pearly gates.

Gallopin' Gertie was taking plenty of punishment too. She was constantly being pinged by flak and stray bullets shot from guns all over the sky. By the time Fanelli dropped her bombs, she was vibrating so much I thought her wings would break off at any second and the wheel shook my hands so hard that my arms and shoulders ached. All the while, all around us, planes were falling out of the sky like burning angels. They would flash past us, trailing long arcs of flame, black smoke, and small pieces of themselves. They corkscrewed and fell until they met up with an immutable, indifferent, and unmovable earth in one last spectacular death spasm and ejaculation.

It seemed a lifetime before we cleared the drop zone and got away— got off that terrible fatal road the big guns on the ground had put up. *Gertie* was still shaking and vibrating, although without the violence she'd shown over the turbulent drop zone. But she was still flying. That was more than most of the squadron could say. Our losses that day were devastating. Of the thirty-something planes in our squadron that took off in the dawning, only fourteen made it back to East Anglia. Our losses were sickening.

We were between attacks, approaching the Rhine River demarcating the French border with Germany, before I had a chance to check the status of the crew . . . and discovered that our radio operator Sol Goldstein had been killed by a chunk of hot steel that took his face and half of his skull off before exiting the opposite side of *Gertie's* body, leaving a gaping six-foot hole. Sol was still strapped in his seat with just his lower jaw and teeth remaining, leaving the fuselage behind him painted in blood and gore.

Smitty, our other waist gunner, had had the middle and index fingers shot off his left hand and was being attended to by Jack Bohn, the tail gunner. Jones, the waist gunner who'd lost part of a leg, had bled to death. He was lying on the floor by his gun position, his sightless eyes staring at eternity, when Jack leaned down and closed them.

We crossed the river into France and vectored to the shortest possible route home. Tommy Norton, our navigator, gave us the heading, and PJ and I turned the quaking B-17 toward home. In my head I estimated we'd make East Anglia in about two and a half hours. Around dusk. Low on fuel. We were alone now, a straggler and prime candidate to be picked off by patrolling fighters. I crossed my fingers and said a short prayer in my mind.

I turned to PJ. "Take over the turret from Blackie. Send him back to help Bohn. The two of 'em will have to run the waist guns."

"They'll figure it out."

"I'm depending on you to keep a sharp lookout. We all are."

PJ climbed out of his seat and sent Blackie back to the waist. He and Jack Bohn were the most experienced and the best gunners in the crew. I hoped they could manage . . . this had been a suicide mission from the start. I gave us about a five-to-one chance against making it back to England at that point, as *Gertie* wobbled her way across the skies of northwest France.

We passed Metz and then Reims without incident, as if the ship and all of us on it were wearing cloaks of invisibility, or been granted safe conduct passes by God himself.

Whatever kind of talisman we'd had, it was revoked and disappeared about forty miles from the coast of France. Fanelli hit the 'comm and said, "Bandit, two o'clock high."

A moment later PJ added, "Bandit, ten o'clock high."

I looked and saw two dots to the left and right, above and in front of me, that turned into a pair of twin-engined Junkers JU-88 fighter planes and very bad news for us. They carried four twenty-millimeter cannons and two machine guns in the nose, a crew of three, and, just for good measure, another thirty millimeter rear-facing machine gun. As if that wasn't enough, it had two eighteen-hundred horsepower twelve-cylinder engines that pushed it to four hundred miles per hour. At five hundred meters they set up in a crossing pattern, and the front of both Junkers lit up with firefly lights that punctuated the total mayhem they were loosing upon us.

"Oh, shit," someone said over the 'comm, then PJ and Fanelli cut loose and all I could hear was the hammering of the twin fifties and the ringing of empty brass casings on the deck behind me. I held the wheel of the wounded B-17, and, jamming my feet on the rudder pedals, hoped to God I'd still be alive in five minutes.

I juked and wobbled as best I was able, trying to make us harder to hit, but *Gertie* was stiff and unresponsive from battle damage. I felt the big plane shudder and heard the plok, plok, plok, plokplokplok of the one-inch diameter shells from the Junkers hitting us as they flashed by below us, and Andy Tensky, down in the ball turret, opened up.

We were under ten thousand feet and I could see the channel ahead, looked for cloud cover, but there was none close enough to help.

"They're crossing below us and coming back," Tensky said.

I figured they'd roll out underneath us and trade the speed they'd gained in the dive for altitude and come right up underneath us. As they did, one of our guns let off a long burst.

"Got 'em, I got 'em, I gotcha you sonofabitch!" someone yelled.

Must've been a one-in-a-million shot, I thought, *better lucky than good.* But as one of the fighters limped away, the second one came up under us like an orca on a wounded humpback, delivering some serious damage.

"Number four is on fire," PJ said from the turret.

I throttled down and feathered it. The flames blew out and *Gertie* listed about fifteen degrees to starboard, and our airspeed dropped down to around two twenty-five or so, but she kept on flying. I almost started to believe some of the tall tales I'd heard about her. *Almost,* I thought, *but not quite,* as I struggled with my bone-tired arms to stay in control of the floundering bomber we called *Gallopin' Gertie.*

While one of the Junkers wobbled away to the southeast, leaving a smoky trail in its wake, the other one came for us with all guns hot. *Gertie* seemed to hunch up like a wounded beast as she took it in the guts. I heard the rounds impacting the hull, making their peculiar noises as they exited, tearing chunks off of her like supersonic piranhas.

The German JU-88 night fighter flashed by in front and to the left of me. I saw his belly and a pair of black crosses with white outlines for a second as he tried to roll out and over at the top of his climb. He couldn't make it—although the Junkers were heavily armed long-range fighters, they lacked maneuverability—so he had to settle for a sloppy Immelmann and wound up pointed away from us. I saw a flash of silver from his wings in the late afternoon sun as he turned and got ready for another strafing run.

I keyed the 'comm, said, "He's going to make another pass."

No one answered. *Busy,* I thought, as I wrestled with the controls, braced myself for his next onslaught. We were far out over the English Channel. *Christ I hope I don't have to ditch in the water. I'd rather do anything than drown.*

I watched him set up, begin his pass at us, saw all the red flashes as he lit those twenty millimeter cannons, tried to accept the fact I was about to die. The green tracers arced out and down from the German warplane, *It'll get to us in another second . . .* horrified, I watched, as the mouse watches the hawk coming down with talons out . . . and then he broke off, peeling down and away, as he headed for France with two of our P-47

Thunderbolts in hot pursuit.

I could see the white chalk cliffs of Dover just ahead. We were losing altitude pretty fast, but I'd clear the cliffs if my arms would hold out. They were numb from flying the damaged bomber by myself.

Jack Bohn came up. He was covered in blood.

"Is that yours?" I said, pointing with my chin.

"Some. Not much. I got the rest tryin' to help the others."

"Didja . . ."

"They're all dead."

"All of 'em?"

"Yeah. It's a slaughterhouse back there . . . Gertie's got more holes in her than a cheese grater."

"You're sure."

"Yeah, Skipper. I'm sure."

We sat in silent shock as the white cliffs passed below us. We were inbound, minus eight souls, thirty minutes and a hundred miles from home, about out of daylight and the ability to still believe in a rational universe. "Get in the right seat," I said, "and put your hands on the wheel and your feet on the rudder pedals."

"I don't know nothin' about flying . . ."

"That's okay, I just need some relief for my arms. Buckle in and pull back on the wheel. I won't let go."

He did as I asked, allowing me to realize how cramped my arms and hands were. It felt like my fingers would have to be broken, one by one, in order to get them pried off of the controls. We struggled on toward home base; the fields and farms and towns of East Anglia never looked so dear to me as they did that evening, passing beneath our wings in the last beams of daylight.

I found the field by dead reckoning and visual navigation. We'd had no radio since we'd let our bombs go over Stuttgart. The same flak had killed both it and Sol Goldstein, our radio operator. Approaching the field, we were out of fuel. I'd have to come straight in and set down; we didn't have enough left to go around again. We fired off every red flare on board and I came straight down out of the evening sky and splattered what was left of my ship and crew all over the runway. My arms and shoulders had given out.

Gertie broke in half on impact. Her aft section cartwheeled off to the right and hit something that exploded and burned, while the front wing and engines plowed furrows in the sod until we skewed off and ground looped, ending on her nose, leaned off and over on her left side. Jack pushed the window out while I tried to pry my fingers loose, one at a time. It was slow going.

"Hurry it up, Skipper. We're leaking the last gas on them hot engines." He saw me struggling, halfway upside down trying to get my fingers to let go, leaned down and kicked me on the right biceps, and my hand came loose.

"Got it," I said, and pulled my other hand loose, released the belts, and, impelled by terror, climbed on my seat to get through the window after Jack Bohn.

With my hands curled into claws, unable to grip, I crawled out and fell about fifteen feet, knocking myself silly. The last thing I saw was a blood-orange moon rising in the sky like an infected, pus-filled boil.

When I came to, it was only moments later. Jack Bohn, with a half-pound chunk of his right thigh blown away and a boot full of blood, was dragging me across the grass, inch by bloody inch. I got up and put my left arm around his and we hobbled away from the smoking fiery wreck.

We fell to the grass as *Gallopin' Gertie* burned. I was on my back, Jack on his stomach. Something in the doomed plane made a long, low moan that rose to a high-pitched whistle . . . almost like a scream . . . then *Gallopin' Gertie* went up in a giant ball of flame. I know it must have been the knock on the head I took, but I swear on Jesus Christ and everything I love, that I saw old Gertie herself in the flames. She was all on fire and she was looking directly at me, right through my eyes, straight into my immortal soul. Then she pointed at me before disappearing in a trail of fire.

But that was all many years ago, more than sixty, I reckon. Now I am old, in the winter of my years, my days are near their end and I think back to England and my time there. It was my first war, first mortal combat, and the first time I came out unscathed. It's as if I've always had a lucky charm, a talisman that protected me, kept me from hurt while in harm's way. I still have the silver Saint Christopher's medal that Chief Master Sergeant Van Horne gave me all those years ago, and I still wear it every day, even though I'm an elder of the Episcopalian Church. It's funny in a way, I've been awarded a lot of medals over the course of my career, seen a lot of combat, seen a lot of good men wounded or dead, like the last time *Gallopin' Gertie* flew, but I've never gotten a Purple Heart for injuries in war. I've never lost a single drop of blood in war. Not ever. Not one.

My old compadre Jack Bohn died a couple of years ago up in Montana. We kept in touch after the war, he and I the only survivors of the last flight of *Gallopin' Gertie*. He was awarded a Silver Star for that, his thirty-fifth and last combat mission. I'll never forget, as we lay on the grass, watching the wreckage burn, trying not to smell the odor of the burning flesh of our fellow aircrew and friends, and waiting for the crash crews, what Jack said.

"I will never . . . never never never . . . get in a goddamned airplane again."

And as far as I know, he never did. He was a gallant man. It was a great privilege to call him my friend.

Back in 1944, *Gertie's* last flight was, as I said, Jack's thirty-fifth and last. He got his Lucky Bastards Certificate and a fistful of medals while laid up at the hospital before being loaded aboard the hospital ship that took him home.

I got a medal too, the air combat medal given to every man who flew five missions. It was the one I treasured the most because it was the hardest for me to get, and paid for with the blood of my fellow crew members. I hold it dear to this very day.

I see the crew from *Gallopin' Gertie* in my dreams. I see them on our last flight together and I see them all dead in the burning wreck that was their funeral pyre. Survivor's guilt? I don't know. I've thought about it a lot. Why was I the only one to come back whole? St. Christopher? Dumb luck? Good joss or the devil's own deal? I just can't say. But the crew isn't the only thing that I see in my dreams . . .

Gallopin' Gertie comes too. I've dreamed of her a lot lately—sometimes I dream of nothing else but her. She just appears, morphs from the blackness of nothing into my dreaming mind. She's nude, and covered in blood, has teeth like a cat, and her hair and her eyes are on fire. She wants me. She beckons me, reaches for me with bloody talons, claws that are her hands. And I feel the heat of her flames as she comes closer,

and closer

and still

closer.

CONCATENATION

Concatenation

EXCEPT FOR WHAT TRANSPIRED a little before closing time, Tuesday was a slow, listless day in Palmer Lake . . . another slow, listless summer day in an unending stream of ennui. Linda hadn't even heard a car pass by on Highway 105 since lunchtime, a couple of hours ago. She sighed and closed the book she'd been reading behind the oak and glass display cabinet and checked the black kit-cat clock in the corner. Kit-Cat grinned the same silly grin he'd grinned for fifty years and his eyes moved left and right, keeping time with his wig-wag tail, counting the seconds and ticking the minutes off on the hands attached to his body. Five minutes had elapsed since she'd last checked. She loved Kit-Cat. His pure goofiness made her smile, *but there're times,* she thought, *that I just hate your message.*

About the only thing to break the monotony was the regular passing of the coal trains that moved between the rear of the small antique shop Linda owned and operated and Palmer Lake itself, about five hundred yards away. There was a steady stream of them, day and night; full ones heading south to feed the power plants in Colorado and Texas and New Mexico and the empties rattling their way north for refilling in Gillette, Wyoming where the massive bituminous fields were dug twenty-four hours a day.

The Denver & Rio Grande Railroad laid those tracks shortly after the Civil War in order to bring visitors from Denver and Pueblo to Little

London, as Colorado Springs was sometimes called, General William J. Palmer's fledgling resort at the foot of Pikes Peak. The eponymous hamlet of Palmer Lake was built twenty miles north of Colorado Springs, at the highest point of the hundred-mile stretch between Denver and Pueblo, to supply water to the 4-4-0 steam engines, but over the years, automobiles and airplanes superseded the passenger trains, and freight became the railroad's main business. The railroads, kings of the nineteenth century, were consolidated in the twentieth as cutthroat competition demanded efficiencies of scale. The D&RG swallowed smaller roads and was in turn swallowed by the monolithic Burlington Northern Santa Fe.

Through all the buying and selling, Palmer Lake had remained a quaint little town three miles off the interstate highway with easy access to the cities.

And that's why, Linda thought, *John figured it'd be a good investment for us to buy and rehab this old building. But I never figured on being bored out of my skull running an antiques store up here.*

She smiled, thinking about how hard John had worked, coming up here after his regular shift selling cars at the Nissan dealership was over. Working at night, he'd gutted and completely rebuilt the old two-story stucco inside and out, and formed it into a wood-fronted store with a one-bedroom apartment upstairs . . . now, the building was in keeping with the historic nature of the town. Instead of an ugly white cube, it looked like a wooden false-front built in the 1870s, complete with an overhanging mini-mansard roof and large wooden corbels John had designed himself.

The Neversink Trading Co. building was even featured on the front of the town's planning commission booklet. She knew John was secretly very proud of that. And she was proud of him. *He's not only good in the bed, he's a good man. A hard worker and good provider. If only it weren't so damn b-o-r-i-n-g all the time up here . . .* She heard another BNSF engineer blowing several long blasts on his air horns as he approached 105 and the County Line Road. It was a nasty intersection where the railroad crossed both highways at once. She counted four long blasts, heard the iron train wheels begin to squeal as the two engines and 125 coal cars entered the big horseshoe bend that circumnavigated the lake. She could feel the floor rumbling under her feet.

She sighed for the umpteenth time and looked at her daily calendar on the counter behind her. The word for the day was "concatenation," a noun, meaning: *a series of links, a chain of events.*

"Concatenation" she said aloud as she looked up at Kit-Cat again. He was still grinning, looking left-right, left-right, left-right and wig-wagging his tail. Ten more minutes his hands said. Linda thought about screaming.

She went to check on Spanky, out on the shady back porch. He was asleep on the glider.

"Hey. What kind of a watchdog are you . . . sleeping on the job."

Linda sat on the glider as Spanky rolled over on his side and looked at her, waved his paws in the air . . . his sign that he'd like to be rubbed.

"Oh, so you want your tummy rubbed, do ya?"

She reached over and ran her nails through the fur on his chest and neck, scratched behind his ears. Spanky sighed and closed his eyes in bliss. She stopped after a few moments. He opened one eye and brushed her arm with his paw, made an erruh-erruh sound in his throat.

"Oh, all right you big pain-in-the butt. If you weren't so cute I'd get a cat. They're not so needy you know."

He rolled over and put his head on her thigh, looked at her with his soulful brown eyes.

"Yeah. You're right. I wouldn't do that."

She stroked his back with gentle pets. Spanky closed his eyes again while Linda felt a slight summer breeze, and rocked the glider back and forth, willing the afternoon to be over . . . thinking about the chain of events that had caused her to be here, being bored out of her mind, one cell at a time.

John's the one with all the ambition in the family, she thought. She remembered how he'd gotten all excited when he'd read about the investment opportunities in small-town real estate adjacent to big cities, started looking right away, and saw old Mr. Kravoc's sign in the front window one night as they were going to a party. That was two years and a lifetime's worth of hard work ago.

They'd been so excited at first. Planned on living upstairs, having the shop downstairs, a more relaxed lifestyle, less stress . . . and they'd be a part of the community . . . appreciated for improving the town, getting rid of an eyesore.

Oh yeah, she thought, *back when our altruism was intact, before the snide comments, the resentment from the entrenched locals . . . and all the trouble from the bar across the street.*

She hadn't told John, but she'd found human feces in front of the door when she came in to open the store, day before yesterday. They'd had one of the drunks put his car over the bank at the edge of their property and abandon it, and a second one who'd been kicked out of his house and was living in his car over on the same side of the property.

John had had the first car towed, told the second one to move or he'd get towed too, and they'd had nothing but trouble ever since.

I never knew people could be so venal, so petty, so downright vicious and cruel. I can't remember the last time anybody from town stopped in the shop. I guess we're being shunned . . .

She remembered other events involving the bar . . . fights, the two men battling in the middle of 105, one of them left unconscious, spread-eagled on the double line, smack-dab in the center of the main road, human vomitus on their sidewalk more times than she could remember

. . . drunks coming in the shop in the midafternoon, leering, making salacious remarks.

Do people come up here and leave their minds somewhere else? Or maybe they were insane to begin with? I know one thing for sure, we'll never, ever, ever, ever own property or any kind of a business near a bar again. What a monster pain-in-the . . .

Her thoughts were interrupted by the thunk of a car door, followed by the tinkle of the bell over the shop's entrance. Spanky jumped off the glider and looked in the back screen door, wagging his tail. Linda went in to greet her customer, Spanky at her heels.

He looked about forty years old, with dark hair and eyes and was casually well-dressed in an Izod shirt, khaki cargo shorts, and Birkenstocks. He spoke first.

"Hi. Are you the proprietress?"

"Yep. How can I help?"

"I was just wondering, do you buy stuff? Old stuff?"

She was going to point to the sign by the register that said "We Buy Antiques" when Spanky ran up to the man wagging his tail so hard that his whole back end was shaking, put his paws on the man's thighs, and, standing on his back legs . . . buried his nose in the guy's crotch.

"Oh! I'm so sorry," Linda said, grabbing air instead of the dog's collar she'd been reaching for.

The man pushed the sheltie away and held his collar, giving her a chance to capture the wriggling dog. He said, "Now that's what I call an enthusiastic greeting. Reminds me of a collie our neighbor had when I was a kid, same color and everything. What's his name?"

"Spanky."

He squatted and held his hand out palm-down, to let the dog get to know him. Spanky, with Linda holding his collar, sniffed and covered it with kisses with his pink tongue.

"You have dogs?"

"Two of 'em, back in Chicago. A poodle and an English bulldog.

The man gave Spanky a few last pets and stood, while Linda put the dog outside, on the enclosed rear deck.

"He's my official store meeter-and-greeter, like the retirees at Wal-Mart? But sometimes he gets too excited."

"He's as enthusiastic a little critter as I've ever seen . . ."

"Yeah. I apologize for his actions."

"You worry too much. You ought to see what it's like at the Board of Trade, where I work."

"What . . ."

"I'm a commodities trader."

"Oh, well . . ."

"What I came for, you buy antiques, right?"

"Some."

"Say, I'm selling the family cabin down in the Glen. And I've got a steamer trunk I want to get rid of. It's been up in the attic since my grandfather bought the place back in the early thirties. It was stuck back in a corner of the eaves behind the chimney. Nobody knew it was there until the home inspector found it a few days ago. I just want to get rid of it so I can close the sales contract and sell the place. It's out in my car."

"Is the top flat, or humped up?"

"It's a camelback. It's full of clothes too."

"Okay. Let's go look. No promises though."

"I understand."

The car turned out to be one of those seventy-five-thousand-dollar Range Rovers made in England that were so popular with the jet-set. The trunk was dusty but in excellent condition with all its metal reinforcements intact and a beautiful double-hasped filigreed cast iron locking mechanism on the front. Linda said, "Do you have the key?"

"I do." And he handed it over.

She unlocked the hasps, *dirty, but functional,* she noted, and raised the lid. "Thanks for pulling it out on the tailgate. I didn't want to crawl up there," she said as the lid came all the way open and locked on the corner hinges to hold it. The lift-out tray was in perfect condition and held small items: handkerchiefs, combs and other personal things. She lifted the tray out, preparing for a thorough search, and looked at some threadbare housedresses that were only good for rags. She replaced the tray and closed the lid.

"It doesn't look like there's much of value in there."

"I didn't think there was any value in old clothes," he said.

"In some, there is . . . wedding or christening dresses, military uniforms, stuff like that."

The man looked at his watch.

"I've got to get going. Would you be interested in it?"

"Depends on what you want for it."

"Jeez, I don't know, how about a hundred bucks?"

"No way. I'll be lucky to get that much, and I've gotta clean it and find someone to buy it."

"Fifty?"

Linda looked at the sides and bottom, checking for damage, found none.

"Okay. If you'll help me get it in the shop."

"Sure. I put it in the car by myself. I'll put it wherever you want."

"I'll get the door. Set it in back please, by the end of the counter."

She went behind the counter, got a two-part sales ticket, and began writing a bill of sale as the man carried the trunk in. He was sweaty, gasping, and red-faced from the effort. "Whew, I'm glad I don't have to move it again."

"You should've let me help. The bathroom's back there if you want to wash your face."

"Thanks," he said and went in.

He came out as Linda finished writing. "Would you sign here, that I'm paying you fifty dollars for the trunk and contents? Oh, and I need your name and address too."

"Here or Chicago?"

"Here's okay. I'm giving you a check . . . I don't keep much cash here. The bank's in Monument, on the other side of the interstate."

"No problem. What's your name by the way?"

"Linda Zabukovic, err . . . Morrisey. Linda Morrisey."

"Which?"

"Both. Morrisey's my married name."

"Ah, explains the blonde hair. Polish?"

"No. My great grandparents came from Slovenia."

"Bojons?"

"Yes. Exactly right. We're the *beau genre* Napoleon mentioned when he was marching his army to Russia."

"Yeah, well that didn't work out so well, did it."

She considered it a statement rather than a question and didn't say anything.

He said, "Your folks work in the steel mill down there?"

"No. My people were coal miners. My grandfather was at Ludlow, in 1915."

"What's Ludlow?"

"It's a place, about a hundred and twenty-five miles south of here where there was a mine disaster that killed some miners. It was owned by John D. Rockefeller. They had the National Guard called out . . . they fought the miners. Killed some. Grandfather Mikhail was one of them. There's a monument down there and a museum."

"Jeez . . . I had no idea."

She took the receipt back, looked at it, and frowned.

"Maybe you'd better let me write your name on here, so it's legible."

"Good idea . . . I write like a doctor."

"It is pretty bad . . . to be honest." She printed the information, gave him the copy and a check for fifty dollars. "Thanks for selling it to me."

"You're welcome. I'll stop if I'm ever out here again, say hello."

"Better do it fast," she said to herself as he let the door close behind him. She watched him drive away, the only thing moving on 105, heading toward Monument and Interstate 25. Linda looked over at Kit-Cat, who looked left, right, left, and told her two more hours to go. She moved to the steamer trunk, opened the top, then changed her mind and closed it again. She got some rags, a sponge, and bucket of soap and water, thinking *I might just as well get the outside of this thing cleaned up before I start on the stuff inside* . . . She pushed out the back screen door as she exited the bathroom, saw Spanky on the porch glider, stretched out on his side, and sound asleep. She thanked the god of small favors, made sure his water bowl was full, and turned to her task.

As the dust of seventy years washed away, she noted that the trunk appeared new. The canvas covering was intact and untorn, the wooden slats that strengthened the trunk showed no sign of being rubbed against other luggage. Even the leather handles were in perfect condition.

A small miracle, she thought, *I've seen a lot of these, but not in this condition. It's almost as if it was bought and never used.*

Finished with washing and drying the outside, Linda dumped the bucket and flushed the toilet, washed the grime from her hands and arms and dried them with a cloth towel she kept in the wall cabinet. She looked in the mirror and patted some stray hairs in place, then went back to the trunk.

This time when she opened the lid she took a careful look at the insides before removing anything. Just like the outside, the inside appeared new.

Pasted inside she noted a chromolithograph of a pretty Victorian woman in a blue full-skirted dress and a high lace collar. Usually they were gone, the weak glue surrendering to the years of heat, humidity, and neglect, but this one looked as it did the day it was put there.

Linda lifted the tray out and put it on an oak table. The tray was divided in half, and was made for smaller items on the lower open side. A taller section with hinged lid stored hats. She started with the lower part.

She found some handkerchiefs with tiny flowers embroidered on them, a dozen or so Battenberg lace doilies, a partly finished cross-stitch sampler, tea towels, quilting squares, a darning egg, and various assorted sewing supplies.

The tall side was full of surprises. A darling pair of red leather baby shoes wrapped in a cloth diaper—tissue paper stuffed inside to make them hold their shape—was the first item. They were like new, showing little sign of having been worn. Next came a used pair in white, also carefully wrapped and stuffed with paper. Other baby items followed: teething ring, silver rattle, silver baby spoon, and a baby dish with Peter Rabbit prancing around the rim. Last of the wrapped pieces was a tiny pink cup with "Grace" inscribed on it in gold and black letters. *I'll check with the price guide, but I think I'll double my money on these things alone . . .* Linda thought . . . *if I ever see another paying customer.*

She put the baby items on the counter, took some shopping bags from the stacks underneath. She put the linens in one and the discarded paper in another. Then she turned to the trunk itself.

Well, it's all gravy from here on with what came out already. Let's see what other goodies are there.

An old coat and half a dozen clean but well-worn housedresses came out.

Cut the buttons off and make dust rags, I guess. Always need more of them, she mused as she put them in a sack.

Two camisoles, socks, slips, and cotton undies were followed by all sorts of baby clothes, including several small pairs of baby overalls . . . highly sought after by collectors for dressing teddy bears and dolls. Linda set the baby things and slips to one side, the undies went in with the rags.

A soft flannel crib blanket came out . . . it was protecting a long white lace christening gown, *Another prized collector's item,* she thought, followed by a hand-sewn crib quilt. It was a rainbow of colors in what she was pretty sure was called the Star of Bethlehem pattern. The workmanship was excellent, six tiny stitches to the inch.

Bingo, she thought, *this is turning into a good day, even without customers.* But another thought began growing . . . *How could all of this get left behind? And where's the daddy?*

Her unease grew with the unwrapping of the next item. A white cotton sheet held a white silk wedding dress with lace and pearls on the bodice and sleeves. Wow, I'd grade this as gem quality, Linda mused as she spread it on the table. *This trunk is like an archaeological dig, a life story being told.*

Her thoughts were prophetic. The trunk had still more to reveal . . . more story to tell . . . a last impression to leave on her heart, and a bittersweet memory of Palmer Lake.

She was close to the bottom; all the trunk had left in it were some flat boxes, like the ones stationery used to come in.

The first and second boxes she opened contained photographs: a smiling woman holding a baby in a long white christening dress and a professional, seven-by-nine sepia-toned one, mounted on heavy gray cardboard. In it, the bride and groom faced the camera side by side, his left arm around her waist, her left arm across her body holding his right hand, her wedding ring prominently displayed for all the world to see. They were a handsome couple . . . she with a smile so radiant it animated not only her face, but her entire body. . . he looking solemn, but with the barest hint of a face-stretching smile about to break out.

Linda recognized the dress as the one she'd just unwrapped from its sheet. A greater sense of unease settled in her as she felt somehow connected to these people, as if she knew them, felt they were like family . . . and suddenly realized the trunk was more than an artifact of commerce, it was telling a story and she'd become a part of it. She didn't know yet, that it would break her heart.

The third box held a newspaper clipping from the *Tri Lakes Leader*. On the masthead, it said,

— A Common Paper for Common People —

The date was April 27, 1921:

Palmer Lake was the scene of a terrible and fatal accident this Tuesday last, when the southbound 3 p.m. Rio Grande train collided with an automobile at the Highway 105 and County Line Road crossing.

Killed and pronounced dead at the scene were Bonnie Cassidy, 20, and her 18-month-old daughter, Grace, of Palmer Lake.

The engineer, Herbert Moffitt, said he saw the Ford sedan on the tracks and applied long warning blasts of his whistle as he approached the intersection, sounding a continuous one for the last quarter of a mile before the impact. The vehicle appeared to be stalled on the intersection according to Moffitt, and unable to move. The impact destroyed the automobile and evidence of the carnage was strewn about, nearly to Palmer Lake itself, half a mile down the tracks. The mangled bodies of the young woman and her baby were found among the various pieces and parts of the flivver. It appears upon investigation at the scene by county marshals and the D&RG inspectors, that the ballast was missing from between the ties at the conjunction of the railroad tracks and county road, possibly due to heavy rains over the weekend. The woman drove the car over the top of the rails and it became stuck between the ties. Trapped there, unable to move, she may have panicked when she saw the approaching locomotive bearing down on her.

*Funeral arrangements are by Feeny's of Colorado Springs, Services 10 a.m.
Saturday at St. Peter's in Monument. Her husband, Stephen Cassidy, was
rushed to the scene and was devastated by what he saw there. He was unable
to make a statement for the paper.*

Linda returned with care the brown and fragile article to its box, feeling
a tangible sense of loss from the aged, and now-unremembered tragedy. It
was as if she'd become part of the story somehow . . . and felt the tragedy
personally.

*How awful, and how terribly sad, two lives snuffed out by a twist of fate,
a concatenation of events resulting in the death of a mother and baby. One
life just beginning and another just beginning to flower stopped dead, just
like that . . .*

She put the boxes on the floor next to the trunk and pulled the last
items from the bottom of it. They were black, hand-knotted shawls with
tassels on the ends and sides that Linda recognized as shrouds. Coffin
covers, placed atop the caskets during the burial service. There were two
of them, one large and one small. Touching them made feelings of grief
well up so strongly that twin trails of tears ran down her cheeks.

She'd refolded the shawls and laid them on the counter when the phone
rang.

"Hey, honey, it's me. I just wanted to make sure you're still there."

She looked at Kit-Cat, who seemed to say "uh-oh" with his shifty eyes
and grin. The hands said six thirty.

"Oh gosh, John, I didn't realize the time. I've been busy all afternoon
with some stuff I bought."

"I just wanted to make sure you're okay. I just got home too."

"Yeah. Tell you about it when I get there, it's a sad story is all."

"Sure."

"Why don't you order a pizza. I should get there at the same time it does."

"Done deal, honey. Love you."

She put the "Closed" sign out as soon as she hung up, retrieved Spanky from the back porch, and locked up for the night. As she went through her nightly routine, Linda was thinking about the steamer trunk and the story it told in artifacts.

So many broken dreams and wrecked lives in those items, so much hope and potential wiped out in an instant . . . !

She clipped Spanky's leash on and locked the front door, turned toward her car, and saw the two men standing across the street at the bar, staring at her.

A couple of locals . . .

She could almost hear their thoughts, feel their resentment about those "rich S.O.B.'s from the city come up here to change things." She waved to them. They didn't wave back, continued staring at her. She got in her car, thinking about "concatenation," the word for the day on her calendar, *a chain of related events.*

She thought then about the chain of events that had put her here, in this place at this time, put an item in her hands that mirrored both her and John's broken hopes of living in Palmer Lake, left their dreams in a heap of smoldering wreckage, their plans and ambitions for a relaxed, casual life up here gone forever.

She sighed and started the car, backing carefully out on Highway 105, past the four-by-four posts the Realtors had put in to hold the big sign, and said the same little prayer to herself she'd said every day since last winter. *Please God, let it sell soon.*

THE RETRIBUTIONISTS

The Retributionists

MELEKI WAS PETRIFIED . . . scared to move, afraid to stay where he was . . . cowering behind the carcass of a burned-out Toyota pickup truck on a war-ravaged street just three blocks from the safety of his home. He sensed his pursuer, straining his nose, eyes, and ears to their limit, trying to smell, see, or hear some little proof that the assassin was inching closer. Meleki knew he was the prey. His hair stood on end as he crouched, heart pounding, breathing in shallow, rapid gasps . . . trying to decide the best time and place to run . . . wishing he'd stayed at home. Tears leaked from his eyes. He was so scared his heart threatened to beat a hole through his chest . . . so scared he knew he could lose control of his bladder and soil himself at any moment. He didn't want to die . . . not here . . . not like this. Not today.

Azziz was the predator . . . the sword arm of the Imam, Ali Muktar. Azziz was the archangel, the invincible one, sent by Muktar to punish blasphemers, idolaters, and infidels. His job was to send them to hell, down into the burning lake of fire and eternal damnation they'd earned by their actions. Meleki would join the forty-two other souls Azziz had shipped there as soon as he revealed himself, God willing. Azziz could see the Toyota from his third-story vantage point, knew Meleki was crouching behind it, but couldn't see well enough to take the shot. He waited.

Meleki also waited . . . in hopes of deliverance. He looked at the oozing scrapes on both hands and wrists. The blood had stopped, but the wounds seeped a yellowish fluid, like a blister. They hurt, as did his left ankle from twisting it when he'd stepped off the curb and gone flat on his face, a fall that saved his life, *Allah be praised*, as the shot rang out and the bullet whanged into the empty building behind him. He'd managed to crawl behind the burned Toyota as two more shots were fired, both impacting the truck with sickening thunks.

He's using lead bullets. Steel jackets would've passed through the truck and hit me.

Maybe, his optimistic-self said.

Maybe my ass, his pessimistic-self said, using a term he'd learned just that week from the foul-mouthed NCO from Colorado. Pessimistic-self added, *You know the filthy dog up there is using lead. It'll tear you apart, take an arm off . . . or a leg.* He shuddered at the thought, remembering his uncle Faoud's weeping, raw stump, him limping around on a homemade wooden crutch.

Look on the bright side, optimistic-self said.

What's that? pessimistic-self said.

After a pause, optimistic-self said, *There's only one of him.*

Meleki found no comfort in the thought. He remained terrified, frozen in place, shivering like a rabbit. He crouched behind the front fender and wheel, hoping for more protection from the engine block, feeling his feet, ankles, and knees going numb, knowing he couldn't stay like this for much longer. He prayed. It was a petitioning prayer, asking *Allah, all praises to him*, for rescue.

Azziz waited in his perch on the third floor, certain *the apostate will show himself and accept the judgment of Allah, all praises to him, all blessings from him.* He watched, and waited. It was only a matter of time. He rubbed his cheek along the stock of the Heckler & Koch seven millimeter rifle, inhaled the bright, bitter smell of gun oil, and watched the truck through the twenty-power Zeiss scope. Experience told him it would be soon, very soon, and Meleki would make his run. His last, fatal run. Azziz sighed, happy in his righteousness. His right index finger resting lightly on the trigger guard, ready to do its holy duty and send the accursed one to hell.

Meleki knew he had to take his chance soon . . . make his run for it. No help was coming. He squinted, guessed the sun was about straight up. *It must be noon. I've been here for an hour and a half, but it seems like forever.* The sidewalk was hot as a griddle. He was sweating, losing fluid, dehydrating.

And it's only going to get hotter . . . pessimistic-self said, *it's a hundred-plus degrees now, no water, no shade . . . no chance.*

Meleki wiped the sweat from his eyes with his sleeve, looked around, trying to conjure up an escape plan. He rolled to his left, so he could survey the sidewalk and the empty buildings behind him. *Careful, don't give him a shot.* He wormed onto his side, keeping his back against the wheel and tire, not letting any part of himself be exposed across the street. He felt the blood returning to his legs, the numbness disappearing as circulation was restored.

Azziz peered through the scope, his attention drawn by movement behind the burned truck. He saw a flash of cloth when the doomed man moved. *Not enough to take the shot,* he thought, but experience taught him that the condemned one would run shortly. He steadied his breathing, tightened his finger on the trigger ,and prepared for the kill shot.

Meleki looked at the looted, wrecked, and abandoned buildings less than thirty feet away. *Not even as far as it is from my desk to the colonel's office,* he thought. *Less than the distance I go every day to get my next pile of papers to translate. I can make it, easy.*

Pessimistic-self chimed in . . . *On a bad ankle? You think so?*

Optimistic-self said, *Yes . . . yes, I do.*

He felt his ankle throb, was working it around in a circle, testing it, when pessimistic-self threw another barb at him.

Wasn't that what you said when you signed on with the Americans at three thousand dollars a month? What got you branded as apostate and an idolater? Put you on your face in the dirt, with a death sentence on your head? I think I can . . .

Meleki ignored the voice in his head, rolled over on his stomach, and, gathering his legs under him in a tight crouch, pushed off with his arms as he screamed, *"Allahu Akbar!"* and ran, intent on diving through the blown-out front window of what was once a coffee shop.

Across the street, up on the third floor, Azziz, seeing Meleki break for freedom, took his shot. *Almost too easy,* he thought as he saw Meleki hit the side of the building, leaving a smear of gore as he fell to the sidewalk, his heart blown out by a seven millimeter hollow point. *"Allahu Akbar,"* Azziz said aloud, God is great. *Retribution is mine. And soul number forty-three is gone to hell,* he thought.

He stood, but as he leaned forward, looking out the window at his latest kill, his head exploded in a burst of bone, brain matter, and blood as a .50 caliber round struck him in front of the left ear.

"Praise Jesus," the spotter said to U.S. Army Ranger Staff Sergeant Cynthia Ann Sauchuk. "A head shot at nine hundred yards must be some kinda damn record."

"Praise Jesus my ass," Cynthia Ann said. "You want to praise somebody, praise Ronnie Barrett, the Model 82-A, and Lady Luck. I couldn't do it again in a million years. Now grab your shit. We gotta haul ass before the gomers get here."

THE PRISIONER OF JANE RUSSELL

The Prisoner of Jane Russell

I KNOW THEY'RE COMING FOR ME . . . I can hear them all the way down the building . . . the big sonofabitch I call Flounder-foot and the little weasel who is always at his heels like a quiet and sinister shadow: his ever-smirking assistant with the metal clipboard, Schlee.

The whup-whup-whup of Flounder-foot's size sixteens is contrapunted by Schlee's smaller, lighter clop-clop-clop. Whup-clop-clop, whup-clop-clop, whup . . . their footfalls come closer, closer. They're here. I watch from my seat on the bunk, wait for one of them to speak. It's Schlee; the little bastard catches me off guard when he says, "Come with us, you have a visitor."

"You sure you got the right guy? What do they want with me?" *Being summoned means I'm noticed. Not good. First you're noticed. By who. For what? Nobody knows. I only know that getting noticed and getting summoned comes just before getting disappeared. You keep your eyes and ears open, Davie, and your mouth shut. You can't trust anyone. Not anyone.*

"We've got the right guy. Move it. *Raust mitt.*"

It isn't a request. With my mouth as dry as hundred-year-old dust, and my legs quaking like a shotgun groom, I follow Schlee out of the room, with Flounder-foot bringing up the rear. As we move down the building I sense his presence back there, imagine feeling his hot breath on my neck, like a giant grizzly bear, wide-open jaws about to clamp his razor-sharp teeth into me, snuffing out my life as easy as switching off a lightbulb.

We walk toward reception like three tin soldiers, or a prisoner being led to the firing squad. *Never surrender*, I think, *Never. Don't give up, don't give in, don't give 'em any information . . .* I shiver, and march on.

A couple of other prisoners loiter by the open area as we march by. A bald guy with a white fluffy beard down his chest smiles at me and flashes a V for victory sign. "Good luck, Davie. Give 'em hell 'n' don't never surrender."

I nod at him and keep walking, prodded on by Flounder-foot's looming presence. I'm nervous. Scared, but be damned if I'll let them know it. *Wonder where they're taking me. And why. More torture? Change is like dying. I'm scared shitless.* The other guy standing there has sleeves of tattoos covering both arms and up his neck to the jaw line. He stares with hate-filled eyes and flips his middle finger at me, mouthing the words at the same time. I stare back at him, "Fuck you too, Ace."

Flounder pokes me in the back with a size-forty index finger. *"Raust. Raust."*

I follow where Schlee leads. Follow orders, move to my visit with the unknown.

I hear Flounder say something to Schlee, and he answers back. Flounder says something else and they both start laughing. I know they're laughing at me, but I can't tell what they're saying, they've switched to kraut.

"Yeah yeah yeah and fuck you too you Nazi assholes. My guys are coming. They're coming, and they're gonna bomb your kraut asses back to the Stone Age. You and your whole country, you miserable *schweinehund* sons of bitches."

I spit at the floor, trying to hit Flounder's shoes, or better still his pants. I brace myself, expecting the big bastard to whack me in the back with the butt end of the Mauser he carries, but the blow doesn't come. I put both hands on my head and keep on marching. *One for the U.S. Army Air*

Force. I may be planeless, but I'm damn sure not helpless. I smile to myself and soldier on.

We get to the admin section and there's a woman waiting there, dressed in civilian clothes. She faces me and an electric charge, sharp as a face slap, goes through me. She looks familiar, like someone I knew from before. *Before the war and before England, before fighter escorts and bombing runs inside Germany, before dogfights, before ME-109s diving at us, coming down out of the sun, before the voice in my ears screamed out, "Davie, on your six he's on your six BREAK RIGHT BREAK RIGHT BRE . . ." And then the whap! tickita-tickita-tick of machine-gun rounds stitching through the fuselage, tearing up my tail section, destroying the rudder, and my Mustang flopping over and pointing her nose at the ground and then I am spinning, out-of-control head down at four hundred miles an hour. I don't know how I bailed out but I did. The next thing I remember was a couple of kraut farmers, old men, cutting me out of the tree where my chute was caught.*

Then I realize . . . the pretty woman smiling at me as I stand there between Schlee and Flounder looks like Jane. Jane Russell the movie star whose picture was gracing the ready-room wall.

Then she spoke, "Uncle Davie . . . it's Kathy, Kathy Ralston, Howard and Carol's . . ." and then she switched to kraut.

Nice try, sister. Don't you mean Uncle Sam? I'm not buying your jive. Not today. Not ever. I turn my eyes back to the front, and stand. My fingers laced together on top of my head, thinking, *She ain't Jane Russell and I never heard of a girl named Kathy Ralston. And Howie, he's just a squirt, building model airplanes in the bedroom we share back in Colorado Springs. She looks about thirty-something, thirty-four, -five maybe? A few years too old for me anyway. Maybe if I was ten years older. She sure is cute as hell though, and it's been a helluva long time since. Quit it, you damn fool. Look at you. You're a prisoner for chrissakes. Snap out of it. She's a kraut officer or spy of some kind. Wake up you dumb bastard, there's a war on.*

I see, out the corner of my eye, a single teardrop slide down her left cheek. See her brush it away with the back of her hand as she turns to Schlee and they start yapping in rapid-fire kraut again.

What an actress, but I ain't buyin' it, lady. I know you'll try to get information out of me and then those evil fuckers in the black uniforms with the steel eyeglasses and the steel surgical tools will come and . . .

I see Schlee hand her the metal clipboard and a pen. He points. She signs and hands it back. Schlee takes the first page, gives her the rest, and a brown envelope and . . .

What the fuck. Are these Nazi bastards turning me over to her? What's . . .

A couple of officers in civvies come out of the hallway and see us. They come over. One of 'em says something to Schlee. He answers *ja*, and the two officers take the beauty who looks like Jane Russell over to the desk where they all tête-à-tête for several minutes. She shows them the paper Schlee handed her and hugs the big brown envelope to her chest, protecting it. The officer says something to her. She shakes her head, no. Then he holds his hand out, palm up. No again, with a shake of her head. She's holding the envelope like it's her firstborn child. I can see the kraut officer getting red in the face, more demanding, louder. The other officer gets involved. The two of them step away, exchange words, and gesticulate at each other. The second officer takes the paper, walks back to Jane Russell, and hands it to her with a slight bow. She comes back to where Flounder, Schlee, and I are standing and says something to them in kraut-speak. We start for the door as the two officers, still arguing, move down the opposite hallway.

I can see sunlight ahead. The door opens and I smell the sweet smell of new-mown grass, hear the sound of a distant wind chime. I'm outside. Still under guard. Flounder is sticking to me like a bad attitude, and we're all following Jane Russell toward a gray vehicle of some kind.

Sonofabitch. I think I'm getting out of the stalag. Yeah, but to what? To where?

Schlee is looking at the vehicle and saying something to Jane Russell, who's fiddling with keys at the door. She drops the keys and Flounder reaches down to pick them up. That's when I break for freedom.

I only make about three or four steps when Schlee, Jane Russell, and Flounder all yell. I get another few paces, going hell-bent for election, before Flounder grabs me in a bear hug, lifts me off my feet, and, oh shit. I'm caught. I kick and scream, curse and spit, but it doesn't matter. I'm still caught. And I'm being carried by Flounder like a naughty schoolboy on his way to the woodshed.

Now I'm fighting for my life. I grunt, try for a heel-strike on Flounder's shin, miss and try again but can't get him. His arms are like clamps. I gnash my teeth, try to bite, get my own damn tongue instead, spitting blood, howl in frustration.

I can see the gray vehicle getting closer. The open door, yawning like the mouth of some prehistoric beast, trying to swallow me whole. I fight harder. I can hear Flounder breathing big in my ear, but I'm running out of energy, I can feel blood dribbling from my mouth as Schlee grabs my right arm.

He's got a hypodermic needle clenched in his teeth like a dog would a bone. I watch, trying to resist as he swabs my arm and slides a needle into my vein and depresses the plunger. It's cold. It stings like hell. Then, nothing. The last thing I remember is the smell of new-mown grass.

I wake slow, sense that I'm moving. I'm in a vehicle, lying on my back, covered to my chin with a light blanket. Comfortable, I go back to sleep.

It's dark when I wake the second time, in spasm.

I try to sit up.

Can't, I'm in some sort of restraint. I start to struggle.

"Sh-sh-sh," a calm voice says, "easy, Uncle Davie, easy. I'm going to stop and get you up. Easy, easy, don't get upset. Sh-sh-sh . . ." She puts her hand on me. It's soft and reassuring, her voice a whisper. I relax, feel calm. She pats me gently, soothing me.

The vehicle stops and she gets out. A light comes on when the door opens. It hits my eyes, scares me. I start to thrash against the restraints, still almost flat on my back. Then the door next to me opens and she's here. Jane Russell is doing something next to me and I sit up. I'm in a car seat, with a belt on. She smiles at me, pats my hand again.

She goes around back and opens the trunk. I hear her doing things, clunking noises, then she's back. She hands me a bottle of something. I look at it, look at her. She smiles and takes it, removes the cap and drinks from it, hands it back.

I take a timid sip, still careful. These krauts are tricky bastards. It's water. It's only water and I'm dry as cotton lint. I tip the bottle up and take several big swigs. It's good, but it's about to get better. Much, much better. She produces an orange and peels it. I don't think I've seen an orange for a long, long time. Years maybe. She hands me a slice and I put it in my mouth. When I bite it my taste buds explode. I can't believe how good it is and we eat the rest of it together. More surprises, we share a chicken sandwich with mayonnaise, and lettuce, and last . . . oh, sweet Jesus, she produces a Hershey's chocolate bar and we each eat half. I feel for a moment as if heaven's gate has opened up and swallowed me whole.

I think for a few seconds about making another break for freedom, then decide against it. It's pitch-dark. I see we're on the side of a big divided highway. *The Autobahn?* I've heard rumors of these and seen them from the air, but never traveled one before.

You'd better hold your water sport, until you figure out where in hell you are.

I tell Jane Russell, "I've got to piss."

She nods her head. "Will you be a good boy if I unbelt you?"

"Yeah. I've really got to go."

"Okay."

She reaches across me and does something to the restraint and it lets go of me. She helps me swing my feet and legs out, then holds my hands and helps me stand erect.

Oh, fuck. The world spins around. My head explodes with bright lights and pain I think I'm gonna ralph.

"Sh-sh, easy. Take a deep breath. It's the shot they gave you. It'll pass in a moment. Breathe. That's it, good. Better now?"

I nod my head. She takes my right arm and we move over to the edge of a ditch. I pull my package out and make water while she holds my arm. I see her looking politely off into the distance. Truthfully, I feel so sick I just don't give a damn who sees my equipment. All I want is relief, and to sit back down so the whirlies will go away. I tuck in and shuffle back to the gray motor vehicle. I sit, pull my feet in. Jane Russell rehooks the restraint and puts the blanket over me. She takes my hand and puts it on a latch that allows me to recline the seat back, or sit it up.

"Okay?"

I nod.

"Drink more water if you can."

I nod again. She puts an open bottle in a holder between us, walks around the vehicle, and gets behind the wheel. As soon as we're moving, I doze off.

My sleep isn't restful. It's punctuated by vignettes of prison camp, the atrocities I suffered there. One Nazi after another steps through my mind as I'm shot down again and again, captured and interrogated, again and again by an SS officer wearing a black uniform with the death's head insignias and round steel spectacles that glint in the light as his assistant, a big smirking torture-meister with a bad attitude and tattoos on both forearms, starts to work on my hands and feet with a carpenter's claw hammer and a pair of general-purpose handyman pliers.

I awake fighting this time. As I emerge from a well of darkness, demons in steel-rimmed eyeglasses come with me. The sweat and the blood, the pain and the terror that accompanies us is as true and real as the sweat on my body and the animal stink of fear I'm giving off.

I moan.

Kick.

Claw.

Scream.

I lash out, connect with flesh, hear the smack, a yell, someone shouts, "Stop. Stop it."

But I won't.

Can't.

Don't.

Then the voice screams again, in German. I fight harder, twisting and turning, gibberish and spittle spewing from my mouth. I'm lashing out with hands, feet, teeth, howling now in rage, fear, and frustration. I don't notice the vehicle has stopped or that I'm alone. I'm too busy battling the phantoms swimming up out of one nightmare after another.

All at once I run out of gas. I'm completely exhausted, sitting with my hands in my lap and staring out at nothing when the policeman opens the door. I try to escape, but I'm held by restraints. I brace myself, waiting for the blows to begin.

Instead of hitting me he squats on his haunches and says, "Lieutenant Corcoran."

"Yes, sir."

"We don't have much time, so just listen. Stop fighting this woman. She's on your side. She's a partisan risking her life to rescue you. She's smuggling you out of enemy territory and taking you to an American hospital."

"She's a spy?"

"We both are. I'm going to go ahead of you and clear the way. We're almost there, but you've got to play along. Can you do that?"

"Okay.

"But you've got to stay calm, or we'll all be back with the Nazis."

He pats me on the shoulder, stands, and closes the door, gives me a thumbs-up. I nod and face eyes front, watch a blood-red sun rising like a malevolent eye in front of me.

When Jane Russell gets back in the vehicle I can see a mouse rising on her face just below her right eye. She has a piece of ice in a hankie she's pressing on it.

You'd better say something, Davie. Don't act like such an asshole.

As she starts the vehicle and pulls up on the highway behind the patrol car I manage to croak out, "S-Sorry. Very sorry."

She pats me with a cold, ice-wet hand. "Goes with the territory," is all she says.

* * *

The rest of the journey passed in a few hours. By midafternoon, less than thirty some hours after leaving the "stalag" in California, David Lee Corcoran, eighty-four years old and suffering from schizophrenia and senile dementia, was checked into the psychiatric section of the Southwest Assisted Care Center at Colorado Springs, Colorado, by his niece and only surviving relative, Kathryn A. Ralston.

That evening, over a Bombay Sapphire gin and tonic, an exhausted, road-weary Kathy Ralston was telling her husband about the trip. "If it wasn't so sad, it'd be funny. He thinks he's a twenty-four-year-old lieutenant. He thinks I'm Jane Russell and he's a prisoner of war back in Germany."

Her husband said, "He's a prisoner of Jane Russell in his own mind?"

"Yeah . . . that's the sad part. He doesn't remember any of his life after the service."

"Good thing you did his estate planning and had his power of attorney."

"And you tracked him down. The nursing home in California was on the verge of having itself declared his guardian. He thought they were all Nazis."

"You're getting a black eye."

"Yeah, I know. Be good, or I'll tell everybody you're beating me."

"Nobody'd believe you. Now if it was the other way around . . ."

"Ha-ha. Would you make us another drink? Then I think I'll be able to sleep."

"How did you get him calmed down the last time?" Dick said as he made fresh gin and tonics.

"When he freaked out, I couldn't. So I called nine-one-one, and a state trooper from the highway patrol stopped and talked to him. He told Uncle Davie I was a secret agent sent to rescue him and take him to an American hospital."

"He went for it?"

"Yep. He was a lamb the rest of the way."

"So now he thinks he's in an American hospital, instead of a POW camp?"

"Yeah. And get this, when I signed him in, I asked the staff to call him Lieutenant."

"Will they?"

"Sure. I told them I'd come see him this weekend."

"I'm gonna find a photo of Jane Russell on the Internet and give it to him."

"I think he'd like that . . . if he remembers who she is."

THE EMERALD PEARL WITCH

The Emerald Pearl Witch

MEL'S BARBER SHOP was a nondescript place, a pass-by-every-day-and-never-notice kind of place, a been-there-forever place, four hundred square feet cloaked in anonymity, over on West Colorado Avenue, in the oldest part of Colorado Springs.

Melquiades Arguedo opened the shop in 1968, after he got back from Vietnam and was honorably discharged. Drafted in the fall of 1965, four months after he'd graduated from Palmer High School, he went willingly and served without protest. Neither a hero nor a coward, his service was unremarkable and best described as indifferent. He made no friends or enemies, passing through unnoticed and pretty much ignored by his fellow soldiers. Mel liked it that way. He preferred listening to talking, the shadows to the spotlight, a supporting, rather than a starring role in life. At five-six and 145, he was a small man with a bad complexion and poor eyesight who'd lost most of his hair by his late twenties. He was a man who went unnoticed in crowds because his only distinguishing characteristic was a face-wide perpetual smile that he wore twenty-four hours a day. He'd be an ideal barber.

So Mel came home in September of 1967, having lived through the war in Southeast Asia. He went to barber school on the GI Bill, married a heavyset girl named Gabriela Pacheco whom he'd known since high school, opened his shop on West Colorado Avenue in April of 1968, and settled into an unremarkable, routine life.

By 1974, his wife was well on her way to becoming the *mamacita* she was always meant to be, and Mel was the father of two daughters: Christina, four, and Constance, six.

He was in the market for a used car. That's how he met Jimmy-Dan Dee, where his life was utterly changed. It's when he discovered his inner man, the man he really was, the why known only to himself and God.

He began his search by looking in the newspaper, reading the classified auto ads, checking prices, trying to find what was out there to buy, and at what prices. After a week or so, Mel headed out to the used car ghetto on East Platte Avenue, where the used car lots went from curb to curb in what seemed like an endless profusion of chrome, fluorescent green, orange, or yellow on black "Buy Now, Deals on Wheels" and "Lower Price" signs that screamed from sparkling, shiny windshields . . . where there were big teddy bears on shiny, waxed, gleaming hoods, helium balloons tied to radio antennas, and flags of every description flapping, flying, and waving to attract the attention of anyone driving through the glitz-choked gulch. East Platte Avenue looked like a circus designed by competing teams of insane chimpanzees. Mel felt like a deer who'd wandered into a preserve, filled with half-wild lions dressed up like car salesmen who lurked in a jungle of used vehicles of every size and shape, color and description.

He worked his way from Union Boulevard to Circle Drive without finding anything he liked at a price he could afford. He was almost to Academy Boulevard, almost out of places to check, when he spotted a dark green Cadillac parked on the next-to-the-last used car lot, a place named DAN-DEE MOTORS. He pulled in for a closer look, and was captured by a hairy-legs.

A hairy-legs, according to Jimmy-Dan Dee, was a meeter-and-greeter, a person whose job was to meet the customer, qualify him, demonstrate a vehicle by taking it for a ride called a "demo," and asking him to buy. At that point the customer would be taken inside to an office, made comfortable with coffee or soft drinks, and a "deal" written up in the form of an "offer to buy." It didn't matter if the offer was realistic or not; the idea was to get the customer psychologically committed to a purchase, then and there. If all those things went as planned, the hairy-legs went to get "the boss's okay," while the customer relaxed in the office. At that point the customer was T.O.'d, or turned over, to the "closer," a sales manager who would appraise the trade-in and whose job it was to make the transaction doable. Doable meant that the trade-in was purchased from the customer for a wholesale price, a down payment was negotiated, the financing was arranged, and the buyer committed to making the payments.

The hairy-legs who captured Mel on the night he first saw the green Cadillac was an experienced salesman named Alvin Poorman. The closer was Jimmy-Dan Dee himself and poor Melquiades Arguedo, Mel the Barber, had no chance of escaping their combined onslaught.

It was past closing time, but Alvin, Jimmy-Dan, and several others were in the back office shooting dice and they'd forgotten to turn the outside lights off.

Mel was bent over at the waist with his face pressed against the driver's side window, hands cupped around his eyes, trying to see inside the Cadillac when Alvin, who'd stepped away from the crap game to step into the restroom, saw him. Mel, who had no intention of buying a Cadillac, and furthermore couldn't afford one, was fantasizing about driving down the interstate, stereo playing, cool air-conditioned air keeping him comfortable, encased in a butter-soft tan calfskin leather seat, was startled from his reverie when a male voice behind him said, "She's a beauty, ain't she?"

"Oh . . . Oh, yeah. She is. She is definitely a beautiful car. Too rich for me, though."

Alvin, whose first dictum as a salesman was "Do your customer a favor and disbelieve everything he tells you," said, "Actually, she's not expensive at all, only about two hundred a month." While that was marinating in Mel's brain, Alvin added, "This is a brand-new color for nineteen seventy-four: it's called Fire-Mist Emerald Pearl. I heard they won't ever offer it again. Too expensive. My name's Alvin, by the way. Alvin Poorman. And you are . . . ?"

"Melquiades Arguedo. But everybody calls me Mel."

"Okay, I will. What'd you say you did, Mel . . . for a living?"

"I'm a barber. I own Mel's Barber Shop on West Colorado Avenue."

"Is that right . . . I've been looking for a good barber. Been there long?"

"Just about seven years."

"Izzat so. Hang on a second. I'll be right back." Alvin darted up the four steps into the square cement-block building that was the office. He disappeared through a doorway as Mel worked his slow and careful way around the dark green Cadillac, checking for flaws in the deep, emerald pearl paint. He found none.

Inside, Alvin motioned to Jimmy-Dan, who'd just passed the dice. Alvin jerked his head around toward the hallway, indicating he wanted to speak privately with the boss. When they were out in the hall, Alvin said, "I need your keys. I've got a live one."

"On the Caddy?"

"Yeah."

"Is he qualified?"

"He's owned his own business for seven years, over on the west side."

Alvin didn't tell Jimmy-Dan that Mel was a barber, thinking, *I'll cross that bridge when I get to it.* He got the keys and hustled back outside to where Mel waited alongside the emerald pearl Caddy.

"Mel—catch," Alvin said as he tossed a set of keys. "Let's go for a ride. The round one opens the door and the square one goes in the ignition."

And just that fast, Mel the Barber found himself driving a car he'd only dreamed about, a luxury automobile he couldn't afford and didn't intend to buy, a car he found himself suddenly wanting with all his heart: an emerald pearl Cadillac Sedan de Ville with air-conditioning, power seats and windows, stereo, and butter-soft calfskin leather. He felt like he was living a dream, a dream come true and, with Alvin's prompting, was able to ignore the little voice inside his head that kept saying, "Don't do it, don't do it" over and over again. Melquiades Arguedo, Mel the Barber, husband, father, and businessman was in the grip of a fire-mist emerald pearl Witch . . . and she wasn't about to let him go. Her spell was absolute.

Alvin Poorman directed Mel on a test drive that took about twenty-five minutes and left him in a daze. When he steered the big Caddy back onto the used car lot, Mel was almost in tears, his emotions wound as tight as a broken clock. He felt the big V8 engine throbbing under his feet on the pedals and under his legs on the seat, and he heard it just below the music playing softly on the stereo speakers, as if she were letting him know her power, speed, and awesome majesty were his to command. He smelled the calfskin leather, rubbed his hand along the smooth seat cushion, saw the reflection of the streetlamps moving across the hood, looking at once solemn and mysterious in the emerald pearl paint, now almost black in the absence of light, moving proudly in the dark, moonless night.

Alvin was monitoring Mel from his perch on the passenger's seat, saw the glaze in Mel's eyes and the smile he had on his face—the one that looked like it couldn't be knocked off with a fire ax, and went right into a close. "So, Mel, whadda ya think? Wanna take her home, make her yours?"

Mel went for it as quick as a starving cat for a fish head. "Oh, yeah. I'd love to, but . . . "

"But what? I'll make this so easy you won't believe it. You can pay two hundred a month, can'tcha?"

"Yeah . . . but."

"But what? Don't worry, I'll take care of everything. We sell more cars than anybody. The bank gives us special deals on financing. C'mon in and we'll do some figuring."

"How much is the car?"

"Fifty-seven hundred is all."

"That's twice as much as I was going to spend."

"Were you gonna pay cash?"

"No."

"Can you pay two hundred a month? You told me you could."

"Oh, yeah. Sure," Mel said, thinking, *That's an extra hundred haircuts . . .* But the other voice in his head followed right up with, *You deserve it. Don't forget tips . . . and you can stay open longer. You'll look good driving it too. One important hombre. El Jefe himself. Go ahead. You know you want it. Just do it.* As he followed Alvin into the office, Melquiades Arguedo was a man in torment, conflicted and transformed in twenty-five minutes of ride and drive to a man whose psyche was composed of equal parts longing and dread by a fire-misted, emerald pearl siren with a 450-cubic-inch motor. He had to have her.

"Well, then," Alvin said, "it don't make any difference what she costs as long as the payment's two hundred a month. Does it?"

"No, I guess it doesn't. It just doesn't," Mel said with a smile as he looked at the big, beautiful Cadillac with gleaming emerald pearl paint and spotless whitewall tires. He shivered, turned, and went up the steps with Alvin.

Alvin stuck to the plan, wrote an offer, got $225 cash and a credit application from Mel and a cold can of Coors beer for him to drink. Then he went in the backroom for Jimmy-Dan Dee's approval.

The craps game was still going strong, with five men standing around a desk that was pushed against a wall so the dice could be rolled against it. Jimmy-Dan had just made his point, a six "Old Henry-Hicks" the hard way, by rolling three-three. He'd picked up the bets and was holding the cash in his left hand. He was fading the next round of bets with his right. When all bets were covered, he picked up the pair of green dice that had been sitting in front of him, and rattled them in his right hand for a second before tossing them across the desktop to the wall. "C'mon, baby. Daddy needs new shoes."

The dice clattered to a stop. "Nine. The point is nine," someone said.

The dice were sent back to Jimmy-Dan, and he placed them in the same spot in front of himself.

"Betcha don't."

"Pass."

"Three-to-two says you don't."

"Pass. Any two-to-one?"

No one spoke.

"Okay," Jimmy-Dan said. "I'll fade the three-two."

Two of the players put three one-dollar bills on top of their first bet. Jimmy-Dan covered each of those with two dollars.

"Bets right? Shooter's coming out," and Jimmy-Dan rolled the dice again.

"C'mon nine. Niner from South Caroliner. Mama needs new shoes."

When the dice stopped bouncing, skittering, and clattering, a five and a four were showing. "Come to Poppa," Jimmy-Dan chortled as he pulled in the cash, about forty dollars, and the betting sequence started again.

Jimmy-Dan's next toss produced another nine and the one after that a seven and he'd crapped out. The dice went to his right and a Chevrolet salesman from Academy Boulevard took over as the shooter. Alvin pulled his boss out in the hall for the second time in less than an hour. "Told ya I had a live one," Alvin said as he handed Jimmy-Dan his order and Mel's cash.

"My new Caddy? No shit. Well, let's go back to my office and take a look."

"It ain't exactly new anymore," Alvin said as he lit a cigarette with his hands cupped around the match, "she's got twenty-seven hundred and forty-two miles on her."

They went into Jimmy-Dan's office at the rear corner of the building where he sat in his high-back black-leather executive chair behind the six-foot-wide mahogany desk. The desk and chair, as well as the credenza behind it, were all on a four-inch raised platform . . . which gave Jimmy-Dan—who was short and thick like a bowling pin—a height advantage. He peered down at Alvin, sitting in one of the two customer's chairs opposite the desk and said, "Izzat so. You been out joyridin' in my car?"

Alvin looked up at Jimmy-Dan, who had his head cocked sideways so he could light the cigarette in the corner of his mouth with the gold lighter in his hand, and said, "No. I ain't. Just stating a fact is all. That's what she reads." He leaned his head back and exhaled, blowing smoke at the ceiling. "You'd better look at the deal, it's pretty good. Said he could pay two hundred a month."

Jimmy-Dan glanced at the purchase order. He checked the inventory card that was in a pull-out file, then did some computations with the big calculator on his desk. After running the numbers and totaling them he looked up at Alvin. "Jee-sus Khee-rist boy, y'all have torn this poor bastard's head clear off."

"Whadda ya mean?"

"Where'd you come up with this fifty-seven-hundred-dollar figure?"

"I dunno. It just popped into my head when he asked how much she was in dollars."

"How'd you price it before then?"

"Two hundred a month."

Jimmy-Dan fished in his desk for a moment and brought out a set of keys in a leather holder with a Cadillac emblem on it. "Here. Take these."

"Now listen," Jimmy-Dan said, "I want you to put them in your pocket and go get the customer."

Alvin started to get up.

"Waitaminute goddamn it, I'm not finished."

Alvin sat back down with his head turned to face the boss, his eyes focused on the sparkle and fire from Jimmy-Dan's diamond pinky ring, and waited.

"Go get the customer, bring him in here. Then go out and get the new-car sticker and my pistol out of the glove box. Don't let anyone else see them . . . keep 'em under your coat or something . . . and put them both in your bottom desk drawer and wait. I'll call you on the intercom. You got it?"

"Yeah."

"Then go get him, and Alvin . . ."

"Yeah . . ."

"You've got a bit over two grand gross on this."

"Better get it done then."

Alvin fetched Mel, who followed him to Jimmy-Dan's office, where he sat in one of the two chairs that faced the mahogany desk on its raised platform.

"So you're the guy who's taking my new Cadillac away from me."

"Yeah," Mel said with his trademark smile. "I guess I am."

"Well, you're getting one helluva car and my favorite of all of 'em, and I've had a lot of cars. I'm Jimmy-Dan Dee. Very nice to meetcha, Mel."

"Melquiades Arguedo," Mel said, still smiling.

"I'm going out to take care of a coupla things," Alvin said. "You want 'nother one?" He pointed to the Coors in Mel's left hand.

"No. I'm good."

Alvin left them and went outside to retrieve the window sticker and Jimmy-Dan's pistol, a .357 Magnum Colt Python with checked walnut grips and a two-inch barrel. *Wonder why he's carrying a hand-cannon like this?* Alvin thought as he stuck the pistol in his waistband and smoothed his jacket down before relocking the car doors and retreating to his office. He put both of the items in the lap drawer of his desk and closed it. After lighting the last cigarette in his pack, he reopened the drawer and carefully wiped the gun off with his handkerchief. He sat. Smoked his coffin nail, staring at the emerald pearl Cadillac, smiling, calculating the size of his sales commission, and he waited for the telephone to summon him.

Twenty-five minutes later, it did. Alvin picked it up on the second ring.

"Alvin," Jimmy-Dan said, "get a temp sticker and holder so Mel can get going."

"Sure. You guys doing okay? Need anything else?"

"Yeah. Bring us two more beers."

Alvin took his right leg off of the desk, stood up, and stretched. He took a temporary paper license tag issued by the State of Colorado out of the locked cabinet in the corner of his office, a plastic-covered cardboard permit holder the size and shape of a metal license plate, and headed back to the corner office where Mel and Jimmy-Dan waited. On his way he took two Coors in brown bottles out of the bottom of the Coke machine in the waiting room, being careful to close and lock it. He and Jimmy-Dan had the only keys. He hummed "Bringing in the Sheaves" as he headed back, one of his favorite Sunday School hymns, *And it sure seems appropriate to me, with that whopper gross,* Alvin thought, *"and we shall come rejoicing, bringing in the sheaves . . ."*

"What took you so long?" Jimmy-Dan said when Alvin entered the inner sanctum with both hands full.

"Took me a coupla minutes to get these, but they're ice cold," Alvin answered as he handed each of them a beer.

"Thanks," Mel said.

They opened the bottles while Alvin filled in the thirty-day tag and went outside to bolt it on after removing the dealer tag.

Mel watched him go, elated with the emerald pearl Cadillac and scared to be so far in debt. He tipped the bottle back, felt the icy brew on his teeth and tongue, bitter and somehow sweet at the same time. He swallowed, felt it disappear down his throat, and swallowed again. He put the bottle down, wiped his mouth with the back of his hand, and smiled at Jimmy-Dan.

When Alvin came back, Jimmy-Dan stood up and extended his hand to Mel, who also stood. "I wanna thank you for buying from me. And I wantcha to know, you're getting my personal ride. I'm sure gonna miss that car," and he shook hands with Mel. To Alvin he said, "You're gonna take Mel's truck home for him. He's gonna get the title and sign it and give it to you . . . then bring you back. You got it?"

"Yep."

"I'm gonna go back there and give those guys a chance to get their money back."

"Are you going to come in for haircuts too?" Mel said.

"Yeah. I always do business with the people who do business with me."

"I will too," Alvin said. "Do I need to call or anything?"

"No," Mel answered. "Just come in. Early morning or late afternoon's the least busy."

"I'll see ya next week."

Jimmy-Dan walked them to the door and watched from the office windows as the emerald pearl Cadillac's taillights disappeared, headed west on Platte Avenue, followed by Alvin Poorman in Mel's old Ford pickup truck. He noticed that the truck had only one working taillight as he locked the front door and turned the outside lights off before heading back to the craps game, which was still going strong in the back office.

In the pickup truck, Alvin was wishing he had another cigarette. He was following Mel in the Caddy, west on Platte, then up Union to always mispronounced Uintah Street, down to El Paso, and finally home on San Miguel Street where he lived in a white stucco three-bedroom bungalow. Mel went down the block and turned into the alley that paralleled San Miguel, stopping in front of a two-car cement-block garage. He dimmed his lights and got out, waving Alvin to a parking place beside the detached garage.

"Be right back. Just leave the truck, the Caddy's open."

"Here's your keys. You wouldn't happen to have a cigarette, would ya?"

"Sorry. Don't smoke."

"Maybe we could stop on the way back."

"Sure."

Mel went up three steps and disappeared in the back door, leaving Alvin leaning against the right front fender of the emerald pearl Cadillac, and dying for a cigarette. He listened to the pops and an occasional boom of fireworks being set off in driveways and backyards around the city; it was two days before the Fourth of July and some celebrants were starting early. Mel came back out in a few minutes with the truck title and his wife, Gabby. She oohed and aahed a couple of times as her husband showed her the car. She said, "This car must cost a lot, no?"

"I can handle it. I can make the payments. Don't worry."

"Are you getting rid of the truck?"

"No. It's collateral."

"What is collateral?"

"It's extra. For the loan."

"Extra . . ."

"What it means, Mrs. Arguedo, is if Mel doesn't make the payments, the bank will take it, and the car," Alvin said, then added, "but Mel ain't gonna let that happen. Are ya."

"No. No, I won't. Don't worry, Gabby. Wait'll I take you for a ride."

"I don't know. We got to buy shoes and clothes for the girls for school, it starts next month. I don't know about this."

Alvin, who could imagine his monster sales commission slithering out the door and away in the tall grass if this kept up, said, "We'd better get back. Jimmy-Dan's waiting. Do you have the title?"

"Yeah," Mel said, handing it to Alvin.

He produced a pen from his shirt pocket and said, "You got to sign it right here," pointing to the correct line, adding "exactly as your name appears."

Gabriela tried one last shot: "You sure about this, honey?"

"Yeah," Mel said as he signed and handed the pen and paper back to Alvin, who was at last able to exhale.

Mel kissed his wife on the cheek. "I'll be right back and take you for a ride. You'll like the car."

"I'd like to, but the girls . . ."

"We'll take them too. Half an hour, I'll be back."

He and Alvin got in the car and headed down the alley, retracing their route to Jimmy-Dan, Dan-Dee Motors, and the craps game in the back sales office.

They were heading up Union when Alvin said, "What's the gas gauge say?"

Mel raised his hand off the top of the steering wheel and said, "Just over halfa tank."

"Tell ya what. If you'll stop at the gas station at Boulder Street, I'll fill 'er up for you."

"That's the Dividend Bonded, I don't like their gas. How about the Skelly on Platte? It's before Circle Drive."

"Sure. That'll work."

They pulled in just as the place was about to close. Mel stayed in the car while Alvin got out and nodded to Frank, the retired highway patrolman who owned the place. "Hi, Frank. Fill it up with ethyl would 'ya? I'll pay. I'm gonna get some smokes before I have a hissy fit."

"Behind the counter by the register."

"I know."

The dour ex-cop started pumping gas and cleaning the windshield, not saying anything to Mel, who watched from behind the steering wheel. Alvin watched them both, standing in the station, puffing away on a filter cigarette.

Frank finished cleaning the windshield, went around to the rear of the car and topped off the gas tank, rounding up the numbers on the pump. Stone-faced, he hung the hose, replaced the gas cap, and came in the office. "You just sell that car?"

"Yeah. I'm delivering it."

"To a Mesican?"

"Yeah."

Frank shook his head in a "what's the world coming to" manner and cleared his throat, spat in the trash can under the counter, and said, "It's nine dollars and twenty-eight cents for the gas."

"How much did it take?"

"Fourteen and a half gallons."

"And two packs of Winston's."

"Ten bucks, eighteen cents," Frank Tulley said as he counted out change for Alvin's twenty. When he'd finished counting, Frank said, "It's a helluva thing when Mesicans is drivin' brand-new Cadillacs."

"Shit, it ain't no worse'n payin' sixty-four cents a gallon for gasoline and forty-five cents a pack for cigarettes."

"Well, brace yourself, buckaroo, 'cause they're both gonna cost ya more. Real soon too."

"Fuckin' A-rabs. We oughta nuke 'em and just take the oil."

"Wouldn't help. It's the big oil companies that're screwin' us."

"Think it'll go back up to a dollar a gallon?"

"Yeah."

"Well, we gotta have gas so I guess we'll just haveta pay. But if these cigarettes go up to a dollar a pack, I'm gonna quit."

"I hear a lot of people say that."

"See ya later, Frank."

"Sure. Thanks for your business."

Alvin went out the door, taking a last drag on his cigarette before tossing it to the driveway and stepping on it. He climbed in the emerald pearl Cadillac with Melquiades Arguedo, the car Gabriela Arguedo would soon christen *La Bruja*, The Witch, the car Frank Tully, the retired Colorado highway patrolman, was thinking was *one pretty sonofabitch* as he turned out the lights and locked his little four-pump gas station for the night. *Imagine that . . . a Mesican in a brand-new Cadillac. Well fuck me for a fool. Now I have seen it all.*

The craps game was breaking up when Mel pulled in the Dan-Dee Motors lot. The night's winners and the losers were coming out the door and heading for their cars. Mel left Alvin off at the street because there was too much traffic inside the used car lot. As he got out, Alvin said, "Don't be a stranger around here, Mel, you're always welcome. I'll see ya next week for a haircut too, and thanks for your business."

"You're welcome," Mel said with a smile.

Alvin, who was bent over at the waist, resting his left forearm on the roof and holding the door with his right hand, leaned in and said, "You think your wife's okay with all'a this?"

"Gabby . . . sure. She wasn't happy about me pledging the truck is all." *And God above knows what she'd say if she knew I also pledged both the new Koken hydraulic barber chairs and the oak backbar in the shop too . . .*

she'd piss blood for a week about it. Mel drove off into the night, trying not to worry about thirty-six payments of $197 and change, or the fact that he'd just spent the last four days of shop income as a cash down payment—money meant to pay household bills and rent on the shop. He tried not to worry. Tried to enjoy Freddy Fender's voice coming from all six stereo speakers, singing *"Si te quiere de verdad . . ."* his heartbreaking song, "Before the Next Teardrop Falls." It would be a smash hit before the year was out. *A guy who damn sure deserves a break,* Mel thought, remembering Freddy Fender's story, the Hispanic rock 'n' roll and country music crooner, the Hispanic whose tenor voice could bring tears to a stone statue, the Hispanic who was busted in Baton Rouge, Louisiana, on May 13, 1960, and sentenced to five years' hard labor in Angola State Penitentiary, the toughest prison in the United States of America for the crime of possessing two marijuana cigarettes, when he was just twenty-three years old.

"Si te quiere de verdad . . ." Mel didn't know if it was because of Freddy's story, his voice, the song, the music and melody, or the fact that he himself was driving his very own dream, but tears were rolling down both his cheeks when he turned on Union Boulevard, the song ended, and he headed on home.

Gabriela and the girls were all waiting when he got there, excited, eager to see what Daddy's new car looked like and anxious to go for a ride in it. Christina and Constance were both turbocharged, bouncing around like two BBs in a boxcar, while Gabby, Mel noted, looked worried. He took them all for a long ride, traversing the city from north to south and west to east, up Ute Pass, down through the Garden of the Gods and up the Cragmor Hill, past the new campus of the University of Colorado at Colorado Springs, then down to Academy Boulevard, Platte Avenue, and home. They all had a great time, even Gabriela. Mel was exhausted by the time he parked alongside his red pickup truck and they all trooped in to bed. The emerald pearl Cadillac waited, kept company by the well-used Ford pickup, serenaded by the pops, booms, and explosive flashes of the Fourth of July celebrants through the short summer night.

When Mel went to work the next day he drove the new Caddy. He parked on Colorado Avenue, in front of a big blue Victorian house that had been converted into five separate apartments. It was directly across the street from his shop, where he could admire her all day. He was happy, had a busy day, and chatted up all of his customers, which earned him an extra few dollars in tips by the end of the day. Life was good.

The next day, Wednesday July 3, business was slow. By four o'clock in the afternoon, Mel had only done seven haircuts, less than half his normal total. And that's when he started to worry about how he was going to make the thirty-six monthly payments of $197 and change.

Truth was he'd been so blinded by beauty and so caught up in his own impetuousness that he hadn't stopped to do some simple arithmetic. Aided and abetted by Alvin Poorman and Jimmy-Dan Dee's psychology and salesmanship, his desire for the emerald pearl Cadillac had overpowered his common sense. He was taking in about $750 a month. His monthly bills were averaging $675 to just over $700 . . . *What the hell was I thinking? I musta had my head stuck square up my ass . . .*

Melquiades Arguedo had come down with a raging case of what Alvin Poorman and Jimmy-Dan Dee called "buyer's remorse." Mel wanted out of the deal. He couldn't see any other solution—he'd have to return the emerald pearl Cadillac, *La Bruja*, and get his money back. It was all he could think of to do.

After one last late haircut, Mel closed the shop and headed for East Platte Avenue to see Jimmy-Dan Dee and rescind his purchase at Dan-Dee Motors, Inc. He wasn't looking forward to it, either.

When he pulled in the parking area in front of the used car lot, the first thing he noticed was a brand-new, lipstick red Mark IV Lincoln coupe.

The Mark IV was the sporty model—the one with the rear-deck spare tire bubble and Rolls-Royce style grille designed by Lee Iacocca himself. The car was just plain smoking hot and screaming for attention. Mel couldn't take his eyes off of it as he mounted the steps into the building.

Inside, Jimmy-Dan Dee and Alvin Poorman were both watching Mel with the intensity a pair of tomcats would give an approaching sparrow.

"Shit. I knew he'd try to crawfish."

"You don't know that, Alvin."

"Betcha ten he is."

"You're on. Bring him back to me if he does," Jimmy-Dan answered, adding, "and I'll betcha twenty I keep it together."

"I'll pass on that one."

"What a pussy."

Alvin stuck a half-assed smile on his face, stubbed out his cigarette in the sand-filled canister ashtray by the front door, and pulled it open for Mel, coming up the steps with a worried look on his face.

"Hi there, Mel. How'ya doin'?"

"Uh, not so good. I gotta talk to Jimmy-Dan."

"Something wrong with the Caddy? 'Cause we'll get it fixed for ya. It's got a new-car warranty on it."

"No. The car's fine. I need to talk to him about something else. Something personal."

"Can I help?"

"No, man. It's personal."

"Okay. Have a seat. I'll go see if he's off the phone or if he's still here."

"His new car's out front."

"Don't mean he's here. Be right back. You want anything . . . coffee, pop, beer . . . ?"

"No."

"Kay. Hang on."

Alvin disappeared down the hall to Jimmy-Dan's office. Mel stood, looking out the window at the emerald pearl Cadillac and the lipstick red Mark IV Lincoln, parked nose-to-nose outside. Unconsciously, he was shifting his weight from one foot to the other, like a boxer getting ready for a fight.

When Alvin got to the inner sanctum, Jimmy-Dan was sitting at his desk with both feet propped up on a middle desk drawer so he could lean back in his big leather chair. He had a telephone hugged to his left shoulder and ear, talking and cleaning his fingernails with a bone-handled six-inch German stiletto. Alvin waited.

"Okay . . . it's a deal. I'll take the pair for forty-five hundred. Yeah. Next week sometime. Sounds good. What? You do? Sure. Hold on." Jimmy-Dan looked at Alvin. "Got a quarter?"

Alvin dug one out of his pocket. "Here you go."

"I don't want it. When I tell you, flip it on my desk." Into the phone Jimmy-Dan said, "Okay. Call it."

He pointed to Alvin and pantomimed flipping. Pointed with the knife at the desk pad with all the notes written on it. Alvin flipped the quarter on the desk, where it bounced a couple of times and stopped. "Call it out loud," Jimmy-Dan said, holding the phone out.

"Tails."

Jimmy-Dan pushed a button and retracted the stiletto blade into the handle at the same time that he took his feet off the desk and sat up. He said, "That's fifty you owe me," and laughed. He listened, then said, "Yes, I am. See you first the week," and hung up the phone. Jimmy-Dan was laughing as he put the phone back in its cradle and stuck the knife in the lap drawer.

"What's so funny?" Alvin asked.

"It was Bobby Lee in Oklahoma City. He said I was luckier than a billy goat with two peckers."

"Well, Melquiades wants to talk to you."

"He trying to crawfish?"

"Big time. Won't talk to me."

"Okay. Bring him in. Wanna take my twenty that I keep him together, now?"

"Yeah. Can't lose either way."

"Smart boy. Bring him in," Jimmy-Dan said as he picked up some papers from the wooden box on his desk and started reading.

Alvin got Mel, who was still gazing out the window, still shifting his weight back and forth. "Okay, Mel. He's finally off the phone. C'mon back."

They went down the hall together. As they got to the big office, Alvin said, "Here's Mel. He wants to talk to you, alone."

"Okay. Shut the door behind you, Alvin."

Alvin went back up front and got involved with a new potential buyer looking at a blue Chevrolet pickup truck. He was outside doing the meet-and-greet thing about thirty minutes later when he saw Mel leave in the emerald pearl Cadillac. He waved, but Mel didn't wave back. He watched as the big car disappeared down Platte Avenue.

When Alvin tried to qualify the man on the pickup, he found out that the man couldn't afford to buy anything; he was unemployed and killing time until his girlfriend got off work at the diner on Academy Boulevard in a half hour. Alvin gave him a business card and wished him good luck, then went inside to find out about Mel and the emerald Pearl Cadillac.

When Alvin got inside, Jimmy-Dan was waiting for him.

"Where were you weak?" he said, pointing at the departing prospect with his chin.

"No job. No money. No hope. Other than that he was a great customer. What happened with Mel?"

"You owe me twenty bucks."

"Ten. You lost the first bet about crawfishing. Nice try, though."

Jimmy-Dan grinned and said, "Mel's keeping the Caddy."

"What'd you tell him?"

"That it was between him and the bank . . . that I'd sold his note to them. That they wouldn't take kindly to owning his truck, two barber chairs, and his oak backbar. Probably ruin his credit forever and the bank would probably go after him in court."

"Kind of hardball, wasn't it?"

"This is the big leagues. I ain't doing this for fun."

"Jeez. You tell him anything good?"

"Yeah. Raise his price a little, and have a happy Fourth of July."

"Speaking of . . ."

"Wait until six o'clock. Not before. I'll see you on Friday." Jimmy Dan went out the front door, trailing cigar smoke and aftershave lotion in his wake, and left in the lipstick red Mark IV Lincoln.

Shit, Alvin thought. *Forty-five dead-assed minutes to go. And I know he'll call here at five fifty-eight to make sure I didn't sky out early.* He sighed and settled in to wait, dealing himself a hand of solitaire from the forbidden deck he had secreted in his desk.

Melquiades Arguedo was smoldering with suppressed shame and anger as he pulled out of Dan-Dee Motors and drove west on Platte Avenue. He was frustrated and ashamed with himself for crawling out of there like a woman, begging like a peon . . . with hat in hand and head down before *El Jefe* . . . angry with himself for acting like such a *cabron . . . a nutless wonder . . . that's me.* He drove on home, where his wife and daughters were waiting for him.

Three and a half months later, Melquiades Arguedo, Mel the Barber, was in financial trouble, falling behind on all his payments including . . . *La Bruja esmerelda perla,* the emerald pearl witch . . . his pride and joy.

He'd been getting past-due notices from various creditors for weeks;

now the phone calls from creditors were coming in at the rate of one or two per day. Mel would be polite and apologetic, explain that his business was off a little bit. "It's been a little slow, but it'll be better in a week and I'll send you the money as soon as I can. Yes, I will. I promise." And so on, and on, and on.

Mel would get one creditor paid at the expense of another going past-due. It was a treadmill going faster and faster, to the point of throwing him off, and he was powerless to stop it.

By the end of October, Mel was out of options. The bank was threatening to repossess his Cadillac, his old pickup truck, his oak backbar, and his two Koken hydraulic barber chairs . . . taking away his business and his livelihood. His house was close to foreclosure, the utilities at the point of shutoff, and a host of other smaller creditors were like hounds, snapping at his heels, baying, barking, and howling for his blood.

Mel's problem was that styles were changing and he wasn't doing enough business to pay the bills. He'd raised his price to two dollars and fifty cents for a haircut but it didn't help. Men were growing their hair longer . . . styling was in . . . barbering was out. It was that simple. Fixing his debt crisis wasn't going to come from working harder, either.

When the solution walked right through his door, Mel didn't even recognize it at first.

Every other Thursday at three o'clock, Mel's oldest and best customer came in for a haircut. He was an older man, in his fifties with thinning black hair that was about half-gray. He was built thick in the shoulders and waist, short and stout with eyes the color of onyx . . . eyes that took in much . . . and revealed nothing. He was a local businessman, owned a small café downtown where he could usually be found sitting at the farthest table in back, smoking his omnipresent cigar, and drinking coffee, or in the afternoon and early evening, grappa, sometimes ouzo from a white china mug, watching the café, waiting for his next real customer—the ones who came to borrow money at five percent per week. His name was Antonio Vincenzo Andolini. Fat Tony to a few of his peers . . . Tony to those he liked . . . Don Andolini to everyone else.

Mel was sitting in one of his barber chairs, holding the sports pages in his hands but staring into space, tired from dodging creditors and worrying . . . wondering how he could turn things around and maybe straighten his life out, get it back on track. He hadn't had a customer since lunchtime, didn't see Fat Tony until he pushed in the door with a Colorado Claro stuck in his jaws.

"Hey, Mel. Wake up, boy. I need my haircut."

"Hi, Tony. Sorry, I lost track of the time." Mel had a hundred-watt smile on his face as he climbed out of the chair and spun it around so the big man could climb in and sit. As Fat Tony eased his bulk down, Mel said, "Got it all warmed up for ya."

Tony made eye contact in the mirror, took the cigar out of his mouth with his right hand, holding it between his index and middle fingers while he picked a piece of tobacco from his tongue with his left. "Yeah."

Mel spread an apron over Tony's lap and chest, put a strip of sanitary paper around his neck, and fastened the snaps in back. He took a fresh comb and scissors out of the sterilizer and put them in his breast pocket, picked up the electric clippers, and began shaping and trimming the sides and back without saying another word. Mel was a good judge of human nature, honing his skills every day in the shop. He could tell something was amiss with Tony.

Wonder what's got him so mad? Mel thought. *I've never seen him so smoking hot, not even when he was having a hard time collecting.* He watched out the corner of his eye in the mirror as the fat man smoldered in the chair. Mel kept combing, kept cutting with the scissors, and kept quiet. He waited for Tony to speak.

The hair cutting was finished and Mel was just about to snip the hair from his ears when Fat Tony, Don Antonio Andolini erupted, "The bitch. The fucking bitch. That fat cunt won't get away with it. She won't."

He threw his cigar on the floor, stood up from the barber chair and pulled the black nylon apron off, threw it on the floor, and stomped out the door, slamming it in his wake with such violence that the front windows rattled and shook.

I wonder who he's talking about? Mel thought as he stepped on the cigar butt, making sure it was out. He picked up the black apron, shook it, and started sweeping the hair clippings off the floor. *It could be his wife . . . Tony's been complaining about her ever since I've known him.*

Mel had just finished tidying the shop when Tony came back in. He had a fresh cigar going, a twenty-dollar bill in his hand, and the hard glare of anger in his face and eyes. "Here, Mel," he said, putting the bill in his hand. "Keep the change."

"Thanks. Thanks very much. Why don't you sit back down and let me finish up. I wasn't quite done." Fat Tony, Don Andolini, sat in the barber chair and Mel respread the apron over him, prepared to finish his haircut. Tony started talking.

"That fucking fat bitch. Thinks she's gonna gouge me for everything I own. I oughta clip her. Sorry bitch that she is. Thinks she can take everything I own. Said so. Told me so. Right to my face."

"Sounds pretty bad."

"Listen'a this . . . sorry bitch threatened to divorce me. Divorce me. Told her that ain't gonna happen. No fuckin' way. My whole family'd be excommunicated from the church. My old momma's eighty-three years old. It'd kill her. Church is very important to her. Important. Hell, it's her life. She goes to mass every day."

"She knows this . . . your wife?"

"Sure. She don't care. Wants the money. Says she's gonna do it. It'd kill my ma for sure. I ain't gonna let that happen. No fuckin' way."

"Sorry to hear of your troubles."

"Oh, I'm gonna solve 'em. I'm gonna solve 'em, all right. Right away."

"Really . . ."

"Listen, Mel. I know you a long time. You're a good boy. Keep your mouth shut. Know what I'm sayin'?"

"Yeah."

"Good. That fuckin' bitch is gonna have an accident. Bad one."

To his dying day, Melquiades Arguedo, Mel the Barber, couldn't explain it, couldn't say why for sure, but when Don Andolini said those words, he turned the barber chair around, looked straight into the Don's eyes in the big mirror, and said, "I believe I can solve your problems." Those seven words changed his life forever.

Eight days later, on November the fifth while the Don was out of town and was observed on video playing blackjack at the Fremont Casino in downtown Las Vegas, Nevada, a small man wearing a black raincoat and a black or navy blue golf hat walked up to the front door of a sprawling ranch house, up on a mesa on the city's far west side. It was a custom house, built in the second quarter of the twentieth century, and sat off by itself on a two-acre lot. It was ten forty-five p.m., and the lights had gone off in the house five minutes before the man in the raincoat came up the walk. He reached up and unscrewed the lightbulb in the porch light and put his right hand back in his coat. He gave a quick look around, saw no lights, reached up with his left hand, and rang the door bell. He waited, rang twice more, longer each time.

The living room light came on and the front door opened.

"Whadda ya want? Why are you ringing my doorbell? Don't you know it's eleven o'clock at night? Who are you anyway?

The woman said it in a rapid-fire way, question after question like machine-gun bursts in a shrill, cranky voice like a shrew's. She clutched her blue quilted bathrobe with her left hand as she glared out the screen door.

"Angie?"

"Yeah. Whoareyou?"

"I've got a message for you. From Tony. It's important. Can I come in? Please?"

The man had a smile on his face and looked harmless enough . . . *And he's a shrimpy little man, smaller than me . . . what the hell,* she thought and opened the door, letting him in, then closed it behind him shutting out the cold night air.

"So, what's the message?"

"This." The man raised the sawed-off twelve-gauge shotgun he'd been holding under his raincoat and pulled both triggers at the same time. It was point-blank range.

The concussion was deafening and the smell of cordite filled the air as the old woman was blown backward over the couch, landing with her head bent against the wall, her feet on the back of the couch, and a huge, blood-filled mess in the center of her chest where her heart used to be.

Melquiades Arguedo, Mel the Barber . . . Mel the Hit Man, was smiling as he let go of the old shotgun he'd bought at the flea market and cut down in his garage, letting it hang from the leather strap looped over his right shoulder. Buckshot and blood spattered and ran down the wall. There was no need to check; she was as dead as dead could ever be. He reached out with a gloved hand, turned off the light, and then turned the button to lock the front door behind him. As he walked back to his truck, parked four blocks away, he realized that he had an immense, throbbing erection. He was still smiling when he started the old pickup and drove carefully home. He was back in the house making passionate love to his wife by eleven thirty. It was so good he did it twice more in the early morning hours before dawn. He hadn't been so randy in years. Gabriela was exhausted. Mel hadn't felt so alive since his last firefight in Vietnam, the day before he came home.

What a rush! was echoing in his head . . . over, and over, and over.

Six days after the murder of Angelica Maria Andolini—Angie to her acquaintances, the wife of Don Antonio Andolini—the widower himself came in for his regular appointment with Mel the Barber. He walked in at three o'clock, same as always, trailing a slipstream of cigar smoke, same as always, he ignored the two customers waiting for haircuts and settled into the just-vacated barber chair like he owned the place. The same as always.

When Tony was seated, Mel said, "Very sorry for your loss, Tony."

"Thank you. We were married for thirty-four years, ya know."

"That's a long time."

"Seems like forever," fat Tony said, puffing out a cloud of blue smoke.

"Funeral?" Mel said as he scissored Tony's hair.

"Tomorrow at ten, St. Mary's."

When Mel finished, he pulled the drape from Tony's front and shook out the loose hairs. Tony clamped the cigar in his teeth and said, "Thanks. Looks good," and handed Mel a five-dollar bill.

"Keep the change."

"Thanks."

As Tony went out the door and one of the men waiting stood up, Mel saw the envelope on the chair seat and stuck it down the front of his pants, behind his shirt, before his next customer noticed. Mel smiled to himself as he cut hair for the rest of the afternoon at two fifty a head.

When he opened the envelope later that day, after he'd put the "Closed" sign out and locked the front door, Mel found one hundred hundred-dollar bills . . . more money than he'd ever seen or held in his hands. He was ecstatic. The money was all his. *Pretty good for two minutes' work and a four-block walk . . .*

He was smart with the cash. Paid all of his past-due bills and brought his payments on the Cadillac up-to-date. He rented a safe-deposit box at the bank and stashed the rest of the cash, used it to accelerate the payments and paid off the emerald pearl Cadillac, *La Bruja*, two and a half years early.

Figuring if you can't beat 'em, join 'em, Mel learned how to do razor cuts, becoming Melquiades the Stylist and raising his price to seven dollars and fifty cents for a cut and style, which included a wash and blow-dry. Now, on an average day his tips ran close to what he used to get for a plain haircut back in the old days. He was happy and prosperous. Working less. Earning more.

But every other Thursday at three o'clock was reserved for the Man himself. Don Antonio Andolini. Over the next fifteen years or so a surprising number of small, letter-sized white envelopes passed from the Don to Mel the Barber. So many envelopes in fact, that the Don, when meeting with his peers, would refer to Mel the barber as his "personal clipper," appreciating the private joke when they all thought the always well-groomed Don Andolini had his own personal barber.

For his part, Mel the Barber was a perfect assassin. He had no conscience about doing the deed, and his ubiquitous, unthreatening appearance allowed him to move in close to his victims. He became proficient at killing with a shotgun, rifle, pistol, and in rare cases specially requested by the Don, an old-fashioned ice pick, which he bought at flea markets and antique shows, and for which his work commanded a premium.

After Don Andolini died of a heart attack in 1990, younger, more hot-headed and vicious members of the crime family took over. The drug wars began and the killings became wholesale slaughter rather than discreet. There was no place for a man like Mel the Barber. His last job was rumored to be the hit on a guy named Jimmy-Dan Dee, but it was only conjecture, never proven. The killing of Jimmy-Dan Dee, like all of Mel the Barber's hits, was never solved.

Melquiades Arguedo, Mel the Barber, was killed in a car crash shortly after the new millennium when he was T-boned at an intersection by a young carjacker fleeing the police in a high-speed chase through west Colorado Springs. He was hit on the driver's door by a new Honda traveling "in excess of seventy-five miles per hour" according to the police report, and the air bags on the driver's door of the new Cadillac Mel was driving failed to deploy.

He left behind his wife, Gabriela, and two grown daughters, Connie and Tina, a paid-for house and new Lexus, a thriving styling salon in a paid-for commercial building on West Colorado Avenue, and an old 1974 fire-mist emerald pearl Cadillac Sedan de Ville under a green cloth cover in the five-car garage he'd built behind their house on San Miguel Street. When the cover was removed, it looked as if it were new. When Gabriela opened the huge trunk, she found forty-three green metal U.S. Army .50 caliber ammo boxes stuffed with hundred-dollar bills and a leather diary written by her late husband, detailing his many assassinations without mentioning names.

Stunned, she prayed for guidance. After three days, she closed the trunk, replaced the car cover, and simply went on living her life. She became a traveler, visiting Europe, South America, and Mexican resorts when cold weather came to Colorado Springs. She always wore new, stylish clothes and drove late-model cars. She put both daughters through college and grad school and made annual donations to Catholic charities. When asked how she could afford it all, her answer was always simple . . .

"Mel had excellent life insurance. He was an excellent provider."

Out in the garage *La Bruja* improves with age. She's a classic now.

JINN: THE CATCHER IN THE ROAD

Jinn: The Catcher in the Road

S O THERE WE WERE: my wife, Sally, my dad, and me. We were back in Colorado Springs, headed home on Academy Boulevard after a day at the State Fair down in Pueblo. We'd had a bunch of fun, and we were still all talking and laughing at once. None of us noticed, nor did I care, that all the traffic was passing us in the right lane. We were too busy having a good time.

That's when Pop said, "Watch it!"

I looked up and saw the guy in front of us jam his brakes on just as he arrived at the Maizeland Road intersection. The light turned pink the moment he got there, and he nose-planted the Lincoln Navigator he drove. I jammed my brakes and turned right, but touched his bumper with a thud.

"Oh, shit."

"Better pull over, son."

"Are you all right, honey?

"Yeah," was all I said as I steered my dually pickup to a dead stop.

The SUV driver sat there, blocking the left lane with his four-way flashers on, backing traffic all the way down to Constitution Avenue. I got out and hurried over to him, glancing at his broken taillight on my way past. The driver's window was coming down as I got to the door.

"Hi," I said, "sorry, very sorry about your taillight. Are you all okay?" I could see the driver, a short heavy man, and a woman dressed in black, with a scarf and veil covering her head and face. She was holding a baby and there were three or four young children jumping about in the back.

The man said, "Yes, I think so," in heavily accented English. He turned to his right and said something to the kids in a language I didn't understand, and they quieted down. Turning back to me he said again, "Yes, I think we are all okay."

"Why don't you pull over then, into the parking lot, so traffic can go?"

"All right."

When the lights turned, I stopped eastbound traffic on Maizeland long enough for him to pull into the Steak Smith Restaurant and park next to my truck. I sprinted after them and got to my truck at about the same time. I leaned in the open window where Pop sat smoking his pipe.

"Where's Sally?"

"She went over to the gas station, use the restroom."

"I'm gonna talk to this guy, see if I can't work something out. They're all okay, but his taillight is busted. They're foreigners of some kind, with a bunch of kids in there. The woman's all dressed in black."

"Be careful," Pop said, "be very careful."

"Don't worry."

Pop didn't reply. He busied himself with emptying and refilling his pipe, his gray eyes looking worried.

Hey, I thought, *this is Colorado Springs. People aren't sue-happy out here, not like New York, where you can be slapped with a lawsuit for sneezing at the wrong time; where the second words out of the mouth were "I'll sue," those usually coming right after "It's your fault." Nah*, I told myself. *It's not like that out here . . . and one of the reasons I don't live back East anymore.*

I walked to the SUV. The driver was on his cell phone, but when he saw me, he hung up. I put a smile on and said, "If you'll come here, I'll show you what happened, try to straighten everything out."

"I don't want trouble."

"No trouble. Thought maybe we could settle this ourselves, not get the cops and insurance adjusters involved."

"Insurance adjuster?"

I noticed he rolled his Rs, spoke in a guttural way that made it seem like he was trying to hawk up a big loogie to spit.

"The guys who estimate the cost of damage and repairs, then jack up your insurance bill two or three hundred percent."

"Yes. I understand." He started to open the door, but before he got out he spoke to his wife in a long string of whatever language he was speaking as she cuddled the baby and nodded yes several times while staring down at the floor.

"She thinks you're going to kill me."

"What? Why would she think that? That's crazy."

"It's what would happen back where we came from. Someone hits the car, you get out to see the damage, get shot to death."

I shook my head as he shrugged and climbed out. He was short, about five feet tall, and round. He wore loose floppy pants and a long shirt that ended at mid-thigh. A pointed beard and mustache made his round face seem more oval. Obsidian-dark eyes and blue-black hair along with his swarthy skin gave him a mysterious air, made me think of Zapata and Pancho Villa. Then I saw the black-and-silver signet ring on his right index finger with the symbol in a raised filigree that looked like a claw of some kind. I don't know why, but it made me uneasy.

Dumb, I told myself. *It's a ring, stupid-ass. Stick to your business and take care of this before it gets worse . . . you could get sued . . . he's a foreigner after all, probably looking for some rich American to fleece. Well, screw him. Two can play that game. After selling used cars for fifteen years I've read the book about who screws who a couple of times.*

I put a smile on my face and said, "Come back here, I'll show you the damage, see if we can't work this out."

The man looked around in all directions, turning in a complete circle before nodding to me. He was muttering something in that language again, and rubbing both of his thumbs against his index fingers.

"Hey, don't worry." I said, "I'm not going to hurt you. Nothing bad's going to happen, honest."

He closed his eyes for a moment and nodded. "I know," he said.

"I thought you were praying. What language is that?"

He opened his eyes then, and stared past me, almost like he was seeing someone creeping up on us. I looked, but we were alone on a three-acre parking lot. When I turned to him, the fat man said, "It's Farsi."

"What's that?"

"It's Persian."

"Persia?"

"You call it Iran."

"Oh," I said, the lights going on in my brain at last. I added, "Were you praying?" *Why the hell did I say that?* I wondered as it popped out.

"I was reciting verses from the Koran."

"Oh."

". . . Calling the Jinn."

I shivered, even though it was an eighty-five-degree mid-August evening and I was wearing a T-shirt and shorts. It was as if cold steel had been pressed against my neck by some unknown felon. But then, the feeling went away just as fast as it came on, and I refocused on the business at hand.

The Lincoln Navigator was black and silver, the same colors as the Oakland Raiders, those perennial tormentors of the Denver Broncos. I noticed the man behind me was still muttering and rubbing his thumb and index fingers together as we got near the damaged area of his vehicle.

"See," I said. "Not too bad. A new taillight lens and it'll be fine." I was hoping he wouldn't notice the bent bumper . . . it wasn't apparent, but it was kinked a little and bent into the sheet metal it was designed to protect. I missed it when I walked by the first time. The fat man didn't say anything for about three minutes as he looked, all the while rubbing his fingers and moving his lips. Calling the gin or whatever. The only gin I know comes from a bottle or with a deck of fifty-two cards.

After awhile he said, "It's more than the light. Look here." He pointed to the long gouge in the bodywork where I must have caught him with an edge of my brush guard or something. Something hard and sharp anyway.

I got down and looked closer, humoring him while my brain was going about two hundred miles an hour calculating, figuring, and sorting out possibilities.

"It doesn't look too bad. The guys at the body shop can putty it up and paint over it, no problem. Won't even know it ever happened. It'll be like new."

"I don't know."

"Tell you what," I said, in my best, most sincere closing voice, the one that usually made the sale. "How about I give you two hundred fifty bucks cash to forget about it? Here and now. How would that be?"

He hesitated. I sensed reluctance, went for a harder close.

"Tell you what, I'll not only give you two fifty in cash, I'll give you the name of a guy I know who does paint and body work in his garage at night. Real good guy, cheap too. Does great work."

"He can fix it? Cheap?"

"Yeah. Be like it never happened. See my rig over there . . . ? He painted the whole thing," I lied.

"He did really?"

"Yeah. Looks good doesn't it?"

"How much?"

"Much what . . . ?"

"How much did he charge you?"

"Oh. Four fifty," I said, grabbing a figure out of the air. I figured this turkey was pretty well basted by now, *time to take it out of the oven and eat it.* I went right for the close. Said, "So how about it? You ready to take my money?"

But he wasn't quite.

"Why so much if he works so cheap?"

"Oh," I said, in full sales mode now, not to be denied, "because it had a lot of dents and stuff to fix, and he had to paint the whole thing."

"I see," he said, and then did what I'd been waiting for: he asked a closing question. "How soon do you think he could get it done?"

. . . Just what I was waiting for. His question told me he'd had taken the bait. He was mine.

"Right away if I ask him to. He owes me a favor."

"Can you call him?"

"We got a deal?"

"If he can do it this week."

"Let me find out."

I went back to my truck for my cell phone while the fat man stood beside his damaged SUV. I made a show of it, walking in front of my vehicle, carrying on a one-sided conversation with myself. I was nodding yes and yes again, said, "Yep. I will. I got it. See ya." All for the benefit of my audience of one. I closed the phone just as I was back in front of him. I waited. I was waiting for him, the fat man, to speak first—I was controlling the conversation, you see.

Finally, he said, "Well?"

"He's booked solid for six weeks. Said he couldn't get to it no sooner, but, and it's a good but, he said take it to the Chevrolet dealer over on Eighth Street, behind the hamburger place, and talk to Steve. He'll take care of you. No problem."

"I don't know. This gets complex."

"Nah. Not complicated. Just a different dude is all. He's maybe even better than the first one."

"You know him?"

"Yeah. I use him when the first guy's busy, like now." I was lying through my teeth; there wasn't any auto body shop in the woods, no Steve, either. All I wanted was for the fat man to take the cash, and let me disappear in traffic. He didn't have my name or anything, and he was gonna be hugely pissed when he found out the true cost of the repair. *Really*, I thought, *it's gonna be more like twenty-five hundred to fix his Lincoln.*

"I'm not sure. Maybe we should not do this."

"Well, you could always keep the money, turn it in on your insurance. You could tell 'em it happened in the parking lot while you were at the grocery store."

"Hmmm . . . Maybe."

I pulled out the stops. Went for the sale right there. Said, as I pulled bills from my pocket, "I only have twenties. From the ATM machine. So I gotta give you two sixty. That work okay for you?"

I held out thirteen Jacksons. He reached out and said, "You give me this of your own free will? You want me . . . to have this?"

He said it so solemn, like an oath, that I damn near started laughing. I choked it down, said, "Oh, yes. It's yours. From me. I give it and I want you to have it, sure."

He took the thirteen twenty-dollar bills out of my hand and said, "In my country when two men make a pact, they spit in their right palm and clasp hands, making the bond unbreakable."

He spit in his hand and held it out to me . . . waiting. I figured what the hell . . . I spit a good one in my hand to show I was open to new ideas, new cultures and such, reached over, and grabbed his hand.

And got the shock of my life.

I expected a Pillsbury Doughboy kind of shake. But when our hands touched, it felt like I was held by an iron fist, with a steel-vise grip. My hand felt crushed. At the exact same instant I heard a sizzle, saw smoke rising from our conjoined hands, and smelled the nasty odor of burning flesh . . . and then the pain hit with the force of an iron bar between the eyes. I started to sink down on my knees while trying to shriek, but the intensity of the pain kept me from drawing enough air into my lungs to do it.

The fat man's face was expressionless as he watched me burn, saw me suffer, and looked like he was enjoying it all. Then, he let go of my hand. I stood there, tears running from both eyes as I tried to swallow the pain and draw some air. I choked, grabbed my wrist, and looked at my wounded hand . . . saw the mark where a claw was seared into the flesh. It was still smoking. I was burned to the bone and the throbbing was unbearable. Through the tears and pain, I said in a moan, "What have you done to me, you little fat bastard?"

"Caught you. And you are marked to prove it."

"Caught me?"

"For the Jinn. You are marked with their mark. It says "Jinn" in Farsi, it marks you as their property. They have large appetites and need much food."

"I'm branded like a steer? Property? For *food*?" I kind of screamed out. "What the fuck are you talking about?"

"The Jinn are invisible, only I can see them, talk to them. They move at light speed and know all. They advise me on the stock and commodity markets where I make much money. Billons in fact. In return I catch for them. People such as yourself. Liars and deceivers, those who are nonbelievers, idolaters, and fools. They told me you were trying to deceive me. Unfortunately, they have very large appetites. They eat a lot."

"You're stark raving mad. A fucking whack job."

He laughed, but it was an evil laugh, without humor.

"I don't blame you. It's what I'd think too, were I you. Gratefully, I am not. But consider. You met me at a crossroad. You asked for and were granted a wish. You gave me something of yours, of your own free will, swore an oath, and sealed it with your own precious bodily fluid, as General Ripper would say. But don't worry, they won't come to collect just now, but will do so later. At their leisure."

"I don't believe you. You're fulla crap. I just don't believe this horseshit."

"You will. You may not believe now, but you will."

Then he got in his vehicle and left, just like that, and you know, I coulda sworn I smelled something in the air, along with burned meat . . . sort of like sulfur. Like the smell you get when you strike one of those old wooden matches. Oh yeah . . . one other thing . . . as he drove away, those three kids had their faces pressed on the back window, like kids will do, and I swear they all looked like they had pointy little sharp teeth and a pair of nubbins on the sides of their foreheads that looked just like little horns.

* * *

The man stopped talking and drained the last of his beer. His companion at the bar signaled to the barkeep, who brought another, took the empties and some bills and change from the diminishing pile. He was the kind of bartender who hadn't much use for conversation. It was the kind of bar that was found only by a special group of patrons, it opened early and closed late, and then only long enough to swamp out the vomit and the blood, the broken glass, and an occasional broken man or woman. It was the kind of place where the hard drinkers went to lose themselves and to stay lost until they were either broke or dead. It was an end-of-skid-row kind of place . . . there was no lower place to go.

The man, whose name was Lyle Steele, reached for the fresh beer and nodded his thanks to his new bar friend before tipping the bottle straight up and taking a long pull that drained more than half. He belched politely and said, "'Scuze me," as he wiped his mouth with the back of his hand. "Damn, that's good. Like mother's milk but spicier, by God."

"Yeah. It's spicy beer. They make it here special, for the barbecue."

"Oh, man. I love barbecue."

"Me too. So, tell me, how'd you wind up here . . . on skid row?"

"Seemed like it happened pretty fast. Seemed like one day, I was just cruising along, selling used cars, and a little time went by, maybe five years, and then, I was here. Broke and selling bullshit for beer and drinks."

"How . . . ?"

The man at the bar fingered the purple scar that covered most of his right palm, with a raised welt. He continued, "I started getting a lot of customer complaints, not long after the thing with the fat man. Started drinking some, slapped ole Sally a few times, she divorced me, took the house and all. My pop died from lung cancer, and bingo. Here am I," said the man. "Here am I."

He tipped the bottle up and downed the last of his spiced beer, put his head on the bar, and passed out. His companion looked at him, and took a sip of his drink as the barkeep walked over.

"Looks pretty well marinated to me."

"I'd say so. Everything ready out back?"

"Yep. Took the sauce out a few minutes ago. Five gallons of it. They're waiting."

"Okay. Let's wake him up."

They shook and slapped the sleeper with a damp bar rag.

"Hey. Wake up. Wanna go to a barbecue?"

"Barbecue? Sure. I love barbecue."

"C'mon then, before all the good stuff is gone."

"You bet. I love barbecue."

The two drinking companions went out the back door while the barkeep tidied up and locked the doors. He was checking himself in the bar mirror, with his upper lip raised, rubbing his teeth with an index finger when the screams started; the butchering had begun. He didn't mind missing it, even though that was part of the enjoyment. He was sure Mr. Steele would taste just fine, despite his name. He gave one more rub with his finger to his sharp pointy teeth, and went to join the others of his kind outside.

The mark of the Jinn

DAMN GOOD FOR HIM

Damn Good for Him

BILLY PEARSON WAS AT DOWNTOWN DOUG'S, playing three-handed cutthroat with Doug Martin and Eddie Fisk. He told his partner, Les Jeffers, that he was out buying cars, but the truth was, it was hot and muggy, unusual weather for early June in Colorado Springs, and he didn't feel much like working . . . so he was screwing off. He figured he'd earned it, and besides which, Mr. Jeffers and the 2360 Car Corral would survive for one afternoon at least without him. Doug was dealing. As he was counting and passing out cards, Billy said, "I ever tell you all the one about Pierre and Franklin . . ."

"Oh, Christ, Billy is this another one of your sorry-assed queer or racist jokes?"

"No, Doug. This one's cute."

"Ain't none of your jokes cute," Eddie said.

"Okay. It's funny then."

"I doubt it," Eddie said.

Billy started again. "So Pierre says, 'It's just not fair. They don't call you a batheball player after juth one game . . . but thuck one dick and they all call you a tok thukker. It's juth not fair.'"

No one laughed as Eddie discarded an eight of clubs. Doug picked it up and ginned, discarding a face card that Billy needed for a run, and caught him with a potful.

"Eighty-five," he said after counting his cards. They were playing

Hollywood, which meant three boxes and cumulative scoring. What it really means is that on a day like today, when Billy was loser, he could lose three times as much. Or three times as fast—take your pick. He was down about fifty or sixty bucks at twenty-five cents a point in less than two hours.

"Eighteen," Eddie said. "I needed one or two more draws to gin."

"One or two more of my discards you mean. Y'all are whipping the crap outta me," Billy said.

"And enjoyin' every minute of it too," Doug said. "It serves you right for telling that dumb fucking joke."

"Give me the friggin' cards and I'll see if I can deal any better than you."

Billy was busy collecting and shuffling up the cards when his cell phone started buzzing in his shirt pocket. He was going to ignore it, then pulled it out and stared at it, then started to put it away when he didn't recognize the caller ID.

"Go ahead and answer. Maybe it'll change your luck," Eddie said.

He flipped it open. "This is Bill."

"Billy," a voice said. "This is Alvin Poorman."

"Hey Alvin. Long time, no hear. What's up? I'm kinda in the middle of something." He stopped shuffling and put the deck facedown on the desk.

"S-Say, baby. I g-guess our old boss done pissed off one guy too many."

Alvin had a slight stutter when he got excited. "Say that again?"

"Our old boss musta pissed off one guy too many. Somebody killed Jimmy-Dan last night."

"No shit?"

"Yeah. Cops found him yesterday morning. He took two rounds from a forty-five or three fifty-seven, s-somethin' big anyway, right between the tits . . . dead center of his chest. He was coming out of the shower."

"Lotsa folks been waiting for it to happen," Billy said. "Where was this?

I lost track of him ten years ago."

"Phoenix, Arizona—Scottsdale, actually."

"Figures he'd follow the money," Billy said. "How'd you find out?"

"A guy I used to wholesale cars to, over by Motor City, retired and moved down there. He knew I used to work for Jimmy-Dan and called me. It was in the Phoenix newspapers," Alvin said.

"Well, it's not a surprise."

"Not really. What's surprising is that took so long."

"I hear you there," Billy said. "I know lots of people have thought about it."

"Listen, I'm at the auction, I gotta go. A car I wanna bid on is about to come up."

"You wanna do lunch tomorrow?"

"Can't, babe. I'm in Kansas City. Be back first of the week. I'll call you then."

"Okay. Say, how'd you get my cell?"

"Les gave it to me. Gotta go." And the line went dead.

Billy shut the phone and picked up the cards.

"Bad news, trouble?" Doug said.

"Not really," Billy said as he shuffled and dealt the cards. "That was a guy I used to work with named Alvin Poorman."

"I know him," Doug said. "He's a wholesaler, works outta his car trunk."

"Yeah. He was letting me know that a guy we used to work for was murdered. Shot in the chest. His name was Jimmy-Dan Dee. He was a used car dealer over on the east side, fifteen years ago. Before your time."

"Friend of yours?" he said.

"No," Billy said. "Anything but. I was a salesman for him, then a sales manager for about six months."

"I knew him," Eddie said. "He was a short pudgy guy. Dark hair and eyes. Had a diamond pinky ring and drove a white Lincoln or Cadillac."

"That'd be the guy."

"I bought a pickup truck from him," Eddie said.

Oh Christ, Billy thought. *Here it comes.* "How was it?" he asked.

"It was a good truck, a Ford Ranger. Drove it for five years. But I still hate that fat sonofabitch."

"Why?"

"Made me a shill," Eddie said. "I got a few other guys to buy cars and trucks from him, guys I worked with at the utilities department. Guys I still work with who turn their back to me, don't talk. Guys who used to be my friends, who're still carrying grudges, years later."

"How many?"

"Five or six. Too many, anyway. One would have been too many."

"How'd you ever get hooked up with him, Bill?" Doug said.

"Youth and ignorance. What happened with your coworkers?" he said to Eddie.

"They wound up deep in debt on pickup trucks that were basically worthless wrecks. One guy started out with a nice three-year-old paid-for pickup. When Jimmy-Dan and his "Dan-Dee" deals was done with him three vehicles later, the poor bastard was driving a ten-year-old piece of shit; it was a hundred-thousand-mile oil burner, and he had a forty-eight-month mortgage payment on it, collateralized by all his household goods and a second mortgage on his house," Eddie said.

"How in the fuck did that happen?" Doug said.

"He traded trucks, three times in five months," Billy Pearson said. "And each time he got a wholesale price for his vehicle and paid Jimmy-Dan top-dollar retail for the one he was buying. I saw it happen to several others."

"Why didn't you quit?"

"Like I said, youth and ignorance are all I can claim," was Pearson's answer. "I had bills, a spendthrift first wife, and it was my first real job out of college. Jimmy-Dan could be absolutely charming when he wanted to. Someone once said he could 'beg a starving cat off of a fish wagon.' I think he could have, too. One of the thugs he brought up here from his old Louisiana stomping grounds told me Jimmy-Dan could cry on command, and used to do it when he was going door-to-door selling vacuum cleaners."

"He musta been a real asshole," Doug said.

"Oh, he was," Eddie said. "I think he was rotten to the core. I think he'd do anything for money."

"He would," Billy said. "When he was pitching vacuum cleaners, he'd tell the prospect he was gonna lose his job if he didn't make a sale that night because he was low man on the sales team, and then he'd start to cry. Truth was, he was the top salesman for the whole South, driving around in a brand-new white Electra 225."

They were still playing cards, but without enthusiasm. Eddie's beeper hadn't gone off, so things must have been slow over at the utilities department, and not a single customer came in to Doug's place looking for a new ride. It was as if the whole city was too sweaty and overheated to want to go do anything.

Doug got up to check on his salesman, an old car jockey named Kenny King, and hit the restroom.

"Jimmy-Dan used everybody," Billy said to Eddie, "you, me, anybody he could."

"I have bad feelings about it," Eddie said. "I can't believe I was so fucking stupid."

"Look at it this way. We were both conned by one of the best."

Doug came back with three cans of cold Pepsi. "Don't say I never did anything nice for yez. Tell me more about this guy."

"Jimmy-Dan was a gold-plated prick," Eddie said.

"He was that for sure," Billy said. "He was also a Mason—a Shriner, in fact. He was sponsored by his banker."

"Shriners, the guys in funny hats and Model T cars?" Doug said. "Who march in parades and sponsor a kids' hospital?"

"Yep. It's called Shriners Hospital. They care for children with burns. No charge. It's all paid for by the Shriners. They help a lot of kids, do a lot of good."

"I didn't think that Jimmy-Dan ever did anything good," Eddie said.

"Well, maybe, maybe not," Billy said. "He did leave a ton of bad car loans at the bank when he went out of business and left town. Joe, his banker who bought the loans, *retired*, so to speak, and his vice president, a guy named Kelly, was fired. He moved back East somewhere. Pennsylvania, I think."

Doug said, "What did you mean when you said 'bought the loans'? Were they full recourse?"

"He had it all. Full recourse, which meant that the bank calls up and says, 'So-and-so missed his payment, come pay it off.' The dealer cosigned the loan in effect. That's what a full recourse loan is, but, he also had partial recourse and repurchase agreements too. With those, the dealer is obligated to repurchase the vehicle, but the bank has to find and go get it, then bring it back to the dealership."

Doug tipped back in his chair and sipped his Pepsi. Eddie looked out the mirrored glass windows at the heat waves shimmering with the sun in the dead air over Doug's front line of used cars. Billy enjoyed the cool air from the big swamp coolers that rumbled away like purring lions up on the roof. He shuffled and dealt a new hand, turning up the jack of clubs as the first discard.

Eddie sorted his cards, picked up the jack, and discarded a four. He said, "Was there a lot of money involved?"

"Oh, hell yes," Billy said. "Millions. I heard fifteen to twenty-five million. That's why Kelly was fired. Joe was the president, so he was forced to retire. The board of directors had to find a buyer and sell the bank."

"Fifteen million was a helluva lot of money back then," Doug said.

"Still is in this town. The bank was afraid of Jimmy-Dan at the end. I thought it was a classic case of the tail wagging the dog."

"Those days are long gone," Doug said. "It's almost impossible to get floor-plan money now."

"I hear you there," Billy said. "Jimmy-Dan had a hand in it for sure. That guy pissed off so many people in Baton Rouge, he was afraid to stay home alone."

"What . . ." Eddie said.

"God's truth," Billy said. "If his wife went out of town with the kids to visit her parents or something, he'd go to a motel."

"What'd he do in Louisiana?"

"Bankrupted his company and screwed a lot of small contractors."

"How many?" Eddie asked.

"I dunno. But a lot. He was building new homes, a couple of hundred the way I heard it. But he cut corners, got sued a lot, and then finally took off with the money."

"When was this?"

"Probably twenty or twenty-five years ago."

"Musta took 'em to the cleaners if he was still worried after all this time," Doug said.

"He did. And he was." Billy said. "But he was a weird guy, hot and cold, up and down. We had a really mad customer one time; the guy barely got home and the transmission fell out. The guy wanted his money back. Came in swearing and threatening, he's gonna tear the place up and all that kinda stuff. Jimmy-Dan takes the guy back in his office and sits him down in a chair. The guy wants his money back, period. Jimmy-Dan tells him that ain't gonna happen. They go on, back and forth for a while, then the guy says something else, like, 'I'll fucking kill you,' raising the stakes, you know, and Jimmy-Dan says, 'Hang on a moment,' real calm and reaches in his desk, like he's gonna take out a notepad, or get a Kleenex. Instead, he pulls a chromed .45 caliber automatic out of his bottom desk drawer and cocks it, then lays it on the desk blotter, right in front of himself. He tells the guy to 'go on with what you were saying.' The poor bastard couldn't get out of the place fast enough. He never came back."

"He really did that?" Doug said.

"Yeah, he did. I was standing outside his door. I heard it all. I think it was the way he said, 'Go on with what you were saying . . .' Jimmy-Dan said it in a normal voice. But there was an implied menace in it. I told you he was a great actor."

"You think he would have shot the guy?" Eddie said.

"I honestly don't know," Billy said, "it wouldn't have surprised me, though. I saw him try to stab a guy in the eye with a fork in a restaurant one night. The man was getting pissed off because Jimmy-Dan was cussing a lot and his wife could hear all the 'fuck this' and 'fuck thats.' First thing you know, the dude's coming over to our table with blood in his eye and Jimmy-Dan goes after him with a fork."

"Then what?" Eddie said.

"The restaurant owner grabbed Jimmy-Dan and stopped it. Put a headlock on him. Could have been an act, I don't know. But the next day, when the third salesman quit—a guy named Richie who was Jimmy-Dan's favorite—when he quit, Jimmy-Dan cried for two weeks. Just sat in his office and sobbed."

"I don't guess it was very good for business," Doug said.

"It wasn't."

"Whad'ja do?" Eddie asked.

Billy picked up Doug's discard, the ten of diamonds, and went down with three fours, five points, and a diamond run from the nine to the ace.

"Well, fuck me," Doug said. "I've got a gob."

"Me too," Eddie said. "Shit-house mouse."

"Just keep counting, boys and quit'cher bitchin'. Y'all have been whipping me like a stepchild."

"We like it better that way. Shit. Eighty-seven," Doug said.

"Sixty-three," Eddie added. "Whad'ja do with Jimmy-Dan acting so weird?"

"Carried on, as best we could. Alvin and I came in and worked at selling cars, same's always. But there was a lot of tension in the air. Then, after a couple of weeks, the thugs showed up and Jimmy-Dan was busy with them."

"You mean Elvis and Denny, those guys from Louisiana?" Eddie said.

"Yeah," Billy said.

"Weren't they collectors, money collectors, for the Mob?"

"Yeah, I didn't know it at the time, though. Jimmy-Dan always said they were old friends that he went to school with. I think Jimmy-Dan was tied up with them somehow, but I never knew for sure. Elvis and Denny were always nice to Alvin and me, but standoffish, and never friendly. Know what I mean? They were polite but didn't want much conversation with those of us who weren't part of their circle. I know they were both street fighters, and I know they were always armed. I heard that once, Elvis stuck a needle in a guy's eye while Denny held him down."

"Who told you that?" Doug said. "You believe it?"

"Yeah. I do," Billy said. "And I'd rather not say who told me. It's true."

"I know it is." Eddie said. "I heard the same story from a guy with a debt to some bad people."

Doug fiddled with his cards, rearranging his hand.

Billy said, "I know those two dragged a guy for about two blocks over in Knob Hill one night, during a beef of some sort. The guy made the mistake of leaning in the car window. Denny grabbed his wrist and Elvis rolled the window up on his arm. Then they took off up the street, laughing at the guy. Denny finally hit the button when they were going about twenty-five miles an hour and let the window down. The guy was pretty busted up."

"Police? Anybody file charges?" Doug said.

"Not as far as I know," Billy said. "The people involved were too scared. I know those two, Elvis and Denny, were always driving new Caddies or Lincolns, always had money and new clothes, and never had jobs like normal people."

"You ever see 'em?" Doug said.

"No. I heard they're both dead, Elvis was in jail in South America somewhere and Denny was killed down in Louisiana by a twelve-gauge shotgun blast at close range."

"Cops get him?" Eddie asked.

"No, I don't think so. I heard it was drug related, but I don't know any more than that."

It was quiet for a minute while Eddie dealt the next hand in his methodical way.

"Khee-rist," Doug said, "this ain't a hand, it's a foot. These cards are plumb nasty." He frowned as he put the last three cards in his hand.

"Hey, man, I deals 'em like I deals 'em," Eddie said. "The cards have no friends and they do no favors."

"Old Lady Luck is a fickle bitch," Doug said as he laid down the king of hearts. Billy picked up his king and went down with five points. He'd been dealt a nearly pat hand.

"You shouldn't talk about Lady Luck that way, she'll bite you in the ass, Dougie." Billy said, and sat back in his chair, getting ready for all the howling and whining, bitching, pissing, and moaning. He was surprised when both of them just started counting up the misery in their hands. Billy could see the score sheet Eddie was tallying and thought he was catching up.

Doug was dealing the cards. "Was it always that bad, Bill?"

"Yeah. It was like the Moscow Circus all the time and it never stopped. I had ulcers after a year and a half, and a divorce in the works too."

Eddie said, "Were you ever in trouble?"

"With the law? Never. I can't say the same for Jimmy-Dan. He was always in court, never in jail so far as I know, but it seemed like he was being sued every other month or two."

"Over car deals?" Doug said.

"Yeah, mostly. Plus the guy he assaulted in the restaurant, and when he got divorced, the first time."

"I didn't know he was divorced," Eddie said. "From Peggy Ann?"

"Yeah. Jimmy-Dan got mad at her for kissing a guy. He was in the front seat with another woman, a friend of his and Peggy Ann's. She was in the back seat with a car dealer from Amarillo, Texas. They were kissing."

"He actually divorced her for kissing?" Eddie said. "I only met her a couple of times but I thought she was a sweetheart."

"She was. The way I heard, it, they kissed a few times. Tongues might have been involved. I do know they were all pretty well oiled. They were going home from dinner and drinks. Jimmy-Dan was trying to line the Texan up as a car supplier . . . he'd buy them on behalf of Jimmy-Dan, ship 'em to Colorado."

"Didn't Jimmy-Dan have a couple of kids?" Eddie said.

"Yeah. A boy and a girl, they were teenagers when their parents split up. I don't know whatever happened to them. Jimmy-Dan divorced Peggy Ann and thirty days after the divorce was final, he married a woman who worked at the bank . . . divorced her forty-five days later."

Doug drew a card and ginned. Billy had two spreads, two players on Doug's hand, and nine points. Eddie had twenty-four. He picked up the cards and started to shuffle.

"Jimmy-Dan fired me right after he got divorced the first time. He and

I were in disagreement about everything. I didn't like the way he treated me or anyone else. One day he told me to 'throw a customer's car keys up on the roof,' so the guy couldn't leave. I said no, I wouldn't do it. He told me, 'Throw the fucking keys, or throw your shit in a box and get the fuck outta here.' So that's what I did. It took me seven months to get my wages."

"He fired you, right there?" Doug said.

"Yeah."

"The guy was a real asshole."

"Yeah, he was. I threw a set of keys on the roof, though, my keys to the building and file cabinets."

"Bet that pissed him off," Eddie said.

"Right royally. Probably why it took so long to get my pay."

"What did you do?"

"I walked a couple of miles up the street and got a job at another car dealership the same afternoon."

"Fellows, it's been fun, but I'm quits after this hand," Eddie said. "I have to get back to the utilities department in time to check out."

We settled up right after that. Billy Pearson's fun for the afternoon only cost him eighty-five dollars. Doug was the day's winner.

Billy went over to Motor City and rolled through the back lots, looking for recent trade-ins, cars that the sales managers might wholesale out, but didn't find anything. He honked and waved at a few guys he knew, then headed for the east side and the used car ghetto where he owned his business.

Les was delivering a car when Billy got there, a sedan that they'd "tote the note" on. The customer was standing out in front of the building watching, as Bob Will, the lot boy, bolted a temporary license plate on. Billy walked up and greeted them, then went inside. Les was in the office.

"Hey, Les," he said. "You won't believe this. Alvin Poorman called me a little while ago and told me that Jimmy-Dan Dee was shot and killed in Scottsdale, Arizona, a couple of nights ago."

"No joke?" Les said.

"Nope. Alvin said it was in the paper."

"Did they catch the shooter?"

"Not yet."

"It doesn't surprise me that somebody shot the sonofabitch, but who'd kill Jimmy-Dan?"

"Who knows? That's the consensus so far. How'd we end up on the Miller deal?" Billy said, pointing with his thumb toward the car being delivered.

"Six hundred cash, and an old beater pickup truck; we're carrying four thousand back at ten percent for three years. Payments are one fifty a month."

"What'd you lay the truck in at?"

"Three hundred."

"How much skin have we got in the game?"

"About seven payments, and Bob might want to buy the pickup."

"What did you tell him?"

"Talk to you," Les said.

"Where's the truck?"

"Behind the garage."

Billy took the keys from the board on his desk and stuck his head around the door to the office.

"What does Miller do?"

"Head custodian at the elementary school over on Chelton Boulevard. He's been there for twelve years."

"Great."

"It's a second car, before you ask."

Billy gave him a thumbs-up and went out back to look at Miller's old truck.

It was a twenty-year-old Chevy S-10 pickup with 185,000 miles on it. It looked like it had a good set of tires and not much else. Bob came around the building with his hand tools.

"Miller delivered?"

"Over the curb and down the road."

"Les told me you wanted to buy this toad."

"Yeah."

"Why?"

"It's cheap. I can afford it."

"You know the engines get weak in these things at a hundred twenty-five thousand miles."

"Yeah. It's got good tires, though."

"Yep. And surely the radio plays loud. Put a dealer tag on it and drive it around the block. Let me know how you can pay five hundred bucks for it." Billy threw the keys to him and went back in the office.

Les was on the phone so Billy went in his office where it was cooler. He sat there with his back to the wall and left leg on the desk, thinking about Jimmy-Dan Dee.

He was a one-of-a-kind asshole, he thought to himself, *and now he's been killed by person or persons unknown. Wonder if they'll ever find "who dunnit," and why.*

"Boss, you look like your brain is out there orbiting the planet Zargon or something."

"Hey, Bob, I didn't see you come in. I was thinking about a guy I used to work for. He was murdered in Arizona a couple days ago."

"Dude. That's extreme."

"Yeah. It is." Billy took his foot off the desk and faced forward. "Did you drive that old toad?"

"Yeah. All the way to Union Street."

"And . . ."

"You said, like, five hundred bucks. Right?"

"That's what I said."

"Okay."

"Okay what? Do you want to buy it?"

"Yeah."

"How're you gonna pay for it?"

"Cash. I'll get it in the morning. At the bank," he said.

"You've got to get insurance."

"I know. I will."

"Okay. I'll sell it to you. But I want to make sure you understand that it's an old piece of crap. No telling how long it'll run."

"Yeah."

Billy could see, Bob was set on buying the old truck, and nothing he said would dissuade him.

"Okay, Billy said. "Go out and get the serial number and mileage."

"Got 'em already."

Here's a blank offer to purchase and an odometer statement. "I'll sign that when you've finished filling it out."

Bob sat on the other side of the desk and did the purchase order while Billy watched. When he finished he surprised his boss by getting a folded hundred-dollar bill from his wallet and handing it to Billy with his paperwork. He said, "I'll get the other four hundred in the morning when the bank opens."

"What about the sales tax?"

"Here," he said, and gave Billy a couple of twenties from the hand-tooled book-style leather wallet he carried in his back pocket, attached to his belt with a heavy silver chain.

"Okay," Billy said as he signed the offer to purchase. "You bot'cherself a truck."

"Thanks."

"It's still a pile of shit. If it breaks in half, you own both pieces. And you still owe me four hundred dollars."

"It's a done deal?"

"Yeah. It's all yours."

"Thanks, boss. You made a mistake about that truck. It's a good one, and it runs like a Swiss sewing machine."

"For your sake, I hope so," Billy said.

Bob's word was good: he came to work the next day with four one-hundred dollar bills. Les worked up the papers and gave him the title. They went on to have a profitable Friday and Saturday, delivering a total of eight retail units, all for cash or preappoved financing. They had totaled fourteen sales that week and marked it as exceptional—and *mas grande* profitable. Les and Billy normally kept about forty-five cars and trucks in stock and ready for sale. With the phenomenal sales run, they'd turned over one-third of their inventory, and by the middle of the following week Billy was really hopping, trying to buy additional vehicles and get the ones in stock detailed and ready to sell. He was so busy that he forgot all about lunch with Alvin Poorman. He called Friday morning. "Hey, baby, I'm getting real hungry, you forget about lunch?"

"I gotta plead the fifth," Billy said. Then he told Alvin about their great week and all.

Alvin said, in his cornpone twang, "Well, shit. If you need cars, ya shoulda let me know. I've got three transport loads I just brought up from Kansas City."

"Okay. Are they front-line ready?"

"Pretty much," he said. "Come take a look. I'll buy your lunch and tell you what all I learned about Jimmy-Dan."

"Who could refuse a deal like that?"

Billy got directions to Alvin's place: on West Baptist Road, north of the city a couple of miles. He called Les and told him where he was going and why, and left instructions for Bob Will about some cars he wanted moved over to the front line after they were detailed.

Billy patrolled through all of the Motor City new car dealers that morning, without any success. He had a near miss on a nice old Malibu Super Sport at the Ford store, but was aced out by another used car dealer who outbid him by $250. *"Oh, well . . ."* he said to himself, and jumped on I-25, headed for Alvin Poorman's.

Traffic was light at first but got heavier as he went north. It was congested at Fillmore, slowing at Garden of the Gods, backing up at North Nevada, and stopped dead in its tracks south of Woodmen Road. There wasn't any lane jumping or creepers on the shoulders . . . traffic was at a complete standstill. Billy put his pickup in park and shut the motor off; there was nothing he could do but wait. He started thinking about Jimmy-Dan Dee again, speculating about who'd want to kill him.

The first one he thought of was Uwe, the inspection sticker guy. Back in the eighties, cars and light trucks had to be safety inspected. This could be an expensive proposition if you were bringing cars and pickup trucks to Colorado from the West Texas oil fields like Jimmy-Dan was. Instead of new ball joints, rebuilt front ends, brakes, mufflers, shock absorbers, and such, Jimmy-Dan found Uwe.

"Oo-Vay the Churmin" was what Alvin and Billy called him. Uwe had a repair garage down on South Sierra Street where he fixed Volkswagen, Mercedes Benz, and Audi automobiles, and he was a licensed Colorado State Inspection Station.

Somehow, some way, Jimmy-Dan bought a briefcase full of brand-new Colorado inspection stickers from Uwe, which Jimmy-Dan and his lot boy slapped on the West Texas oil field units. They dolled up, had the body shop paint the pickup truck beds so all the dents and scrapes from oil field tools wouldn't show, and put new floor mats in that come wholesale at six bucks a pair from the Superior Auto Shine truck, which came around to all the used car lots in town every other week. Last of all, they sprayed flat black paint by the gallon in the engine compartment and wheel wells to make the tired old iron look decent, but it was really the same old lipstick that con men have used on the same old pigs for years.

It didn't take long for the complaints to start piling up at the Colorado Department of Revenue. And it didn't take long after that for the revenue agent to stop by for a little tête-à-tête with Jimmy-Dan Dee about such-and-such inspection sticker on this-and-that pickup truck, and so on and so forth, each offense being punishable by a fine of up to five thousand dollars and/or two years in the State Penitentiary at Cañon City.

As there were multiple complaints and multiple provable offenses that would no doubt result in multiple fines and many, many years in the pokey, Jimmy-Dan did what any self-respecting criminal would do: he ratted. He gave up Uwe, his coconspirator, and promised never to do it again, confessed most of his bad inspection sticker acts, and threw himself on the mercy of the Colorado Department of Revenue, crying, begging, and pleading like an Arab rug merchant in the souk.

It worked. Jimmy-Dan stayed out of jail and kept his used car dealer's license after paying a five-thousand-dollar fine. Uwe, "Oo-Vay the Churmin," got thrown under the bus. He stayed out of jail, but was put on probation for a few years, and paid an identical five-thousand-dollar fine. He lost his business and went bankrupt paying lawyers, and his wife divorced him, taking his last few dollars and whatever shreds of self-respect the poor bastard had left. *Yeah,* Billy thought, *I could see Uwe getting even with Jimmy-Dan.*

"*Whaa-Wap, Whaamp,*" an air horn blast from a green Kenworth tractor-trailer driver two feet behind him let Billy know traffic had started moving. He started his pickup and scratched rubber taking off.

Alvin's current place of business was an old Conoco station on Baptist

Road, about five miles north of the city limits. It had a two-bay garage with a lift, an office, and plenty of parking on pavement. The place was surrounded on three sides by a high chain-link fence with two big swinging iron gates in front, and cars standing in neat rows across the front and sides. Billy pulled up by the office and parked. Alvin was at his desk doing paperwork.

"Billy Pearson," he called through the open door. "I was about to give you up for dead."

"There was a car versus truck fracas at Woodmen Road. Had traffic to a complete standstill."

"Woodmen Road's been futzed up since dirt was discovered."

"Yeah," Billy said. "It has."

"Chinese okay with you?"

"Sure."

Alvin went into the garage where two men were detailing cars, said something to one of them who looked over his shoulder at Billy, then nodded and went back to work, polishing the trunk lid of a white Ford Mustang.

"Come on," Alvin said. "I'll drive."

They got in a late model red Corvette Coupe and headed up I-25.

"We're going to Fat Fang's in Monument."

"Good?"

"Best Chinese I ever ate. Try the Crab Rangoon. But it's all good," Alvin said.

He got on the on-ramp and floored it. The Corvette hit ninety-five by the time they merged into an empty northbound land.

"Sporty."

"Oh, yeah! I just love doing that," Alvin said.

They got to the restaurant, and the food was every bit as good as Alvin predicted it would be. Fat Fang was a congenial host, and they lingered for a while, drinking tea.

Alvin lit a cigarette. "I found out about Jimmy-Dan."

"I've been wondering about him," Billy said. "Found myself thinking about 'Oo-Vay the Churmin' on the way up here, thinking he'd be a prime candidate for turning Jimmy-Dan's lights out."

"Yeah, Uwe would be a good guess. But it wasn't him, or the goofy bastard that lost his gas station that night shooting cooked dice with Jimmy-Dan and the thugs in the back of the car lot. Funny, I can't remember his name."

"It was Joey Small," Billy said, remembering the confrontation at the car lot the day after, when Joey sobered up and realized he'd gambled away his business on a pair of dice that were shaved smoother than a newborn baby's ass and passed in and out of the game slicker and faster than the first man in line at a thousand-seat mess hall.

"Yeah, that's it," Alvin said as he put out his cigarette. "Shit. I forgot you couldn't smoke in restaurants anymore. Come on, I'll tell you the rest of the story. You drive."

He tossed the Corvette's keys to Billy as they went out the door into the parking lot. Billy put his sunglasses on so he'd look cool driving Alvin's red rocket. Then they headed out Highway 105, toward I-25.

"Go north, and we'll ride for a little."

"You just want me to fall in love with this badass car," Billy said as he made the light at the northbound entrance and ran down the ramp to merge with traffic, the sports car responding like a thoroughbred at the slightest touch of the gas pedal or steering wheel.

"Maybe," Alvin said.

He cracked his window and lit a cigarette, looked out at the town of Monument. The silence lasted for a few minutes while they crested Monument Hill at eighty-five miles per hour and gaining, headed under the County Line Road underpass, then on to the long straightaway leading to Greenland and Larkspur. About when Billy ripped past two semis, feeling like Dale Earnhardt at Talladega, Alvin said, "It's not hard to get a ticket in this car."

Billy looked down, saw that he was "doing the ton"—one hundred miles per hour— and let off the gas, tapped the brake pedal, and got it down to seventy-five.

"Jeez, is this a ZR?"

"No, just fuel-injected."

"Damn. She's a racy little bitch."

Alvin didn't say anything. He lit another cigarette from the butt of the first one. Billy could see that something was making him agitated, pensive, reluctant. He was squirming in the passenger seat. "I'm gonna turn around at the next exit," Billy said, "the one after Larkspur."

"Yeah. Good idea."

Billy was southbound before Alvin spoke again.

"A-about Jimmy-Dan."

"Frig, Alvin. Just spit it out."

"Well, it's not like you think."

"So somebody he screwed over . . ."

"No. It's not like that. Has to do with sex."

"Yeah, so . . ."

"With a seventeen-year-old." Alvin lit his third cigarette since lunch and took a deep drag. Then said, "boy."

Billy couldn't believe it.

"No shit?"

"No shit. Turns out ol' Jimmy-Dan was what the gays call a chicken hawk—an older man having an affair with a younger one."

"So Jimmy-Dan was a chicken hawk and fudge packer," Billy said. "That's wild."

"The boy was a young gangbanger. He shot Jimmy-Dan and took off for the border in his new pickup truck."

"They catch him?"

"He was intercepted north of the border, but he ran, hid out in the desert, truck and all, and escaped."

"No police helicopters?"

"Shit." Only the way Alvin said the word, it came out as two syllables. "That's only in the movies and tee-vee, Billy."

"So he's in Mexico?"

"Yeah, but that ain't all." Without waiting for Billy to speak, Alvin said, "Elvis and Denny are involved. They're in Mexico, hunting for the kid. Probably kill him."

"They'd be the boys for the job. I thought they were dead?"

"Yeah, well, they ain't," Alvin said. "Elvis speaks the lingo too; he spent a few years in a Colombian penitentiary."

"You think Elvis and Denny are queers?" Billy said.

Alvin looked straight ahead for a full minute before he said anything. Billy could see out the corner of my eye that he was blinking rapidly, and that there was sweat on his upper lip.

"I'll n-never say so outside of this car. I'm not positive, but, yes, I believe they are."

"Why?"

"Simple. I never seen 'em with any women."

"You worried about them?"

"Just don't need any more grief in my life. Especially from them two. And you, my friend, need to be smart enough to be damned well afraid of them two assholes. They'd just as soon kill ya as lookatcha. And for Christ-fuckin' sakes, don't you go telling nobody what was said just now. The only reason I told you is so you won't go talking or nosing around and stir up a bunch of shit that could come back on both of us."

Billy was quiet for a while. Alvin was too. They pulled up the ramp at

County Line Road, crossed over, and parked on the entrance ramp. Billy left the motor running and the air conditioner blowing cool air. As he put the car in park, he finally spoke. "You're serious."

Alvin looked him in the eye and took a last puff on his latest cancer stick and said, "Brother, I'm as serious as a bullet in the chest. Them two faggots, or queers, or gays, or whatever you want to call 'em, you do so at your own peril. I'm telling you they're hitters. Stone. Cold. Killers."

The color drained from Billy Pearson's face as he processed all that Alvin had told him. He put the Corvette in drive and headed down the ramp with a new reality aborning in his head.

"I hear you there," Billy finally said, as he pulled into Alvin's place and parked next to his pickup. They didn't mention current events, or their old boss, Jimmy-Dan Dee, again that day. Billy bought six cars and a pair of Ford pickup trucks from Alvin. Sadly, the Corvette wasn't one of them. When he got back to town to make arrangements to ferry all of them home, the first thing he saw was a shiny old pickup with chrome wheels parked alongside Bob Will's workshop at the back of the Car Corral lot. Bob was just finishing up on a white Toyota four-door as Billy walked in.

"Bob, grab the transit tags and come over to the office, We've got eight units up in Monument to go get."

"Okay. I can probably find us a driver, too. Dave the fireman is off today; he was just here."

"Call him. Pays ten bucks and one beer." Billy nodded at the pickup out back. "Is that the old beater I sold you last week?"

"Uh-huh," and a happy grin told him everything he needed to know, but Bob added, "and it runs as good as it looks, boss. Told you, you were missing the boat on it."

"It's okay, Bob. It's okay. I'd much rather be screwed by a friend than someone I don't know," Billy said with a smile. *So the little bastard outtraded me. Well, good for him,* he thought, *damn good for him, and too damn bad for that asshole, Jimmy-Dan Dee* . . . Billy decided he had better develop a whole new respect for the alternative lifestyles of the Gay and Lesbian communities. He didn't want any late-night visits from the two thugs named Elvis and Denny . . . and hoped to hell that he hadn't spouted off with any antigay jokes in their presence. *Oh, shit,* he thought, *what if I* . . .

A MISCHIEF OF RATS

A Mischief of Rats

My name is Jake McKern.
I've been a cop for most of my life.
During that time I've seen the highest of
human ideals and the worst of human depravity.
These are my journals of those events.

Oklahoma State Penitentiary
McAlester, Oklahoma
9 a.m. CST, Wed., Nov. 2, 1955 . . . forty-nine hours remaining

The mantrap thudded shut behind them and a pair of men stepped across the short distance to the outside door. The prisoner stood . . . motionless . . . expressionless . . . impatient . . . waiting for the hack to find the key that unlocked the steel door in front of them. After what seemed like forever, he inserted the key and pulled back the outer portal. George Phelps hesitated, trained not to move until the jailer gave permission. The guard smirked and made an exaggerated sweep with his right arm. As the prisoner started moving, the guard cleared his throat. "Good-bye, convict. We'll see you again. Soon."

The prisoner squared his shoulders and stepped through the doorway into the bright early morning and drew his first lungful of free air in more than five years. *No fucking way,* he thought, *not a chance. I'll die before I go in a hellhole like this again.* He meant it too. He had no idea that in less than forty-eight hours he'd suffer a violent and painful and horrifying death.

U.S. Highway 64 West
Woodward, Oklahoma
9:15 a.m. CST, Thurs., Nov. 3, 1955 . . . twenty-eight hours remaining

Two men in a blue '49 Ford sedan rolled down U.S. Highway 64 toward Guymon, Oklahoma. To the casual eye, they looked like two ordinary Joes on their way to work, and the car looked like any of the tens of thousands of similar ones made in Detroit and sold to the motoring public. But that was to the casual observer.

To the eyes of law enforcement officers and experienced man hunters, those who were familiar with cons, criminals, and recidivists, the two men had a furtiveness about them that drew the attention of the captors, jailers, and executioners of the miscreants of the world. Then there was the car. It, too, was a wolf in sheep's clothing. It had been purpose-built by hard men who worked at night in anonymous shops hidden in the Appalachian Mountains, and tucked into an obscure corner of western North Carolina. It had a reinforced frame and springs, double shock absorbers, and oversized tires. The back seat was shortened and the trunk was larger . . . large enough to accommodate the sixty gallons of untaxed and illicit alcohol it was built to carry. But the car's crown jewel was the motor. The factory flathead had been yanked out. It was replaced with a big overhead-valve V8 from a stolen '54 Cadillac El Dorado. It displaced 354 cubic inches and with twin four-barrel carburetors, it made three hundred horsepower. Fully loaded with moonshine, it could go from zero to a hundred in less than ten seconds and topped out at more than a 150 miles an hour. It was the fastest car in all the southern territories.

The driver idled through Guymon. With the car's oversized exhaust pipes walloping the pavement, they were watched through the squinted eyes of every cop they passed. Both occupants of the vehicle stared straight ahead . . . watching with their peripheral vision, the cops watching them as they passed the town limits and headed on west.

"How much longer before we get outta this miserable state, George? All these fuckin' cops are giving me the willies."

"It ain't too far—about seventy-five miles to Boise City and we'll turn north. It's only fifteen or twenty miles to the state line from there, and we'll be in Colorado. There ain't many towns after that. It's pretty wide open. Speaking of which, how're we doin' on gas?"

"Just under half a tank."

"Plus the three jerry cans in the trunk?"

"Shit, no. I put them in last night in Woodward . . . while you was inside, fuckin' ole Melinda, or whatever her name was. I would've gone to a filling station, 'cept you told me not to. And besides which, I ain't got no money."

"Nothing?"

"Naw. I spent the last of it back in Lawton on cigarettes. Which I'm also running out of."

"Well, don't worry. I'll take care of it. We got enough to get to Boise City?"

"Just barely. This thing don't go real far on a tank with that big motor. You've got cash, aint'cha? They gave you your walkin' money when they released you, didn't they?"

"Twenty dollars is all. I give it to Melissa yesterday evening."

Ray Matthews took his eyes off the road and looked over at George Phelps. "Really?" was all he said.

"After five years in McAlester State Penitentiary I'da fucked a rock if I thought there was a snake under it. I knew she was a sure thing. Got my money's worth too. And she fed us supper and breakfast, didn't she?"

"Still. She's a little old and a lot fat for my taste. Whatta we gonna do for gas?"

"Don't worry about it. I got a plan. Just let me know when you get below a quarter tank," George said, "and I'll take care of it. You just be goddamn sure you mind the speed limit."

"Sure," Ray said as he flicked his eyes back onto the roadway. After Guymon, traffic was nonexistent, and he had the road to himself for the most part. He reached up and pulled his wire-rimmed aviator-style sunglasses from under the visor and put them on. In the mirror he could see the sun rising into a blood-red sky. Ahead, the two-lane road went to the horizon in a monotonous straight line that never seemed to get any shorter. He sighed and settled into his seat.

Beside him, George Phelps was staring out the passenger-side window, thinking about yesterday, his last day in prison and his first day of freedom in five years, three months, and thirteen days. He'd gone down on an eight-to-eleven-year jolt for aggravated armed robbery. He'd held up a liquor store one night, drunk, armed with a .22 caliber Derringer and his bad intentions. The store owner, having been down that road before, had other ideas. He also had an eighty-five pound Doberman pinscher and a .44 caliber Colt Peacemaker. In the dustup that happened after George said, "Stick 'em up," the Derringer went off, with the bullet hitting the wall behind the cash register. The owner pulled the Peacemaker and cocked it, aiming the monster weapon at George's forehead, while at the same time, the Dobie came out from behind the counter and took what felt like a five-pound bite out of his ass. When the cops showed up a few minutes later, George was facedown on the floor, with his hands on his head and his legs spread. The dog was standing in the V with her snout only a few inches from his scrotum. George could still feel her hot breath and the rumble in his nuts from her growls, still feel her bites, the blood, and the fifty stitches the docs put in his legs and ass at the hospital . . . just before they took him to jail. Sometimes, George shivered when it was cold and damp, his ass hurting so much that tears would dribble out of his eyes. Thinking about it made his face burn with humiliation. *You can bet your last thin dollar that that ain't never gonna happen again*, he thought. *Next time, I'll shoot first. Just take the friggin' money. Ain't never going back to the joint neither . . . I'll shoot my way out: Blam! Blam! Blam! Oh, yeah. Like that. I sure as fuck will.* He felt the nine millimeter Luger he'd tucked in the back of his waistband and smiled. He looked out the window at the unchanging scenery, with its endless, repetitive flatness, and sighed. He reached in his shirt pocket, dug out his pack of Camels, and lit one, turning his head sideways and squeezing his eyes down to slits to keep the smoke and sulfur out of them. Sucking down a lung full of smoke, he sighed again; wished he was in Colorado.

"Gimme one of them, would ya?"

"Sure, Ray." George passed the one he'd lit and reached for another. "How far to Boise City?"

"A few miles. Less than ten."

"How much gas we got?"

"About half of a quarter."

"Thought you were gonna let me know when it got down to a quarter?"

"I forgot. Thinkin' about cigarettes."

"Here, take these and pay attention. Boise City's not very big. Stay on this road. We're gonna turn right about halfway through town. Got it?"

"Yeah. About halfway. What about gas?"

"I'll tell ya when we get there. I got it handled."

The car slowed at the edge of town, careful and observant of the speed limits, and Ray used both hand and the electric turn signals on the steering column when he turned north on Highway 287. A mile and a half later George said, "Pull into that Phillips station," and pointed to the big orange-and-black chevron-shaped sign with "66" emblazoned on it.

"Sure."

Ray pulled up to the high test pump and shut the motor off. He could hear the ding-ding-ta-ding of the bell inside the office as he ran over the rubber hose that announced another customer had stopped.

"Now listen, and do what I tell ya, and do it exactly like I say."

"Okay, George."

"All right then. Tell the guy you'll check the oil yourself. Open the trunk and have him fill the jerry cans first. Then fill up the car. Have him check the tires too, while you wash the windshield. Got it?"

"Yeah."

"Tell him I've got the money and I'll pay him inside."

"Yeah. Inside. Sure."

"After he fills it and goes inside, pull up front. Keep the motor running."

They got out of the car and stood, stretching themselves as a pudgy teenager in a white shirt with a black bow tie, a gray jacket, and a billed hat with the "Phillips 66" patch on it waddled out to the pump island. "Fillerup?" he said.

"Yeah," Ray answered, "Start with these here," as he opened the trunk and pointed to the three jerry cans.

"Then fill the car," George said as Ray got busy under the hood. He added, "You got a pisser in there?"

"Sure. Back past the soda machine."

George nodded. He noticed as he turned to go that the oval patch on the kid's pocket said "Herbie" on it in red chain-stitched cursive letters. He saw the red-and-yellow pimples blossoming on his neck and face and the eight or ten whiskers erupting from his chin. *Kid wouldn't last two weeks in stir,* he thought as he went inside to case the office and work bays. He looked over his shoulder to make sure the kid and Ray were both occupied. *So far, so good.*

Ray creeped the place with the stealth, practiced ease, and efficiency of long experience. He checked out the back door, saw nothing but wind-blown desolation. The big garage doors were closed, which was good. The car in the bay had black-and-white Colorado license plates . . . which was very good. He checked outside, saw that the kid and Ray were still busy. He grabbed a screwdriver and pliers from the workbench, removed the plates, and put the tools and nuts and bolts in his jacket pocket. He stuck the plates under his shirt and went in the bathroom, urinated, and came out as Herbie came in the door, blowing on his hands. "Jeez," Herbie said, "it's colder than a well digger's ass in the Klondike out there. I'm freezin'."

"I'd think," George said, "with all that lard you're carrying, you'd be warm as toast with just a shirt on."

Herbie's neck and ears flushed red and he looked down at his feet. "It don't work like that," he said. Then he turned to the green McCaskey cash register and started punching the rows of green-and-white keys. As he reached for the lever on the right side to open the drawer, he said, "She took thirty-three gallons and the feller outside got two quarts of ten-weight oil. Comes to twelve dollars and sixteen cents . . . best sale I made in the past three days."

"Is it now?"

"Oh, yeah. It's slow this time of week, won't see but three, four cars go by for the whole afterno . . . " he stopped midword, with the register lever pulled halfway, as he heard the slide racked back and released, loading a live round into the Luger George had pressed to the back of his head. He'd stolen it that morning, along with a dozen extra shells from Melissa's closet while she made breakfast. It was the one her absent husband brought home from Europe, after the war. George had lifted it when he prowled the room while Melissa went to the bathroom, and cleaned herself off from the first couple of times they'd screwed, then waddled on out to the kitchen, yawning, scratching, and farting.

"Nice and easy now, take your hands off there. Put 'em on your head."

Herbie did as he was told. With his lip quivering he said, "Are you holding me up?"

"Yeah."

"I won't be no trouble. Please don't hurt me. The deposit money's in the pop machine. In the underneath."

"Where's the key?"

"In the register. Back part of the drawer. The key and crank are in there together."

Kid looks about to piss himself, George thought. Out loud he said, "Get down on your knees. Keep your hands on your head."

Herbie, shaking now, fell to his knees with a moan. "Don't shoot.

P-p-please don't kill me. I don't wanna die."

George, who had the Luger pressed to the kid's head said, "I ain't gonna fucking kill. . ." but the rest was cut off by the sound of a gunshot as George, startled by the clang of the station bell when Ray ran over the hose laid across the driveway, flinched and pulled the trigger. The nine millimeter parabellum entered Herbie's skull, where it mushroomed before exiting below his right eye in a splattering of bone and blood, hair, chunks of brain matter, and most of his face. He was dead and pitching to the floor when a second round, fired as George's shaking hand touched the hair trigger again, sent another bullet ripping through what was left of the kid's head. Herbie's body lay face down, convulsing in a spreading lake of gore as pieces of his head and face dripped from the cash register.

"Oh, *fuck! Fuck. Fuck. Fuck* me with a fence post. Oh fuck me to tears," came from George's mouth. George felt like puking and screaming at the same time . . . did neither as a low moan escaped his trembling lips. His heart raced and he was breathing in rapid shallow gasps, the room spinning out of control when the door crashed open.

"Hey! What's going . . . oh, no. What the fuck have you done?"

"It just went off. Fuckin' thing's got a hair trigger. I . . . I dunno. It just went off, I was just gonna rob the place."

"Well then, you'd better fuckin' do it. I'm gonna wait three minutes and I'm outta here." Ray closed the door and went back to the car.

George snapped into action. He reached over Herbie's body and opened the cash register. He took the bills and silver, stuffed it in his coat pocket and grabbed the key and crank that opened the pop machine. His hands shook as he inserted the key and removed the lock from the upright cooler and dropped it on the floor. He stuck the crank in and opened the door, saw the vinyl bank bag lying on the bottom. He grabbed it and turned to go, then reached in and stole two bottles of Coca-Cola. He set the bag and the bottles on the counter, reached down and took the ring of keys from Herbie's belt. Breathing more normally, he rifled the keys until he found what looked like the one to the front door. Tried it. It fit. Realizing his time was about up, George turned the lights off and flipped the "Open" sign to "Closed." Remembering Ray's request, he went behind the counter and took a carton of Camels, stuck them under his arm, grabbed the Cokes and the bank bag. As he pushed through the door he heard a clunk when Ray put the car in first gear. "Wait up," George yelled, then turned the lock in the door and ran to where the '49 Ford sat with the motor running. He threw the keys on the roof of the station, jumped in the car and slammed the door.

"Drive," was all he said.

U.S. Highway 287 North
Sixty-five miles south of Lamar, Colorado
1 p.m. MST, Thurs., Nov. 3, 1955 . . . twenty-two hours remaining

Each man being a prisoner of his own thoughts, there was only silence in the car as they fled the murder scene and the state of Oklahoma. Ray Matthews chain-smoked his way through the pack of George's cigarettes as he kept flicking his eyes from the road, to the rearview mirror, to the road. Back and forth, back and forth, watching for the flashing red lights of the law . . . fearing it was only a matter of time. Almost paralyzed, he operated the car more by instinct than control and concentration. *What a stupid, stupid sonofabitch . . . I can't believe he turned a simple stickup into aggravated homicide in the first. I agreed to be the wheelman for whatever job it is that Lee Roy's got planned . . . but not this. Not this, I don't know whether to tell Lee Roy or not. I do know I'm ditching this stupid fuck the first chance I get.*

Beside him, George Phelps stared out the window, numb with denial and disbelief. Inside, he was full of self-pity and a desire to blame Herbie or Ray . . . anyone but himself . . . for what had transpired back in Boise City. *What rotten-assed luck. If that pistol hadn't gone off, an' that kid wasn't makin' me talk . . . If that pistol . . . Piece of shit German engineering. Ha. What a fucking joke . . . The fucking thing goes off just lookin' at it . . . Whatever am I gonna do . . . How'm I getting outta this one . . . Maybe blame it on Ray. No way . . . Wouldn't ever work . . . No way to connect him . . . Ooh fuck me . . . Whatever am I. . .* "Pull over, Ray. Up there, by that old gas station. Go around back."

Ray pulled into an unpaved lot in front of an abandoned building with peeling whitewash that was flaking off in chunks from the square facade. Faint blue-and-red lettering spelled out what looked like "Albert's Service," and a dilapidated sign promised "Last chance for service next 70 miles." It was impossible to tell the brand of gasoline or much else about the place because most of the front and one side were pushed into a pile inside what was left of the charred and scorched walls. The roof, windows, and doors were all long gone. Ray pulled around back next to a pile of rusted metal and fire debris, turned around, and pointed the Ford toward the highway and parked. Behind them, the ever-present prairie wind ruffled the wild grasses, and a flock of small dark birds took flight from the telephone wires strung between poles that marched to the horizons. It was the essence of desolation . . . at the edge of nowhere.

Ray smoked, listened to the ticking of cooling metal, and watched a line of gray clouds scuffing against a cold November sky. He took a last drag on his cigarette and crushed it out in the car's ashtray. "Now what?" he said.

Ray tensed when George reached inside his jacket, then relaxed after he pulled out a pair of black Colorado license plates with white lettering on them. Next came a vinyl brown bag with a zipper on it. It was larger than a letter envelope, but the same rectangular shape. It had "Boise City Bank" printed on the side of it.

"You can count the money or put these plates on," George said.

Ray zipped his leather flight jacket. "I'll do the plates," he said, and started to get out.

George reached in his pocket. "Here," he said, as he handed over the pliers and screwdriver and the nuts and bolts he'd taken off of Herbie's car, "you're gonna need these." Ray had everything in hand and the door opened before George added, "And don't leave them old plates on. Take 'em off."

Ray made eye contact with George and held it, his eyes flashing hot and his jaw muscles tight. He put the tools in his pocket and pulled the key from the ignition. He got out and slammed the door. George watched him go with a slight smirk on his face and barely controlled prison rage in his eyes, then relaxed his grip on the Luger in his waistband. *After that first one, it don't matter how many more there are. They can't electrocute ya but once, so don't try me motherfucker, don't even think about it.* George turned his attention to the money in the bag. Accepting in his mind the fact that he'd murdered someone, George's brain was already busy rewriting and making himself more heroic. He was already liking his new, self-appointed self as a steely-eyed, stone-cold killer. He liked the feeling of power it gave him . . . and he liked seeing the fear that had formed for just an instant in Ray's eyes. *Yessir, I like it just fine,* he decided, *and I'm done bein' somebody's bitch. That's done forever.* George focused on counting the money. From the heft of the bag it wouldn't take long.

Ray kept a surreptitious eye on George as he knelt in front of the car and took the Oklahoma plate off and replaced it with the one from Colorado. He was careful to put the spare bolts in his pocket, just as he'd done the half-dozen times he'd already switched them out as he traveled from east to west. He moved around to the back and changed that plate, then opened the trunk.

After sneaking a quick peek to make sure George was still occupied, Ray moved a toolbox, lifted the rubber floor mat, and exposed the lid to a hidden compartment by the wheel well. He unscrewed two sheet-metal screws, reached in, and pulled out a Colt .357 snub-nosed revolver with grips wrapped in black friction tape. It was formerly the property of a North Carolina deputy sheriff who was killed in the line of duty after stopping a suspicious looking Ford sedan on a remote back road one night. It was a dirt road, a shortcut into Tennessee, and a known route for moonshine runners. The lawman's killer had never been found. Neither had his sidearm, or the .410 shot pistol that blew out his heart and most of his left lung as he stepped up to the driver's window in the dark. His patrol car had been driven into a nearby ravine and ditched, his body dragged into the woods and abandoned. There, it had been savaged by a host of wild creatures. A couple of crows, some skunks, buzzards, and possums, as well as raccoons, a fox, and even a bear all dropped by for a taste before the body was found three weeks and a couple of days later. When he saw the remains, Sheriff Dwight Haverkorn, his voice choking with emotion, vowed to never stop looking for the lawman's killer. His badge and gun were missing, along with several items of police tactical gear that were kept in the vehicle. The case was still in the Open-Unsolved file, but there wasn't much hope of clearing it . . . all leads had been exhausted. Ray flipped out the cylinder and checked the load, rubbed his thumb over the raised scar on the frame where the serial number had been ground off and arc welded over, making the weapon untraceable. He tucked it into his jacket pocket as George got out of the car.

"What's taking so long?"

"Toolbox was tipped over. I was pickin' everything up," Ray said as he shoved the compartment cover down, pulled the toolbox on top, then threw the license plate bolts, machine screws, and tools in before closing the lid. He came out wiping his hands on the oily rag the gun was wrapped in and slammed the trunk lid down. George was slouched against the front fender, smoking and drinking a Coke. "Hey, buddy, shake a leg. I told Lee Roy we oughta be there by three, four o'clock. You're gonna haveta haul ass to get us there before six. We still got two hundred miles to go, and all them little towns will slow us down."

"An' just who the hell put you in charge, George?"

"Me, myself, and I," George said, feeling all of his newfound courage and authority tucked into the wristband of his prison-issue denim dungarees, "I'm the new honcho around here."

Ray stared at him for a long hard moment, still wiping his hands with the rag until George took the cigarette out of his mouth and concentrated on grinding it out with his heel. "Well, okay then," Ray said, thinking, *First chance I get, he's gone. One way or another. If it takes a bullet in the head, so be it. This dumb bastard's too stupid to live.* The corners of his mouth were turned up in a subtle sneer that George never even noticed. They buried the old license plates and bank bag in among the burned timbers and metal debris. George had stolen a total of thirty-seven dollars, some silver coins, and a carton of cigarettes. For that he'd committed murder.

It was a few minutes after two o'clock as Ray pointed the '49 Ford north and headed for their rendezvous with Lee Roy. There were nineteen hours remaining.

CSPD Headquarters, 212 East Kiowa Street
Colorado Springs, Colorado
3 p.m. MST, Thurs., Nov. 3, 1955 . . . twenty hours remaining

I was dog-tired, weary past reason, and beat right to the bone. All I could think about at the moment was walking two blocks to my room at the Albany Hotel for a few hours of shut-eye before I had to go back on shift at midnight. But as I sat there, with my back to one wall of lockers and my face to another, relaxed for the first time since I'd gone to work two days ago, I had to admit that sleep wasn't the only thing I was thinking about. No. Not by a long shot.

I was thinking about all the overtime I'd racked up since Tuesday. Close to twenty-three hours' worth. At time and a half, I'd damn near doubled my wages, and there were still eleven days to go before payday. I was thinking about my new car: a 1955 Chevy Bel Air deluxe convertible. It was my dream ride and it was waiting for me a block away at the Daniels Chevrolet dealership. I'd ordered it special with the help of Ron, a salesman I knew over there. We'd spent hours together, fretting over details like gear ratios and engine options, tires and transmission, as well as a host of other details and minutiae. By the time we were done, it was a honey-dripper for sure . . . and as well equipped as the White Owl girl. I couldn't wait to get my hands on her. I thought about Ma and my little sister, Annie—wondered if I'd made a big error in judgment with the purchase of an expensive new car while Ma was struggling to keep the bills paid up in Palmer Lake, running her little diner. It used to be a Harvey House, one of hundreds of medium-priced restaurants built alongside the railroad tracks by a man named Fred Harvey back in the last century. Palmer Lake had been a place where the old steam engines stopped for water. But, with the railroad converting from steam to the new diesel-electric locomotives and the passenger trains disappearing, being replaced by freight trains, and the way the public was now traveling in automobiles, business for Ma was just plain bad. And it was getting worse. On top of that, Annie had contracted scarlet fever as a child. Hers was a severe case and she suffered from a damaged heart and other problems. Sometimes her medical bills were enormous. She was almost twenty and still living with Ma and would always be dependent on her, so I gave them some money every month to help out. I hoped I hadn't made an error in judgment by buying the car. It was paid for with the cash I'd saved since becoming a cop, but now my savings were pretty well used up. I guessed there wasn't anything to do about it at this point—the deed was done. I had to live with it. Just like I had to live with the sad creature who inhabited my dreams at night . . . the one I'd lived with for some fifteen years now . . . ever since I'd discovered that a monster, born of rage and nurtured by violence, lived inside me. The one I try to keep locked in a mental prison in my subconscious.

On top of all those things racing around the neurons and synapses of my brain, I still had room to think about the reason for all the overtime: the forty-four souls who'd perished two days ago up in Denver. Rumor had it that it was a bomb. Whatever the reason, United Air Flight 629, a DC-6B outbound from Denver to Portland, Oregon, had gone down in a ball of flame a few minutes after takeoff. All forty-four people aboard, passengers and crew, were lost. Pieces and parts of human bodies, luggage, papers, books, and clothes, as well as airplane seats, engines, wheels, props, fuselage, wing pieces, and all kinds of unidentifiable wreckage and burning fuel were scattered all over a Longmont beet farm. The FBI was at the scene within hours, and most every cop in the state had been called in and put on high alert, watching for crime or fifth column subversive activity. The Red Scare was at its height back then, and we were all mindful of the possibility of Communists trying to overthrow the U.S. government. Me personally . . . I thought it was all horseshit. I reckoned the Soviets had enough of their own problems to deal with. They didn't need ours too. I thought that guy, Joe McCarthy, was a jerk. His pal Richard Nixon was too.

I thought, *Where were they when I was getting my ass shot off on Guadalcanal, or when all the other marines and GIs were leaving their blood and guts all over the world, fighting the Japs and Germans or Italians? I didn't have use for any of those shirkers. Chickenshits. Every damn one of them.*

Christ on a crutch. I had to get some sleep. I had no idea, as I pulled my khaki pants and sport shirt on, slipped my feet into a pair of brown loafers, and stuck my arms into my old navy peacoat, that in the next twenty-four hours my life would undergo a transformative event that would leave me forever changed; annealed once again in a furnace of violence and reforged on the anvil of time and place. No idea at all. I pulled my 1911 Colt .45 caliber automatic pistol from my locker, checked the clip, and stuck it in the back of my waistband. I'd picked it up on the beach at Guadalcanal and never went anywhere without it. It had saved my life more than once.

I went up front to log out, saw Mad Ed was on the desk reading some kind of men's magazine. They were pulp magazines sold at newsstands with black-and-white photos of women posing in their underwear, and some short stories and articles of manly interest. "The Blood Red Beaches of Baatan" and "My Lost Weekend of Lust with Two Nurses." Stuff like that. And tame as a lawn croquet match by today's standards. But in 1955, they weren't seen in polite society . . . or the front desk of the cop shop.

Sergeant Greene, Mad Ed to his friends and fellow officers—because he was always angry at something, or someone—was so engrossed he didn't see me coming.

"Ain't you taking a helluva chance reading that in the middle of the shift?" I said by way of greeting.

Mad Ed, who looked like, acted like, and talked exactly like Andy Devine, the cowboy actor, said, "Aw shit, Jake, I heard ya from the time you shut your locker door back there. And 'sides which, I got this thing behind the counter and stuck in a newspaper."

"Well, I wouldn't let Lieutenant Hoffman catch you."

"Oh, Christ no. I'd be on school traffic duty."

I laughed. "Now that would be something worth seeing."

"Yeah. Well don't worry about it, 'cause you ain't gonna."

Not ready to give it up, I said, "I'd pay two dollars to see you out there, all sweaty and *mucho* pissed off, directing those kids in their hot rods."

Mad Ed snorted and shook his head. "Not a chance in hell. But for the same two dollars I'll play the spoons and sing a few bars of 'On Top of Old Smokey' for ya."

I signed the log-out sheet on the clipboard Mad Ed handed me, noted the time, and said, "It's mighty tempting, Ed, but I've gotta get some sleep. I've been up since Tuesday night's graveyard shift and I'm back for tonight's as well."

"Plenty of overtime?"

I nodded. Pulled out my pack of Luckies, shook one out, offered it to Ed. He took it, and I shook another for myself. We lit up, and I said, "Yeah."

Mad Ed stuck his cigarette in the corner of his mouth, cocked his head sideways, and squinted to keep the smoke out of his eyes. "Well, do it while you're young, boyo. Your eyes look like a couple of piss holes in the snow . . ."

"Why, Sergeant Greene, you old reprobate. I didn't know you cared."

Mad Ed took the cigarette out of his mouth and stared at me. "You'd better quit while you're ahead, son."

I turned to go. Bantering with him had its limits. I knew it was time to knock it off. I left the building by the side door and crossed Nevada Avenue. All I could think about was the smell of clean sheets and the feel of a soft pillow under my head. Ron Theisman and my new convertible would have to wait until morning.

U.S. Highway 50
East of Pueblo, Colorado
5:30 p.m. MST, Thurs., Nov. 3, 1955 . . . fifteen hours, forty-five minutes remaining

Late-afternoon sunlight crashed into the dimness of the juke joint as the man entered, but only for an instant, as his bulk filled the doorframe before the door closed again.

What a shithole, he thought, as he stood waiting for his eyes to adjust to the lack of light and sized up his surroundings.

It was a side-of-the-road kind of place, full of end-of-the-road people. It was stuck up under the ass-end of the Colorado Fuel and Iron Works and just a couple of stone throws from the rail yards of the AT&SF and the Denver & Rio Grande Railroad lines. It was where the lights stayed low, the liquor was cheap, and you found the one-stall crapper by following your nose to where the smell was the rankest. The patrons were shot with beer-back serious, heads down, elbows up, and mind-your-own-business types . . . dedicated to their mission to crawl into a liquor bottle and stay there until death did them part. On most nights, between the cowboys and the steelworkers, the young bucks and the biker hard-asses looking for a fight usually found one . . . generally left blood at the scene . . . most always had a scar or two for a souvenir. It was the kind of place where a sawed-off Louisville Slugger with fifteen ounces of lead drilled into the business end was kept within the bartender's reach at all times, ready for whatever urban combat might transpire.

But then too, the man mused, as he took possession of a table halfway between the jukebox and the pool table, sitting with his back to the wall so he could survey the bar scene and the front door, *it looks like the kind of place where a man can talk business without a bunch of assholes trying to listen in.* Someone slid a handful of quarters into the battered old Wurlitzer, punched the red plastic buttons, and the neon-washed sounds of a pedal steel guitar and the voices of Hank Snow, Kitty Wells, or Webb Pierce, together with the click of pool balls, were all that could be heard. The stranger at the middle table laced his sausage-sized fingers together and sat there, watching the front door with the intensity and barely controlled malevolence of a feral cat eyeballing a sparrow.

That one could be a whole bushel basketful of trouble, Dougan thought as he checked the leaded billy under the bar. He noted the buzz cut hair and bull neck on the stranger, saw the huge shoulders, and the corded, muscular forearms with crude tattoos slithering out of sight under his rolled-up denim sleeves. *He's one big, mean, tough-looking sonofabitch,* Dougan thought as he washed and rinsed a couple of bar glasses and put them on the drying rack, watching the stranger the whole time. Dougan sighed as he dried his hands on an old bar towel. He touched the billy again for reassurance, slapped the damp towel over his left shoulder, and made his way to the middle booth while Kitty sang "I'm in Love with You" for all of them.

The stranger looked at Dougan as he approached, but remained silent, giving the barman the first word. "Getcha something?"

"Coors."

"You want a bottle or draft?"

"Draft."

Dougan nodded an acknowledgment, headed back to the bar thinking, *Cold as a mother-in-law's kiss and trouble in the making.* He rechecked the billy before taking a glass of beer to the man, who watched his approach. As Dougan put the glass on the table, the stranger said, "You ain't gonna need that scattergun you've been checking on up under the bar. I ain't looking for trouble . . . just waitin' for a couple of business associates is all."

Dougan took the beer money off the table, rattled the coins in his hand like dice. "It's gonna get busier in a while. I won't be able to bring you your drinks—you'll have to come over to me. I won't have a barmaid until later."

"No problem."

Dougan returned to his post behind the bar. The stranger looked around the room as he picked up the glass, drank half of it in two swallows, and set it down with the exaggerated care of a man who finds that things get broken easily in his presence. He turned his outward gaze back to the front door and sat with his hands clasped in front of him, his innermost feelings known only to himself . . . an aura of silent menace emanating from him. The drinkers went on romancing their drinks, while the jukebox poured another round of pastel yellow and green, orange, red, and blue heartbreak over the whole room and everyone in it.

U.S. Highway 50 West
Two miles east of Manzanola, Colorado
7 p.m. MST, Thurs., Nov. 3, 1955 . . . sixteen hours remaining

George Phelps took a last, deep drag on the cigarette butt he'd been smoking, pulled it out with his thumb and middle finger, and flicked it into the empty field he stood beside. In the dark, it made a bright tangerine arc before exploding into a shower of sparks as it hit the ground. He turned, jammed his hands into his pockets, and, hunching his neck into his coat against the cold, walked back to where the car sat on the road with the right-front tire in shreds.

He was bored. Tired of waiting for Ray. *Where is that asshole? He's been gone a coupla hours or more . . .* There wasn't much to do out here in the sticks, even when there was still some light. But that was gone. *Ain't nothin' to do in the dark. Not a fuckin' thing . . .'cept wait. I did enough of that in prison.* He shivered. Sat in the car and lit another cigarette. Tried to get warm. Couldn't. Kept waiting. In the dark. And cold. He was so busy being pissed off and bored he didn't even notice the faint yellow headlights in the far distance, coming east. The first vehicle since dark. Headed his way.

U.S. Highway 50
One mile east of Pueblo, Colorado
Side of the Road Bar
8:55 p.m. MST, Thurs., Nov. 3, 1955 . . . fourteen hours, fifteen minutes remaining

The bar was busy. Even though it was only Thursday the joint was packed with serious drinkers. The barmaid, who came to work at six, barely had time to take her coat and scarf off before she had people wanting drinks. She hadn't had time to take a break, smoke a cigarette, or pull up her fishnet stockings and straighten the seams since. Her name was Jewell. She was single, widowed in the war, no kids, a forty-three-year-old woman who was a little past her prime, but still attractive in an ordinary sort of way—especially to a certain kind of man who preferred a certain kind of woman: one with some meat on her bones. She never lacked a social life whenever she chose to have one, but could take men or leave them, and did so as she felt like it. Her biggest shortcoming was that she was kind-hearted and as a result tended to pick men who were losers.

She came up to her station at the bar with a tray full of empties. When Dougan came over to pick them up with a Pall Mall hanging out of his mouth, Jewell put her tray down, reached over, pulled the cigarette from his mouth, and puffed on it.

"You quit buying your own?"

"Haven't had a chance to do much of anything since I got here. Are you giving away free turkeys or something? This is a helluva crowd for a weeknight," she said as she took a second drag and handed the smoke back to Dougan.

"First of the month. Social Security, VA disability, and retirement checks all come in then. It'll taper off next week."

"Gimme three Buds, three Coors, Coors draft, four shots of bourbon, and a tequila."

Jewell was counting bills out when Dougan returned with the shot glasses and bottles. As he set them up and began pouring, he said, "Have you been paying attention to that big guy at the middle table?"

"Yeah. His name's Lee Roy. He's waiting for someone."

"Any trouble?"

"Nope. Not a bit. Though he did evict a couple of claim jumpers who tried to grab his spot when he went to the bathroom."

"I've been watching him all night. I didn't see that . . . what happened?"

"Not much. He came back and two young guys were sitting there. He leaned over the table and asked, real calm and quiet-like, if they'd rather move elsewhere, or get a chair stuck up their asses and then moved. He was real nice . . . kind of matter-of-fact about it . . . like it didn't matter one way or the other to him. One kid started moving. The other pulled a knife. Lee Roy grabbed his hand and squeezed 'til the kid's eyes started to pop and he dropped the knife. Lee Roy caught it with his other hand and, you ain't gonna believe this but, still holding the kid's hand, he put his thumb against the side of the blade and snapped it off . . . easy as I'd snap a string bean. Lee Roy said, 'You two little peckerheads get the fuck outta here before you piss me off.'"

"Did they?"

"Hell, yes. Wouldn't anybody?"

"He say anything else?"

"Sorry for the ruckus, Miss Jewell."

"Can't believe I didn't see it."

"You were probably in the back, going after beer. It happened really fast. I was right there bringing him a new glass of draft, else I wouldn't have seen it myself."

"Seem like he's getting drunk?"

"No. Not at all. He leaves a bit in every glass, and he's eaten just about all the peanut butter crackers in the place."

"Think he'll turn mean?"

"As far as I can tell, no. But I'd hate to be the guys he's waiting for. They were supposed to be here a couple of hours ago."

"Keep your eyes open. Let me know if his mood starts changing."

"You bet. I think I'm falling in love."

Dougan grinned, shook his head, and watched her prance off with the tray of drinks. He thought about calling in some reinforcements—a couple of heavies from the sheriff's department—thought better of it, decided to wait and see.

Lee Roy sat, all 265 pounds of him, on a hickory bar chair with a hoop back; the kind American factories had been turning out by the tens of thousands for the last fifty or seventy-five years; the same ones found in eateries and dance halls, churches, grange halls, auditoriums, and buildings of every size and condition ever conceived by human creativity. Other than the shape, the only things they had in common was that they were cheap, easy to find, and uncomfortable. And the larger the user, the greater the discomfort. Lee Roy was tired of waiting, tired of sitting here with his lower back hurting like a bastard. He was almost ready to pack it in. Almost. But not quite. Not after all the months of watching, timing, and planning.

Where are those two fuckers? I know that little weasel George is as crazy as a shit-house rat, but Ray's generally as regular as taxes. I know George was released as scheduled. Maybe they broke down or something. Melissa told me they left at eight o'clock this morning. They should have been here two or three hours ago. Where are those two assholes . . .

U.S. Highway 50 West
Outskirts of Pueblo, Colorado
9:20 p.m. MST, Thurs., Nov. 3, 1955 . . . thirteen hours, fifty minutes remaining

The two assholes in question were about five miles away. Ray was tired, squinting in the headlight glare from oncoming cars. Traffic increased as they approached the Steel City, as Pueblo was called—a reference to the giant open-hearth furnaces that turned out rail for the railroads and oil-well casing for the drillers twenty-four hours a day. Now it was an unbroken line of cars and the stress of driving all day, plus the tire blowing and then the two-mile walk into that little hick town, knocking on doors to find the service station owner, and hunting for a tire. The only one they could find was used and the wrong size, so now the car pulled to the right and he was fighting the wheel, making it hard to drive . . . all of that, plus the anger he felt toward the dumb fucker he was transporting had given him a blinding headache, and caused him to start clenching his jaws and grinding his teeth 150 miles ago. *I cannot wait to get shed of this ignorant fuckhead . . . one way or another.* He thought about George, what the .357 in his pocket would make his head look like, and smirked to himself in the dark. *One way or another . . .* The smirk stretched itself into a lopsided kind of grin. It made his face look sort of feral . . . vulpine maybe . . . but cunning and deadly for a fact. He slipped his cigarette out of the wing window, thought once more about the man staring out the window beside him, saw him in his mind's eye, down on his knees with Ray pressing the .357 to his head, the sound and the feel of it going off. The thought came close to making him giddy with pleasure. *Yessir, one way or another. So help me God.*

George was quiet. He hadn't said much of anything since they'd left Manzanola. He was trying to come to terms with the fact that in just few more minutes he'd be in the presence once again of his protector and cellie for the last four and a half years . . . the man who had been his tormentor . . . the man who'd raped him on multiple occasions every week for the entire time they were caged together on the third tier of Cellblock A at Oklahoma State Penitentiary. The man, named Lee Roy Morgan, was waiting for him and Ray just a couple of miles and a few minutes away. The very man George had sworn he would kill at the first opportunity that presented itself.

He'd thought about it time after time throughout his humiliation; fighting back his tears and the searing pain, trying to ignore the blood, the tearing of his flesh, the damage to his most personal parts—as well as the utter devastation of his spirit, the shattering of his self-respect as Lee Roy, bigger, stronger, and a hundred pounds heavier than George, huffed and pounded his way to a groaning, sweaty, and disgusting climax behind him, all the while holding Ray by the back of his neck like a tomcat fucking a tabby. *I was his bitch all right,* George thought bitterly, *but that was then, and this is now. And my new associate, Herr Luger, along with his little brass buddies are here to back my play.*

I think I'll put one in his kneecap first—then two or three in his crotch—shoot that pecker he's so proud of right off. Fully invested in his daydream now, George imagined himself as Cody Jarrett, James Cagney's psychopathic tough-guy killer in the film *White Heat,* which he'd seen in 1949, just before he himself went to prison.

Blam! Blam! Blam! George could smell the smoke and gun oil in his head as he imagined Lee Roy rolling around in the dirt, not knowing whether to hold his knee or the place where his balls used to be. George could almost hear the screams, see the blood and that big fucker in agony, begging for mercy.

George imagined himself as Cagney, playing Cody Jarrett, eating a chicken leg and walking behind an old sedan, on his way to commit the robbery of the century: a chemical plant payroll. In the film, Jarrett has a hostage named Parker in the trunk of the car. Parker complains that it's stuffy in the trunk. Cagney, as Jarrett says, "Stuffy, huh? I'll give you a little air," whereupon Jarrett, chewing a bite of the chicken leg, pulls out a .45 caliber automatic and *Blam! Blam! Blam!* shoots the poor bastard in the trunk.

Yeah, George dreamed for the hundredth time, *just like that. Blam! Blam!* . . . His reverie was interrupted.

Ray said, "This the place?" pointing with his chin at the ugly dark building on the other side of the road. It had a couple of red neon Coors Beer signs on what passed for front windows and some red, blue, and green Christmas-tree lights nailed around the front door.

"Yeah," was all George could say for all the cotton that suddenly filled his bone-dry mouth.

"Looks like it's jumping."

"Yeah."

Ray found a place to park in the back, pointed the car toward the highway, and shut it off.

They got out and headed for the front door with George leading the way. He reached into his jacket, making sure the Luger was tucked in his belt on his left side, all thoughts of Cody Jarrett gone from his mind. He reached for the brass door handle with a sweaty palm and pulled.

Jewell saw them right away. She'd just put four bottles of beer and a couple of shots of Southern Comfort down on a table filled with old steel mill workers sitting by the door. When the cold air hit her, she looked up and saw two men come in. The first one looked like a kid. *He's not more than his early twenties,* she thought, *and small, not quite five foot six I'd bet.* He was wearing a heavy denim coat, faded dungarees, and thick-soled shoes. *And he looks like he's scared to death.* The second man had a seamed and weathered face. He was tall and thin, all sinew and stringy hard muscle, with dark eyes that flicked around the room like searchlight beams, checking relentlessly for potential threats or perceived enemies. He had a cigarette in his mouth, a brown fedora with a snap-brim pulled low on his forehead, and a brown leather bomber jacket with the collar turned up. Between his hawklike countenance and catlike gait on the balls of his feet, he exuded menace with every step he took. He nudged the smaller man and nodded his head—then they headed straight for the big stranger, the one who'd been waiting all afternoon.

Jewell saw him glaring at them as they crossed the floor, then the hawk-faced man sat down with his back to the wall next to the man who said his name was Lee Roy. The little one had no other choice: he sat with his back to the crowd. Jewell hurried over.

Dougan was also watching. He saw the two newcomers and felt his gut doing a little flip-flop in anticipation of the violence he was sure was coming. He thought about calling Hernshaw and Barton, the pair of moonlighting deputies, but decided to let it play out for a bit longer. No one had done anything yet, but that could all change in the blink of an eye or the words of a song. He'd seen it happen before.

As if reading his thoughts, someone started playing Kitty Wells singing "Making Believe," probably the most heartbreaking song on the whole goddamned jukebox according to Dougan, over and over again:

> *Making believe that you still love me*
> *Making believe,*
> *I'll spend a lifetime*
> *Loving you and making believe.*

Dougan went straight to the pay phone in the corner, closed the door, and dropped a couple of dimes.

Ray made eye contact with Lee Roy, touched his hat brim, and said, "Well, hello, cousin."

Lee Roy nodded in recognition and indicated the chair to his left. Ray sat, took a last drag on his cigarette, then dropped it on the floor and ground it out with his brown cowboy boot. Lee Roy turned and zeroed in on George with a gaze that was intense enough to pin a common moth to a specimen board. George's revenge fantasy, so real only a few moments ago, disappeared in a splash of red neon light as Lee Roy said, "Where the fuck have you been . . . what the fuck took yez so. Fucking. Long?"

George, who'd been on the wrong end of one of Lee Roy's rages before, and had the scars to prove it, sat with a thump on the opposite side of the table, thinking, *His face looks demonic in the red light. He couldn't look more evil if he had blood dripping from his teeth . . .*

Ray started to answer, "We had a blow . . ." but stopped as the barmaid came to the table.

"What can I getcha? You ready, Lee Roy?"

"Three drafts."

"Make it two," Ray said. "I'll have a soda and some aspirins, if you got any."

"You mean soda water or a pop?"

"Coca-Cola."

"Sure. I'll find ya some aspirins too."

Jewell headed to the bar and Ray took up his narrative again. "We blew a tire a coupla-three miles outside some little shit-assed town. I had to walk in. Knocked on doors until I found the gas station guy and got him to open up, find a tire, and take me back. It took about three hours."

Watching Lee Roy's eyes narrowing down to slits, George said, "Manzanola," without being asked. Looking at the huge red face, the throbbing veins in his neck and forehead, the prison rage that still flared like burning butane in Lee Roy's eyes, George felt sick to his stomach . . . and he flashed back to the end of his first week in stir. Stir was different from jail. Jail was where you were held by the cops and the courts while your guilt or innocence was decided. It was temporary. Stir was where you went to live out your sentence. Stir was prison, the joint, the big house, or the pen—and it was life-and-death serious. Some would die there. Others would serve their time and leave. All who entered were forever changed by it.

He'd been housed with a huge convict named Lee Roy Morgan. George, small in stature and ten months short of his nineteenth birthday, was terrified. He'd heard all the prison horror stories while he went through his arrest, trial, and conviction. By the time he was sentenced, he was almost numb with panic. But, for the first few days, George thought he'd lucked out. Lee Roy was on his best behavior, helping George learn the ropes and introducing him to the old cons, letting others know that if they gave George any problems, he'd be their problem, and they wouldn't much like it. George thought he was going to be okay. The feeling lasted for three more days.

On the fourth day Lee Roy introduced George to pruno, and the nightmare began. Pruno is a kind of crude prison moonshine. It's made by throwing some fruit, yeast, and water into a plastic bag and letting it ferment for a few days. The resulting product is then strained and slugged down like alcohol. It's coarse, can have high proof depending on how long it's aged, and it can damage internal organs. The stuff Lee Roy gave George that night was all of the above and lethal as cobra venom. George was dead drunk after the first two shots . . . sick as a dog halfway through the third one. After he'd puked his guts out in the toilet, he leaned over the sink to rinse the taste out of his mouth and wash his face. That's when he got slammed head-first into the wall.

George had cupped his hands and taken a mouthful of water when Lee

Roy grabbed his hair and drove his face into the wall like he was trying for the world record in the hammer throw. George's nose was crushed. Blind with pain, he felt blood geysering like a broken water main over his face and chest, started to choke on the water he'd sucked into his lungs, felt himself being spun around by the arm, crashed over the side of the bunk bed, and pinned there like a scab on a specimen slide. He moaned and tried to fight as the skivvies he'd been wearing were torn off and his face was pressed into the mattress with the strength and enthusiasm of the totally insane, while something that felt like a utility pole was being shoved up his ass with the force of a steam locomotive.

George felt a tearing of his anus and violence being done to his rectum, fought harder, thrashing and screaming with pain, horror, and shame . . . was almost unconscious with asphyxiation after being choked and smashed face-first into the prison mattress. Then, Lee Roy reached a grunting panting climax and, after a final thrust that nearly broke the smaller man in half, withdrew. George didn't have the strength to move. He lay there in the soiled bed, sobbing, bleeding from both ends of his body and vowing to kill Lee Roy Morgan with every breath he took, and every beat of his heart. Thus began, he remembered, *four years of horror, degradation, and abuse.* He had to put that pain to rest, had to right that stain on his manhood . . . had to regain his self-worth. Killing Lee Roy Morgan would do it. It was the only reason George had agreed to take part in whatever scheme Lee Roy and Ray had planned . . . and the only reason he'd come back to Colorado.

George sat. He looked across the table at Lee Roy and remembered. All of a sudden he had an overwhelming need to vomit. "Where's the shitter?" His tormentor pointed with his thumb and George bolted. After he was gone, Lee Roy didn't waste time. He said, "What else kept yez?"

Ray took a moment before answering. He wasn't afraid of Lee Roy . . . they fought countless times as kids with both of them claiming an equal amount of wins, but he was wary of Lee Roy's temper . . . knew his solution to loose ends was to cut the thread permanently. Ray's problem was that he needed the money so he could get to California. His plan was to go there and start over. He'd change his name, ditch the car, and start a new life. Put his troubles back East behind him and shake off old Sheriff Haverkorn, known to all the moonshine trade as the most relentless law dog from the Piedmont to the Cumberland. A man who'd vowed never to rest until he caught the person who'd killed his deputy, a promising twenty-eight-year-old man named Nolan Mayhue, who'd left behind a wife and two young children.

Ray needed the money from whatever heist Lee Roy had organized. Experience told him that three men were the bare minimum necessary to pull it off. And with three like George there was probably no way. After that, they could cut cards or throw dice to see which of them turned George's lights out for all he cared. *He's too dumb to rely on, would fuck up a free lunch. And besides, a two-way split is better than a three.* Ray chose his next words with care. Lee Roy was not only mean and unpredictable . . . he was ruthless. Ray didn't trust him at all. He said, "I stopped and changed plates and all those little towns slowed me down. I can't afford to get stopped."

Lee Roy's glance was so malevolent that Ray looked away . . . a sign of weakness. Lee Roy said, "What happened in Boise City?"

"What are you talking about?"

Lee Roy thumped the table with a jumbo index finger. "Don't. Make. Me. Ask. You. Again."

Ray bought some time by lighting up another cigarette off of the one he'd been smoking when they came in, while he tried to decide what to say, then thought, *Aw, fuckit,* and started to speak. "What happened was I'm out of dough. I left Carolina in a hurry, wasn't able to collect for my last run. Your pard in there . . ." He stopped when he saw the barmaid coming.

Jewell set two glasses of beer and a bottle of Coca-Cola on the table, then a tin of aspirins, "There you go, hon'—hope they help."

Ray nodded and said, "Much obliged," as he reached for it.

"Anything else, Lee Roy?"

"Thanks. No. Check back after awhile, though."

Ray leaned closer, pointed with his thumb in the general direction of the back, "Your pard in there gave his walking money to the woman in Woodard. He also stole a pistol from her, but I didn't find that out 'til we were in Boise City. It's where the stupid fuck robbed a gas station and managed to shoot a kid to death. Put two rounds in his head by accident. Claims it's got a hair-trigger. Far as I'm concerned he's dead weight."

It was Lee Roy's turn to nod. "Oh, he's dead weight all right, but only after we pull off the job I've got in mind."

Ray leaned back, took a swig of Coke, and swallowed four aspirins, then put the tin in his shirt pocket. Lee Roy was looking for George, so he didn't see the two men come in the door. Ray did. And he didn't like what he saw. He put his foot on Lee Roy's and nodded almost imperceptibly at the big men heading for the bar. Both of them were over six feet and looked to weigh 250 or more. Both wore black leather jackets and thick-soled shoes, both walked with the heavy tread of authority, and they were both armed with snub-nosed revolvers on the left side of their belts, with the butt facing forward. "Heat," Ray said. It was all that needed saying.

Butch Hernshaw and Wes Barton had just arrived at the bar when Jewell came over with a tray of empties.

Butch said, "Darlin', where have you been all my life?"

Jewell grinned and said, "Same old Butchie. Still as full of shit as a Christmas turkey."

Butch put both hands over his heart in mock sorrow. "I am shocked and heartbroken that you would talk that way to me."

"Same way I've been talking to you since the seventh grade. Hello, Wes.

How's the law-and-order business these days?" she said as she set empty beer bottles on the bar.

Wes Barton leaned over on the padded bar rail and took the ever-present toothpick out of his mouth. "Same as ever, Jewell. Crime never sleeps you know, keeps us busy day and night."

Butch and Wes stood on either side of her as Dougan finished serving some drinks farther down the way, dragged money off the bar in front of his customers that he put in the register before grabbing a bottle of Wild Turkey, a pair of shot glasses, and heading their way.

Wes was surveying the room in the backbar mirror, watching for signs of trouble, and Butch was looking at Jewell like a fox scoping a prairie hen. Dougan poured a shot of hundred-proof bourbon for each of them and said, "Glad to see yez. It's been quiet so far, but I think the war drums are starting to sound. Some idiot keeps playing tearjerker songs on the jukebox, and I think it's only a matter of time before some heartbroke Romeo knocks his neighbor on his ass."

"Anybody in particular?"

"I've been watching the big bastard beside the Wurlitzer. The one with arms the size of my legs and all the jailhouse ink running up them. He's been here all afternoon, staring at the front door like he was trying to burn it down. He got reinforced a little while ago. That's why I called yez."

Butch was attentive and fully focused on Dougan in an instant. In spite of his salaciousness, he was an excellent cop . . . and tough as a three-foot steel crowbar. He was fearless in any kind of a fight, to the point of being foolhardy, but the kind of partner everyone wanted backing them up. He said, "You want us to shake him down?"

Wes, who had already noted them in his mirror surveillance said, "No, Butch. Not yet. They haven't done anything so far."

"That we know about."

"Just hold your fire, hoss. I ain't sure we could take 'em without backup. Then we'd have to explain what we're doin' here.

"Oh. Yeah. That's right."

Wes looked at Jewell. "Have you heard anything out of them?"

"Not that I can think of. They stop talking when I get close, but I think they're up to something . . . they are a mischief of rats for a fact . . . although the big guy's nice . . . he calls me 'Miss Jewell.' His name is Lee Roy, by the way."

Dougan said, "What in Christ's name is a mischief of rats?"

Jewell, who read more books in two weeks than all three of her companions had in the past two years, said, "It means 'a group of rats.' It's called a collective noun and it's one of the oddities of the English language. Groups of rats can also be called a plague, hoard, swarm, colony, or pack. But I like the word 'mischief' the best. It's more fun."

"Glad I asked," Dougan said as he put the last drinks on her tray. Jewell smiled and left with a swish of her hips to deliver the new rounds.

Butch watched the twitching of her ass as she walked away. He picked up his shot of bourbon and threw it back, swallowed it in a gulp, shook his head, and wiped his mouth with the back of his hand. He set the glass on the bar and, still watching Jewell, said, "*Hot damn,* that woman is so smart she gives me a woody just talking to her. I've got a hard-on I could pound nails with."

"Best keep it in your pants until you get home," Wes said, "or your old lady will cut your balls off."

"You've got a point there, Wes."

Dougan shook his head and moved away to wait on the drinkers at the other end of the bar.

Butch kept thinking about what he wanted but couldn't have and would never get . . . while Wes, in his quiet and professional way, kept flicking his eyes across the big mirror behind the bar, waiting for the trouble he knew was coming. He just didn't know when.

Lee Roy watched George make his way back to the table through the dancers and drinkers and pool players and the others who were just milling around. He watched as George sat down and then said, "You doin' better now?"

"Yeah."

"Because we need the three of us to pull this caper off."

"Yeah, Lee Roy. I'm okay. Musta got some bad food or something. Fine now. All okay."

"Well, listen up then. Here's the deal. I figure we'll clear six to seven hundred thousand or more, see, 'cause it's payday for all those construction men building that air force college north of town, plus all the workers at the railroad and the city workers too. They all get paid in cash and it goes through the same place."

The three men were leaning over the table with their heads close together, listening to Lee Roy lay out his plan. They were so intent for a while that they didn't notice Jewell, going back and forth, carrying drinks.

Lee Roy paused to let Ray and George absorb the details, and took a short breather so they could ask questions. George seemed to know his job, which was mostly to watch the front door while Lee Roy did the heavy lifting inside. Ray tipped his chair back on two legs against the wall and thought about the escape routes Lee Roy talked him through. He wished he was a little more familiar with the place. *Maybe get a chance to check them out in the morning* . . . George and Lee Roy were both looking at him as Ray leaned back into the table, putting the chair down with a thump. He leaned close and said, "We've been made," in a voice that was only a whisper.

Jewell came up to her station where Butch and Wes were talking to Dougan. She put the serving tray down just as the jukebox started pounding out a tune called "Cry! Cry! Cry!" by a new rockabilly singer named Johnny Cash . . . a man with a bass voice that was so deep and resonant it sounded like forty miles of gravel road. With twangy guitars and a rocking beat, it had the whole place on its feet. Jewell had to almost shout to make herself heard by Dougan and the two cops. ". . . I said, all I could hear were the two words: 'Bank. Job.' That's all. 'Bank. Job.' Nothing else."

Butch and Wes both turned and looked at the same time, but it was too late. They were gone. The mischief of rats had disappeared to who knows where.

Butch Hernshaw asked his partner, Wes Barton, "What now, boss?"

"Now nothing. It ain't our problem anymore."

Butch looked at the door, looked at his partner, then the door again. He shrugged his shoulders and slumped back against the bar. He watched the dancers and the colored lights that changed the atmosphere of the room with each revolution of the old jukebox light columns, and he tried with all his heart not to think of anything.

Eleven hours and forty-five minutes to go.

Daniels Chevrolet
105 North Weber Street, Colorado Springs, Colorado
9:30 a.m. MST, Fri., Nov. 4, 1955 . . . one hour, forty-five minutes remaining

I was sitting in the six-by-six-foot cubicle the auto dealership somewhat ostentatiously called an office, drinking coffee and eating a cake doughnut that tasted like lard, even though it was covered in sugar. I tossed it in the trash, wiped my mouth with the paper napkin it was wrapped in, then tossed it in with the rest of the trash. I sipped coffee from the white china mug with the Chevrolet logo on it, while I waited for Ron Theisman so I could take delivery of my new convertible, something I'd been looking forward to for more than six weeks. There wasn't anything I could do until Ron got there, so I lit a smoke and gazed out the glass wall of the office that looked into the showroom, thinking about the night shift I'd just completed.

It started out pretty routine. I drew a patrol car from the motor pool, checked the lights and siren, made sure it was full of gas, then headed out. My sector was the south side, which was known as a hot zone, then and now. It's an area with an extensive number of bars, liquor stores, and cut-rate motels, all catering to the soldiers at Camp Carson. The place keeps expanding and it's now designated as a fort. It's an infantry post, so it gets a lot of soldiers coming back from Korea. They're tough, many with combat time in World War II and Korea, and looking to blow off steam and just have a good time, glad to be home in one piece. But, you know how it is . . . mix randy young men in their prime, a lot of alcohol, throw a few young willing women into the mix, and you have all the ingredients for a whoop-de-do, otherwise known as a brawl.

The one I dealt with this early morning was mediocre at best. The call came at about 1:45 . . . a fight at a south-side saloon the cops all referred to as the "Bucket of Blood." It was well known to all of us on patrol and usually declared off-limits by the Fort Carson commanding general. I got there at the same time as a young patrolman named Conroy Jinkins, who was barely out of his rookie stage. We went in together.

Inside, two or three local toughs were fighting with an equal number of GIs. They had the place pretty torn up, and it didn't look like any of them were ready to surrender yet. Then I heard the snick of a switchblade knife, a tinkle of broken glass, and didn't hesitate. I waded right in, swinging my baton like Mickey Mantle going for the fences.

I saw the guy with the knife in his outstretched hand and swung the baton hard. I heard bone snap. He dropped the knife and started falling to his knees. The baton swung again and caught him on the right kidney.

I put my weight into it and connected with a hard smack that would leave him pissing blood for a few days. He fell to the floor with his mouth working like a fish as he tried to suck enough air in to scream. The guy was some of our local talent; I recognized him from other run-ins. I hadn't personally busted him, but I'd seen him in the drunk tank after being arrested by a fellow officer. I kept swinging the baton, as did Officer Jinkins. About thirty seconds later it was all done.

The instigator was the one I'd clocked—the guy with the knife. His main opponent was a young soldier with buck sergeant stripes. We separated the two groups, kept them sitting on the floor with their hands on their heads. I collected driver's licenses from all of them and motioned to Jinkins. We stepped to one side where we couldn't be overheard, but were still in easy reach in case any of the pugilists got a second wind and tried to renew hostilities. I said, "I'm gonna let you call this one. We can get the paddy wagon, and bust all of 'em. Then we'll be up to our asses in paperwork for six to eight hours for no pay. Or, you can take the one holding his arm and moaning and book him in for drunk and disorderly, attempted murder for use of the knife, striking an officer, resisting arrest, and whatever else you can think of on the way to the station. The guy's a known repeater. You can have the collar all to yourself. It's a righteous one too."

"That's an easy one, Jake."

"Smart. You'll go far in the department. Is this your first bust?"

"Yeah."

"Good. Glad I could help. Don't forget to search him after you cuff him."

I gave Jinkins the one license and he took charge of the prisoner while I talked to the others.

With the help of the bartender and a bouncer, we got the onlookers back to their tables and bit of order restored. I commandeered a table and a couple of chairs and began interviewing the fighters. I started with the sergeant. I pointed him to a chair and made a show of writing his information down. I said, "How long have you been in the army?"

"Five years and six months."

"Korea?"

"Yeah. January nineteen fifty to fifty-two."

"See much action?" I said it with the ease of one combat veteran to another.

He didn't take offense, said, "Plenty. All the way to the Yalu River and back. I was at the Chosin Reservoir."

"You marched out?"

"Yeah. With the help of a big marine sonofabitch . . . about your size. You?"

I took out a pack of Lucky Strike cigarettes, offered him one. He took it and we both lit up off my old Zippo lighter with the USMC anchor and the world on it before I answered. "Guadalcanal. August seventh, nineteen forty-two. I came ashore under fire with the rest of the First Marine Division. It was my eighteenth birthday. So how come you're only a buck and not at least a staff sergeant or more?"

He took a long pull on the Lucky, sucked it in, and exhaled while we both reflected on the other's combat record. All three battles were already the stuff of legend, the memories etched deep into the souls of all who'd been there and survived.

"Because I keep getting busted back to private because of shit like this."

I looked him in the face for a few moments before my next question. He was a little bit worse for wear, had a cut over one eyebrow and a bruise on his left cheek to go with the split bottom lip. I remembered a scared fifteen-year-old boy in a marine recruiting office back in 1940 who was a lot more torn up than this kid, and I thought about a highly decorated gunnery sergeant named Millsap who took a chance on that kid . . . and gave me a chance at redemption. I said, "These other two guys . . ."

"They didn't start anything. They got in to help me when the other three jumped me. They're good troopers. I don't think they deserve to get Article Fifteens put in their jackets because of me."

"They're in your squad?"

"Yes, sir."

"Korea?"

"Yeah. Both of 'em. But only the colored guy fought. The other one was a peacekeeper up on the demilitarized zone after the cease-fire."

"What started the fight tonight?"

"A girl I was trying to get to know better. A lot better. I was drinking beer and buying her mixed drinks. They're kinda expensive. When it came closing time . . . time to get to know her a lot better . . . she disappears and her asshole boyfriend shows up, tells me to 'fuck off.' I tell him, 'Try and make me, fuckhead!' You know the rest."

"Are you planning to re-up?"

"Yeah. I was anyway. This hits my jacket, I'll be lucky to fill out my full enlistment period."

I decided to take a chance on the man, the same as Gunney Millsap had on me, all those years ago. "Okay," I said, "here's the deal. I can run yez in and book yez for drunk and disorderly, which you all deserve, or you can pool your money with the other two troopers and pay the bar for the damage. I figure about a hundred dollars or so ought to do it. Then the bunch of yez clear out and stay outta this dump. These kind of places have been running the same bullshit scam forever. Young horny GIs meet these bar girls and buy 'em drinks thinking they're gonna get some pussy after the joint closes. Then the boyfriend or bouncer shows up and gives ya the bad news. There's a reason this place is off-limits."

The sarge went to his two buddies with the proposal, while I gave the same one to the pair of bikers, who went for the deal immediately. I told them to get their dough together. I went to the bartender, said, "Each group is willing to pay a hundred bucks for the damage, if that would be okay with you."

"Two hundred? Shit yes."

I took him to the bikers who handed up the money and left. Then the sarge came over.

"We've only got eighty-five bucks between the three of us. Will that do?"

The bartender nodded yes and the money changed hands. He walked away while I escorted the three servicemen outside. I wanted to make sure there wasn't a bunch of gang members waiting in the parking lot. "Where's your car?" I said.

"We ain't got one."

"How'd you get here?"

"Taxicab."

"Do you have any dough stashed?"

"Nuh, sir. We give it all up in there. We can walk."

I thought about letting them, but decided against it. I loaded them all into the backseat of the patrol car and took them to the main gate at Fort Carson. I got out and opened the back door so they could climb out. I shut the door and said, "Here's your IDs back. Be advised that your good luck charm has just expired. I get called out and see any of yez again I'll not only throw the book at yez . . . I'll see it gets stuck so far up your asses that every time you sneeze, pages of the criminal code will flutter. You understand?"

They all said they did. I didn't know if it did any good or not, but I said, "One last thing. If you want to meet girls, nice girls, try the library, or the hospital. There's lots of nice girls working there who're looking to meet nice young men such as yourselves." I know it sounds kind of arrogant for me to be lecturing men who were almost my own age, but sometimes, when you're young like that, far away from home and lonesome . . . you just need a little friendly Dutch uncle or big brother advice to get back on track. I don't know if it helped or not. I like to think it did. When I told Gloria, the nurse I was dating, she liked the idea . . .

Having done my good deed for the day, I went back on patrol. I decided to swing by the Bucket of Blood, just to check on things. It was past closing time and all the patrol officers in the sector were supposed to be on the lookout for what the duty sergeant who briefed us before each shift called "extracurricular" activity: prostitution, drug dealing, and gang-related criminal behavior. That decision to drive by the earlier callout resulted in one of the most unusual collars of my entire career in law enforcement, and changed my whole outlook on it at the same time.

I cruised down South Nevada Avenue and spotted a big, over-the-road truck at the saloon—the kind that go from state to state carrying everything from produce and groceries to pig iron and drilling pipe. It was parked in back where the shadows were deep black. I wasn't sure if it had or hadn't been there earlier. I turned left at the next street and pulled into the alleyway with my lights off and parked facing the street between a couple of buildings. I had a perfect view across Nevada Avenue, and settled in to watch the truck and the saloon for a little while. I lit a smoke and sat back, listening to the radio calls and watched as a few snow flurries danced on the night winds. I wished I had a hot cup of coffee, was glad I'd left the motor running and the heat on.

I didn't have long to wait. Before I'd finished my cigarette, the lights went out on the bar and two men and a woman came out of the back door. The woman got into an old thirties model sedan and left. The two men talked for a couple of minutes, shook hands, and one of them drove off in a dark-colored Cadillac. The other one fired up the big rig and sat there waiting for it to warm up and build air pressure in the brakes. When he pulled out and headed south, some inner voice compelled me to follow. I dropped my cigarette butt out the window and eased in behind him.

I could not, to this very day, give any reason for following that big rig. It was just an instinct, a gut hunch, and I don't know where it came from, or why, or how. It just appears every now and then; it's usually right. On that night, the driver crossed the center line a couple of times in quick succession and had no brake lights on the trailer. I drove up behind him and hit my bubble gum light and siren. He pulled over and we both parked, about half a mile before the city limits. It turned out to be the most incredible traffic stop of my career.

I buttoned up my coat against the cold, called in my location to the dispatcher back at the department, and grabbed my ticket book. The icy night air hit me as soon as I got out, biting at my face and searing my lungs with every breath. I could see the driver watching me in the big west coast mirror as I approached the cab. He rolled the window open and looked down at me from his seat. I could smell the alcohol fumes from where I stood. I said, "I need to see your license and registration, please. I pulled you over because you don't have any brake lights and you're weaving."

He had the oddest look on his face as he handed his papers down to me—sort of dread, fear, and embarrassment, all at the same time. Maybe resignation as well. "They told me not to come through here. They said I'd get caught in Colorado Springs. Goddamn it all. Why didn't I listen . . ."

"What's your problem," I said. "Caught for what?"

"There's a murder warrant out on me in Clarendon, Texas. Up in the panhandle."

I stepped back a couple of feet, unsnapping the safety strap on my holster at the same time. I put my hand on the butt of my service revolver, a Smith & Wesson .38 and said, "Okay. Put your hands where I can see 'em in the window." He complied. I pulled my gun. "Okay now. Open the door, slow and easy, and climb on down here."

He did as he was told. When he was out, I turned him around and did a quick pat down for weapons. He was clean. I put him in the backseat of the cruiser and shut the door, locking him in. I holstered my weapon and went back to the truck and retrieved my clipboard and his driver's license, then reached in the cab and shut the motor off and pulled the keys. It was then I noticed that my heart was pounding like a trip hammer and I was breathing in short gasps through my mouth. I took several deep breaths and went back to my patrol car. I turned the interior light on and looked at the man in the backseat. He was average height and weight, bald on top and blue-eyed, and appeared to match the driver's license. "Is this your real name?"

"Yeah. Lamont Sims. Everybody calls me Monty."

I got on the radio and gave his name and description, then added, "He says there's a murder warrant on him in Texas."

The dispatcher's name was Ross Thomas. He'd been hurt in a car chase and the chief was letting him work the dispatcher's job until he could retire in another year and a few months. He was permanently on the midnight shift because all of the line officers thought he was a pain in the ass and didn't want to work with him. He came back on in a few minutes and said, "I don't see nothin' on a guy by that name."

We went over all the information again, and Ross's answer came back the same.

Monty stirred around in the backseat and pulled his billfold out of a back pocket. He dug around in it for a moment and extracted a brown newspaper clipping. He said, "Hey, I ain't shittin' y'all. There's really a warrant on me. Look here," and he pushed the folded article through the wire mesh so I could retrieve it.

I scanned it briefly and got back on the radio. "Ross, he's got a newspaper clipping here. Says he's wanted in Clarendon, Texas, for a double homicide. The sheriff's name is in a crease. I can't make it out. Why don't you just call down there on the telephone and ask."

"I can't do that, Jake. It's four o'clock in the morning."

"Who gives a shit. I'd sure as hell want a call if it was me."

"If you curse on the radio again, I'll write you up. I still ain't gonna call long distance. It costs too much."

The sudden burning in my stomach wasn't from drinking too much coffee. I wanted to reach through the radio and slap the old bastard until he couldn't breathe. I took a deep breath and said, "Tell you what, Ross, why don't you put it out on the teletype?"

"Sure. I can do that."

I heard the keys clacking in the background as Ross had left his mic open. Three minutes later, I heard the teletype spring to life and start pounding away. Then the phone rang. I heard Ross answer it. A minute later he was back on the radio. "I'm patching through Sheriff Wondall Luttrell from Clarendon, Texas."

The radio had a slight echo to it. A hollow voice said, "Hello, Officer? To whom am I speaking?"

"McKern. My name is Jake McKern."

"Well, congratulations, Officer. You've apprehended a fugitive we've been seeking for almost three years."

"Just doing my job, sir. You're on an open circuit. Monty Sims is in the back seat. He can hear us."

"Monty. Can you hear me?"

"Yessir."

"Time to come home, son. You'll have to face the music."

"Yessir. I know that."

"Well, I'll see you soon. And McKern?"

I'm here, Sheriff."

"Great work. I'll be sending you a letter of commendation. You ever want a job or are in the area, ever need a favor, look me up."

"Will do."

I heard the connections being broken. I said, "Ross, I'm bringing the prisoner in. You need to send a tow truck out here for this tractor and trailer."

"I can't do that. It'll cost a lot of money. Who's gonna pay for it?"

"It ain't my problem, Ross. I'm just a humble patrolman out here apprehending the miscreants and dragging them in to face the blindfolded scales of justice." I turned the radio volume down to the lowest possible setting, put Monty in handcuffs, and started for the station.

In the backseat, Monty Sims said, "Jesus Christ, boss. It do make a man wonder about the state of law enforcement, don't it."

. . . And that's just what I was doing . . . wondering about the state of law enforcement, when Ron Theisman walked in. It was nine a.m. There was a little over two hours to go.

"Good morning, Jake."

"Ron. Glad you could make it. Did the bed fall down or something?"

"No. My Bible study class ran a bit long."

"You are so full of shit. You haven't seen the inside of a church since the day you were christened."

He grinned and went to get both of us a fresh cup of coffee. He was a good lad, as Ma would say, but suffered from the young man's preoccupation with members of the opposite sex. He'd been out most all night chasing pussy. He was neat and freshly shaved, but I could tell by his face and eyes that he hadn't had much sleep.

He came back with two cups of fresh coffee and we got down to business. He said, "You ready to get that car?"

"Naw. I'm here to renegotiate the price or get my money back," I said.

He looked up sharply and saw I was kidding. "You asshole. Give me your license so I can make out a temporary registration and plate for ya. I always wanted to say that to a cop, by the way. 'Gimme your license and registration.' It's kinda fun."

"Yeah, well, I wouldn't get too used to it, if I were you," I said as I handed it over and watched him write out the information on a paper license plate that he put in a plastic holder. "C'mon," he said, "and we'll get this beauty delivered to you. I had half a dozen chances to sell that thing to other buyers, ya know."

"I'da shot ya."

He grinned again. "It's in the wash bay. You look it over while I bolt this on the back. Then I'll show you a few things and you can go."

When he took me back where the new cars were serviced and cleaned and inspected for delivery, I could hardly believe my eyes. There was my beautiful new convertible, and what a honey-dripper she was. All gleaming chrome, shining white paint, and red leather seats, she was everything I'd ever dreamed about in a car. It was something I'd wanted since I was a kid, but never dared have any hope of owning. I couldn't wait to take my girlfriend, Nurse Gloria, Ma, and little Annie for a ride. I stood there and just stared, anticipating the pleasures of driving such a gorgeous car.

Ron finished fussing with the temporary tag and stood next to me. He said, "That. Is one good-looking car."

"I call them honey-drippers because they're so sweet."

"Well, let me show you a couple of things and then you can go."

Ron's idea of showing me a few things involved a bolt-by-bolt explanation of each and every piece and part of the car, three trips to the parts department for just the right set of free floor mats, and finally, a trip to the gas pump out back for a complimentary fill-up. The whole production took quite awhile. Then he said, "Let me run in and get a shop rag and some wax to fix that little swirl mark on the paint. It'll only take a sec."

At this point, I had to put a stop to it. I said, "Thanks, but it's almost eleven o'clock. I've gotta go."

"You sure? It'll only take me a little bit . . . "

"Thanks. But no. I gotta go," I said and took the keys. As I got in, I thanked him again. It made the little hairs on the back of my neck stand up when I turned the key and the motor rumbled to life. It was ten minutes before eleven. I had about twenty minutes left before the gates of hell got knocked down and my life was hanging in the balance.

West Colorado Springs, Colorado
10:35 a.m. MST, Fri., Nov. 4, 1955 . . . thirty-five minutes remaining

It had been a long and fucked-up night. George hadn't slept a wink. He'd bunked on the floor with his back to the wall and the nine millimeter Luger in his right hand, waiting for Lee Roy's nocturnal cycle of predation to begin, vowing to himself to "shoot the fucker dead" if he tried to pull any of his old shit.

During the night Ray had slept fitfully, thinking about all that could go wrong with the job. If he hadn't needed money so bad, he thought, *I'd tiptoe out of this sorry-assed little trailer the big guy calls home and be over the state line before dawn.* He sat up in the bed and put his feet on the floor. Some inner sense was screaming at him to get away from these fools. He'd never been so conflicted about a job before. *Always worked with pros. Guys who went in, did their business and got out, and we left. Never got caught. Never did time. Banks take four or five men to pull off. Not two. And not dipshits like these.* He smoked and thought about going back there and putting one in Lee Roy's ear, than doing that idiot George, just for meanness and good measure. Make it look like a murder-suicide. Ray took some pleasure from the thought . . . even went so far as to check the

.357 and listen at the bedroom door for a moment. He could hear Lee Roy snoring like a hog in the rear bedroom and a rustling from the living room where George was bedded down. That was followed by a thud from a heavy metal object, more rustling, then a snick of lubricated machine parts and a faint whiff of oil. He knew what it was. "George, I gotta go piss. Put that goddamn pistol down," Ray said through clenched teeth.

"Okay, Ray," came the hoarse reply.

Ray stepped into the small toilet and ran water in the sink, watched a cockroach crawl across the mirror, and flushed the toilet. It looked like it hadn't been cleaned since before the war. He heard Lee Roy make a wet squarking sound in the middle of a snore, then the bed creak as he shifted positions. The snoring resumed and Ray slipped back into his room, his plan aborted. *If only I didn't need the cash . . .*

Lee Roy slept the restful sleep of the untroubled, the innocent, and the young . . . as well as the sociopath . . . those like Lee Roy Morgan, born without a conscience. He'd decided, on the forty-five-minute drive from the bar to his lair up in the foothills off of Twenty-Sixth Street, that he was gonna kill George as soon as the robbery was done. He fell asleep with a smile on his face, trying to decide how: a bullet, knife, maybe just choke him to death with his bare hands.

Now it was midmorning. All three of them were squeezed into the front seat of Ray's Ford coupe. They'd been up since seven, drinking coffee and going over and over Lee Roy's plan.

Ray was the wheelman.

"I wantcha to pull up right here," Lee Roy said, tapping his pencil on the hand-drawn map of Colorado Avenue and Tejon Street, "in front of the bank."

"Okay, then what?"

"Stay put. Keep the motor running."

"Sure."

"Me and George will go in. George, you'll stay at the front door and watch for the cops. I'll go in and grab the dough."

Ray said, "It can't be that easy. You're telling me that they're gonna have all that payroll money and no extra guards or nothing. Something don't sound right."

Lee Roy turned and shined his electric glare on Ray. Ray didn't flinch or look away. Lee Roy said, "Stop thinking like an asshole. The beauty of this setup is it's got a big city payroll, but the guy who runs the bank thinks like a hick. Acts like it's still a small town, and they're only catering to rich, genteel customers . . . like they know the face and name of everyone who walks in there . . . and that they're all honest, upright citizens. They keep a rollaway cart piled with stacks of money in a small filing room just to one side of the teller cages. It's not even guarded. I'm gonna walk in, blast the dead bolt off with a twelve gauge, and take the money while everybody's screaming. In and out in under two minutes. Easy."

Ray looked down at the floor, unconvinced. He said, "I'm gonna go check the car while you all get ready."

George, who hadn't spoken much all morning, said, "I'm ready too. I'll go with ya."

Ray went to the car, parked to one side where it couldn't be seen from the street, and opened the hood. He checked the oil and water and looked at the fan belts, added some oil, and closed the hood. He checked the tires by kicking them, got in, and started it up. He lit a cigarette and smoked, listening for noise from the idling Caddy motor, keeping his thoughts to himself.

George sat on the passenger side, fiddling with the stolen nine millimeter Luger. He stuck it in his waistband when he saw Lee Roy come out the front door of the trailer, buttoning up the front of a blue tweed overcoat. He wasn't quick enough to keep Ray from seeing the sawed-off twelve gauge pump shotgun hanging from a leather strap that looped around his right shoulder. *Looks evil,* Ray thought as he dropped the car into first gear when Lee Roy got in and shoved George into the center, where he wedged up against the wheelman.

Ray dropped his cigarette butt out and started toward downtown Colorado Springs. He said, "When you all come outta the bank, one of ya will haveta get in the back. Dive over the seat. I can't drive like this. It's too crowded."

Lee Roy said, "That'll be you, George. You're a real good diver as I recall."

Burning with shame and rage, George didn't say anything, but under his breath he renewed his vow to kill Lee Roy.

Downtown Colorado Springs
10:53 a.m. MST, Fri., Nov. 4, 1955

I pulled out on Weber, made a left on Platte, and another left around the bronze statue on its massive plinth of General William J. Palmer of Civil War fame: the founder of Colorado Springs and the D&RG Railroad. I headed south on Nevada Avenue, intent on an early lunch at the Busy Corner Café. It was on the southwest corner of Nevada and Colorado Avenues, and my favorite place to eat. I was starving, running on high-octane coffee and not much else, because I hadn't eaten since sometime yesterday. I think my stomach thought my throat had been cut.

When I got there, the place was packed. I could see through the windshield that every seat was taken, and several people were standing by the door and register waiting for seats. I went down the street and turned on Vermijo by the courthouse, then north up Tejon Street.

That simple act changed my life.

Downtown Colorado Springs
10:59 a.m. MST, Fri., Nov. 4, 1955

They had driven around the business district to give Ray a sense of its network of streets, avenues, and potential escape routes. Now they were headed north on Cascade. Lee Roy was in charge. "Turn right at Colorado, then right on Tejon. Park in front. Keep both windows down and the motor running."

"Yeah," Ray said.

Lee Roy looked sideways at George. "You ready?"

"Yeah."

Ray stopped. Lee Roy and George went in the front door. George had his pistol drawn, holding it next to his right thigh. Lee Roy entered the bank unbuttoning his overcoat with his left hand, while his right was bringing the sawed-off pump to bear through a slit cut into the right side of the coat, and leaving no doubt as to his intentions.

11:03 a.m. MST, Fri.

As if it was waiting for me, a curbside parking place was open in front of the Grand Café. It was The Springs' best, and only, Chinese restaurant. *What the hell, good as anything,* I thought as I parallel parked my shiny new convertible, being careful not to brush the curb with the whitewall tires and leave scuff marks on them. Now I was sitting at the first table on the right, in front of the big plate-glass window with the mighty red-and-green dragon painted on it, waiting for Mr. Louie to bring out my moo goo gai pan, and drinking a pot of green tea. I was admiring my car and watching a '49 Ford coupe that was double-parked across the street. The driver was wearing sunglasses. He had a fedora pulled down on his forehead and was smoking a cigarette. I couldn't quite tell from where I sat, but it looked like he was being extra vigilant, looking in all directions without seeming to. He had his window down and was flicking cigarette ash onto the street. Mr. Louie brought me my food and a fresh pot of tea. He was arranging them in front of me, when the window exploded.

11:01 a.m. MST

Lee Roy had terrorized every person in the bank with his menacing size and the twelve gauge shotgun round he'd fired into the wall over the teller cages. He roared out, *"This is a holdup! Everybody on the floor!"* and punctuated his remark by jacking a new round of double-ought buck into the gun's breech.

George stood by the door with arms extended, pointing the Luger pistol with both hands in the general direction of the tellers and customers.

Lee Roy didn't hesitate. He went straight over to the closet door by the teller cages and blew the doorknob and deadbolt lock off with two deafening blasts. He kicked the door and went in, pulling a pair of pillowcases from inside his coat as he entered.

The three-foot steel cart was piled with money in all denominations, and seemed to almost glow in the shine from the overhead light that had been left on. Lee Roy was transfixed for a moment by the sight of it all. He smiled and laid the shotgun and pillowcases on the stacks while he fished three fat red-and-brass shotgun shells out of his pants and reloaded. Then he filled the sacks with the largest denominations of cash, shoving Franklins and Grants in the first pillowcase, Jacksons and Hamiltons in the other, until the bags were full. He grabbed both of them in one hand and the gun in the other . . . all in less than two minutes.

Lee Roy came out of the closet and back to where George waited. They each took a bag and backed for the door. And that's where Lee Roy made his fatal mistake.

Eager to escape, the big man went out the door first. He took three steps toward the waiting car before George shot him. He was aiming for Lee Roy's head, but missed, hitting him in the back instead. The bullet entered his neck, severing the spinal cord at the junction of his fifth and sixth cervical vertebrae, putting Lee Roy flat on his face . . . as if he'd been poleaxed by God almighty . . . paralyzed from the neck down. The shotgun discharged from an involuntary twitch of his finger and sprayed the top and side of the white convertible parked across the street, with a stray piece of shot breaking the front window of the restaurant behind it. Someone jumped out of the window yelling, "Police!" and was immediately engaged by Ray, who cranked off two shots at the guy as he took up position behind the white Chevy and returned fire.

George ran for the getaway car, threw the money bag in the back, and dove in the open window screaming, "Drive! Drive! Drive!" Ray took one last shot as he popped the clutch and the three-hundred horse engine snarled into action, smoking the back tires as they fought for traction and George tried to wriggle in the window. Hit in the gas tank by Ray's last shot . . . the Chevy convertible burst into flames.

11:04

It all happened fast after that . . . but events slowed down for me at the same time . . . as sometimes happens in mortal combat. "Call the cops, Louie. Tell them there's a 10/74 in progress," I yelled and jumped out the window with my .45 automatic in hand.

The Ford driver shot at me twice with what sounded like a .357 Magnum. The first bullet whacked into the stone facade of the building behind me, and the second one grazed me in the left triceps muscle under my arm. It felt like a blowtorch had hit me and the pain was mind numbing. Blood was flowing down my side as I fired back at my assailant. His third shot boomed out, and I heard it hit my new car and the whoosh of the explosion as a fire started.

When the car started to burn, the rage monster inside of me broke out of the cage I keep him in; I started seeing everything through the red haze of battle lust. I ran down the sidewalk, chasing after the fleeing bandits and firing bullet after bullet at them. One hit the driver in the head. He died instantly, but convulsed in his death throes and pulled left on the steering wheel. The car skidded up the curb, onto the sidewalk, collapsing the undersized right-front wheel and tire. The Ford rolled on its right side and slid along the sidewalk . . . which ground most of the lower legs off the man hanging out the window. His screams started before I got to the overturned wreck. He was trapped.

The trunk had sprung open when the car rolled, spilling tools and other junk in an arc across the street, but the big problem was the three broken jerry cans of gasoline that were disgorging their contents in the car and underneath it. When the high test gas hit the hot tailpipe it smoked for an instant before going off in an explosive ignition that knocked me on my ass, fifteen feet out in the street.

Stunned, I sat up with my face, arms, and hands burned. I realized my eyebrows, lashes, and face were singed, and my shirt was smoking. I still had my pistol in my right hand. I got to my knees and felt the badge wallet under my hand. *Musta fallen out from the blast*, I thought. I stuck it in my front pants pocket and staggered to my feet. Something was wrong. I fell again. Got up again and dropped in agony to the street.

I tried to approach the burning car with just my hands and arms pulling me, but the heat was too intense. The screams inside the car were even louder, higher in pitch. They went on, and on, and on. The smell of burning flesh permeated the air, filled my nostrils with soot and horror.

"Shoot me, man. For the love of God, kill meeeee . . ." But, I couldn't move—could only hear the screams and the sirens coming fast.

Then, everything was in someone else's hands and out of mine. I was in an ambulance and someone was tending to me. I felt something stick me in the arm and then nothing. Time ceased for me.

Time had run out for George Phelps too. His forty-nine hours had passed into infinity, as had his poor tortured soul. But sometimes in the late early hours, just before the gray light of the false dawn, I awake from dreaming about the Whim-Wham Man, and hear George Phelps screaming . . . begging me to kill him.

Epilogue

I woke up on Sunday evening with my head, hands, left arm, and chest wrapped in gauze bandages. My right leg was taped up and elevated . . . it seems I had taken some shrapnel there that broke my femur when the explosion happened. A stainless steel rod was clamped through the lower part of the broken thigh bone and attached to a stirrup-looking thing that in turn was hooked by ropes and pulleys to a bunch of weights. It was the damndest looking contraption . . . and to be honest . . . it hurt like such a sonofabitch that I forgot all about the burns on my hands and face for a while. Nurse Gloria, who was sitting in a chair next to me when I woke, told me it's called "traction." She also said I wouldn't be going anywhere for at least ninety days, with another thirty or forty after that for rehabilitation. "You'll lose strength and muscle tone from inactivity. But don't worry, honey, I'll take real good care of you while you're in here."

Ma was standing on the other side of the bed with her hand on my good shoulder. Even in my groggy state, I could see that her eyes were red and puffy, with a couple of stray tears leaking out them . . . whether from joy or sadness I never knew. In her lilting Irish brogue she said, "Welcome back, my foine young son. Ye had me so worried, boyo . . ." Her voice trailed off for a moment as she brushed her hand across her cheeks, then she continued, "But ye and Annie are all the family I have."

Ma's accent got stronger whenever she was upset. I'd never heard it any more apparent than just now, even on the day I had to leave home and join the Marine Corps at the age of fifteen. I said, "Ma. Don't you worry so much. It'll be fine. And if nothing's happened to me so far, I'll be here for a long while yet."

"Ach, Jamie, if ye weren't so hurt, I'd beat ye with me broom, so I would."

It was then that a nurse in white shoes, stockings, and dress, and wearing a starched white cap denoting her nursing school, came in carrying a metal tray with a towel covering something. That something was a pair of hypodermic needles. She said, "One is for pain and the other's penicillin for infection." Her name tag said "Mary Gene Lynn" on it. She was brisk and efficient, with a fast jab in the arm and one in the ass. As she was fussing with one of the two IV bags dripping into my right arm, I must have gone out again, because the next thing I knew it was daybreak. Blood was being drawn from my arm and I was dying to eat something.

The parade of visitors began that afternoon. Seems I was now a hometown hero. The chief came in, shook my hand, and congratulated me while the flashbulbs popped from all the reporters and photographers who were there for the story. Chief Bruce also pinned a gold shield on the pillow next to my head and told me it'd be official as soon as I was out of the hospital.

The bank got back a substantial amount of their cash. Lee Roy Morgan had the largest bills in the bag he was carrying. It was recovered intact on the sidewalk, lying next to him. The other pillowcase had the smaller bills. It burned up in the car fire on the courthouse lawn. The bank was insured for the loss.

The new convertible? My brand-new Chevy with all the options? It was a total loss. Unlike the bank's money, however, it was uninsured. I hadn't even driven it two miles. I kept trying not to think about it, or get too depressed . . . Sure.

As for the mischief of rats, as Jewell so aptly named them, Lee Roy Morgan is in the state penitentiary in Cañon City, Colorado. He's doing life without parole for his part in the crime spree. He's paralyzed from the neck down and permanently consigned to the infirmary, where he's bedridden, and dependent on trustees to feed and keep him from soiling himself, as well as his daily bathing and dressing needs. I'm told he suffers from horrendous bedsores and various skin conditions. His outlook is not good, but however long he lives will depend on the charity of others. I find that to be the most fitting of ironies.

George Phelps was burned alive in the wreck of the '49 Ford. He was found in possession of a nine millimeter parabellum pistol of the same type that killed a teenage boy named Herbie Hill in Boise City, Oklahoma. The Hill boy was found by tracing the stolen license plates on the Ford coupe that was Phelps's funeral pyre.

Ray Matthews died when I hit him in the head with a .45 caliber hollow point during the shootout. His body was incinerated in the car with George Phelps. I saved his case for last because it directly impacted me.

When the car exploded and blew me backward, I was knocked senseless for a bit. When I sat up, I thought I'd dropped my badge wallet and stuck it in my front pants pocket before the medics got there.

Only it wasn't my badge wallet. It belonged to a deputy sheriff named Nolan Mayhue from Madison County, North Carolina. He'd been found in the Blue Ridge section of the Great Smoky Mountains along a back-road smuggling route used by the moonshiners who ran between Ashville, North Carolina, and Knoxville, Tennessee. The badge holder, a pair of handcuffs, and a leather sap belonging to him all fell out of a secret compartment built into the trunk, where the spare tire used to be. That stuff all came loose when the car rolled, because the screws that normally held its lid in place had somehow been removed. Otherwise, it all would've burned up in the fire, leaving the case forever unsolved. The investigating officers and Lieutenant Hoffman were more than fair; they gave me full credit for the takedown and case. That resulted in another commendation letter from Sheriff Haverkorn in North Carolina. He considered it proof positive that Ray Matthews had murdered Deputy Mayhue, because a search of the woods had turned up a single shot .410 shotgun, sawed down to just twelve inches in length . . . the weapon believed to have killed Mayhue when he approached a vehicle he'd stopped on that notorious and lonesome back road. It was a cheap single shot model that still had the empty shotgun shell in it. The gun was rusted junk. The shell, however, yielded a perfect left thumbprint on the brass end, where it was tamped into the barrel by Ray Matthews. Taken together with the evidence recovered in Colorado Springs, Sheriff Haverkorn was able to move Deputy Mayhue's homicide case out of the Open-Unsolved file and close it. Cop murders are special, and every cop killer deserves an extra-special toasting in hell.

I came out of the affair in pretty good shape. I spent a total of fourteen weeks in the hospital and rehab before I went back on duty, as a grade three detective. I had my gold shield . . . just as the chief promised. The hospital stay was a long slog of pain and reconstruction that aren't worth mention. The monotony and boredom was bearable because I used the afternoons to begin writing the journals that tell the stories of my exploits. The nighttime stresses were promptly and efficiently relieved with the help of Nurse Gloria—and a kind, compassionate, and sanguine nurse corps. That's all I care to say of the subject, excepting this: It's positively amazing what acrobatic activities can be done when one is immobilized, with the aid of an energetic and willing partner. Nurse Gloria was.

Fame of course, is fleeting. I was only a hero while the publicity lasted. Now I'm back to the workaday routine, trying to nab the badasses. A job that, thankfully, will never be done.

Since my new Chevy convertible was an uninsured total loss, I started saving for a new one. It's gonna take awhile, but things are already looking up. After recovering about three-quarters, or $435,000 of the stolen money for them, and causing my brand-new car to burn to ashes in the process, the folks who run the Colorado Commercial Bank have given a fifty-dollar reward to me, to assist in the purchase of another new car. Kinda takes your breath away, doesn't it?

I think I'll call Sheriff Haverkorn down in North Carolina. See if maybe he can put me in touch with those guys who built the '49 Ford coupe with the Caddy engine. That'd be some real fun . . .

Acknowledgments

No mortal work of creation takes place in a vacuum. It is an elaborate and combined effort of a dedicated team, many of whom toil in anonymity without public recognition, but are nevertheless critical in equal parts of the equation.

I'd like to thank all the regular members of the Rhyolite Posse for their help and hard work in the nurturing, creation and production of *Colorado Noir*:

Donald R. Kallaus, whose print book design and formatting skills are constantly evolving into something newer, better, more special and amazing; **Lora Brown** for her unflagging dedication to getting it right, as well as her energy, spirit, enthusiasm, endless good cheer . . . and for keeping me on track and on time; **Alison Auch** for all the 'we need it yesterday' editing jobs, for her boundless perseverance, precision and perspicacity . . . and, as always, for making me look smarter than I am; **Susan McKenna** for her awesome web wizardry, computer strategies and marketing skills; to newly sworn member **Dwight Haverkorn** for all things police department as well as many historical details of Colorado Springs; a special thanks to **Sally Lemmon** and **JD** at Rhyolite Press for keeping everything running smoothly; all of our friends and associates at Ingram and Lightning Source; as well as **Jonathon Scott** at Middleton Books for his digital artistry in formatting our eBook designs. Thank you always to beautiful **June**, whose name is carved on my heart.

A huge thank-you to the following irregular Posse Members for all of their technical advice, suggestions, commentaries, readings and fact checking, including: Bob Will, Dick Ralston, Kathy Ralston, Ron Theisman, Dr. Richard Blade, Jan McGraw, Susie Miller, Mike Curley, Skip Mooney, Larry Cary, Betsy Cary, Caywood Lindsey Jr., Mike Hillman, Mary Gene Lynn, Carol Millsap, Linda Cirullo, Jeanie Redding, Shannon Chase and Cynthia McKenna, Ann and Wondall Luttrell.

As always, all errors are mine and mine alone.

One last note: historians and long-time residents of Colorado Springs will know that Busy Corner was at Pikes Peak and Tejon, and the Busy Corner Cafe was at 102 North Tejon Street. In the story *A Mischief of Rats*, I moved the whole corner to Colorado and Nevada Avenues, so Jake would have a reason to park across the street from the bank.

--John Dwaine McKenna

About the Author

John Dwaine McKenna is the author of three fiction novels, two of which have been awarded EVVYS for excellence in fiction by the Colorado Independent Publisher's Association, or CIPA. He writes a weekly newspaper column called the Mysterious Book Report for the *Tri-Valley Townsman* in Sullivan County New York where he was born and raised in the beautiful southern Catskill Mountains. During his career he was a salesman, serial business owner, an investment advisor, and a compliance officer for a nationwide investment firm headquartered in Boulder, Colorado. He retired in 2000 and reignited his writing talents, which had lain dormant since his college days. He currently serves as the General Manager of Rhyolite Press, LLC and is hard at work on his next novel. You can receive his weekly book reviews and blogs by liking him on Facebook.

He and his wife June have lived in Southern Colorado for nearly five decades.

About the Type

Colorado Noir is set in Adobe Garamond Pro. Garamond is another of the old-style serif typefaces. It was designed in the mid-sixteenth century by Claude Garamond and refined in the early seventeenth century by another French punch-cutter and printer named Jean Jannon. Unique to the Garamond letter forms are the small bowl of the letter a and eye of the letter e; as well as it's sense of fluidity. Garamond is one of the most legible and readable of the serif typefaces . . . and is noted as one of the most eco-friendly fonts for its very precise, sparing and efficient use of ink.

Have you seen
our other
Rhyolite Press
Publications . . .

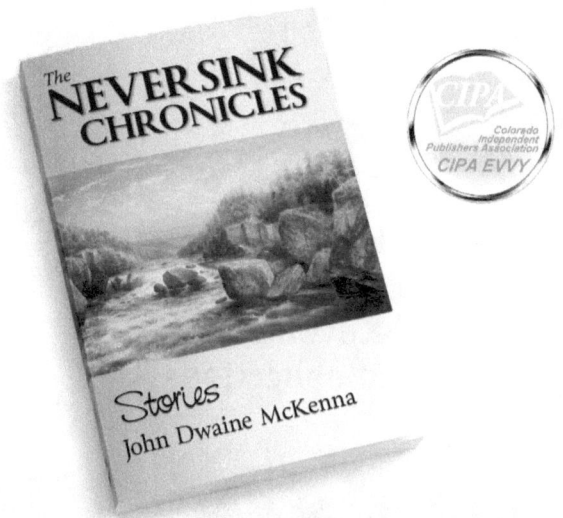

The Whim - Wham Man

A STORY THAT HAS IT ALL . . .
A CRIME YOU CAN'T FORGIVE
A PLOT YOU COULDN'T IMAGINE
AND A CHARACTER . . .
YOU'LL NEVER FORGET!

There's no sanitary way to write about murder.
"The Whim-Wham Man," ia a gut-punching novel of a teen-aged boy whose idyllic life in rural Colorado comes crashing down when reality and adulthood rush in after the brutalization and savage killing of two young girls . . . **It's a helluva yarn.**

CIPA EVVY Award Winner, 2013
2nd prize, Best Fiction

$15 at bookstores everywhere, or direct from the publisher:
www.rhyolitepress.com

ISBN 978-0-9839952-2-7

Praise for *The Whim-Wham Man*

"It's a helluva yarn."
—Dick Kreck, Author of *Murder at the Brown Palace* and
Smaldone

"Great Job! It got my blood boiling! Then it got my mind
thinking."
—Linda Comando, Publisher and Editor of *The Tri-Valley
Townsman*

"It was like eating popcorn . . . I couldn't quit. Congratulations.
I am looking forward to more Jake McKern novels."
Bill Calls, Scottsdale, AZ

"This short book with the odd title is the hard-to-put-down
story of a 15 year old youth who grows up in a hurry when a
grisly tragedy strikes his family."
—Mary Jean Porter, *The Pueblo Chieftain*

"Well written, so compelling I couldn't stop reading until the
last page."
—S.M. Albany, NY

"The Whim-Wham Man is the most thought provoking novel
I've read in a long time. Thanks for writing it."
—Kathy Hare, *The New Falcon Herald*

". . . and the silver award winner for fiction 2013 is . . .
The Whim-Wham Man."

19th Annual CIPA EVVY Awards, Denver Co
May 10, 2013

THE BOY WHO SLEPT WITH BEARS

Pulled from the pages of history, The Boy Who Slept with Bears is a fiction novel that tells the heart wrenching and heartwarming story of Tomas Dequine, or Sak-wa-ma-tu-ta-ci, 'Blue Hummingbird' in his native tongue, a thirteen year old Southern Ute boy whose family and way of life is being crushed by the onrush of white European settlers in 1880s Colorado . . . a time when the Utes were being driven off of their ancestral lands to be resettled on reservations. Told in a warm, grandfatherly voice, Douthit's novel is a past winner of a coveted golden CIPA-EVVY award for fiction. It has been read and loved by ages eight to eighty, and contains a reader's guide and bibliography.

One of our hottest novels!

CIPA EVVY Award Winner, 2005
1st prize, Best Fiction

$15 at bookstores everywhere, or direct from the publisher:
www.rhyolitepress.com

ISBN 978-0-9839952-8-9

Praise for *The Boy Who Slept with Bears*

I loved this book. The author, George Douthit, does a beautiful job of taking a young Ute boy and "brother bear" paralleling their lives and trials. This book made me feel like I was right their in the tepee with Tomas and his mother. This book also made me think about the Ute Indians and the many hardships they had after they were forced to move to the reservations. I love how the writer begins to blend history, culture, and symbolism all into one story. Being a Colorado native I really loved the use of historical fact mixed with fiction. I rarely read a book that I want to not end and this was one of these books. I grew to understand Tomas and his relationship with the earth and brother bear. This book is a great book for young and old alike.

Valorie R. Hornsby, Interior Designer

George Douthit's book *The Boy Who Slept with Bears*, is the moving story of a Southern Ute boy coming of age at a time when the Ute traditional territories were being overrun by non indians during the gold rush and the Utes removal to reservations. The author captures the boy's desire to avenge his father's murder at the hands of white soldiers. He steps from boyhood into a man's world while struggling to hold onto his traditional beliefs. Though fictional, Douthit weaves true historical details of the Southern Utes and a legendary grizzly bear named "Old Mose" into a masterful story that leaves the reader enthralled and captivated.

Vickie Leigh Krudwig, Author, *Searching for Chipeta*

A terrific read for both young and old! Outstanding! *The Boy Who Slept with Bears* is the best book about native Americans I've ever read. Please send two more copies for my nephews.

Leonard Foxworth,